Murder
in the
Christmas Tree Lot

Books by Judith Gonda

Tory Benning Mysteries

Murder in the Secret Maze
Murder in the Christmas Tree Lot
Murder in the Community Garden (coming in 2021)

Murder
in the
Christmas Tree Lot

JUDITH GONDA

BEYOND THE PAGE
PUBLISHING

Murder in the Christmas Tree Lot
Judith Gonda
Beyond the Page Books
are published by
Beyond the Page Publishing
www.beyondthepagepub.com

Copyright © 2020 by Judith Gonda
Cover design and illustration by Dar Albert, Wicked Smart Designs

ISBN: 978-1-950461-85-1

For my late parents, Marge and John Gonda, whose unconditional love and support fostered the creativity, curiosity, and persistence that have served me well as an author.

Acknowledgments

I'd like to thank, as always, my wonderful family, Victor, Jennifer, Heather, and Matt, for their constant love and support, and my two Pomeranians, Izzy and Ollie, for keeping me company in my office while I write.

I'm indebted to my fabulous agent, Dawn Dowdle, for her wealth of knowledge, wise guidance, and encouragement, and also to my wonderful editor, Bill Harris, for his insightful suggestions, publishing wisdom, and generosity of spirit. I am very grateful to Dar Albert, my talented cover artist, for once again producing cover art that so well expresses the essence of my book. A big thank-you also to the amazing Beyond the Page Publishing and staunch writer advocate, Jessica Faust.

Lastly, thanks to my many writer friends and colleagues who inspire me, and to the great readers who buy my books and write reviews. Big virtual hugs to you all!

Chapter 1

"Sorry to bother you so early, Tory. I left a message for Fuji but never heard back from him." Matt Ortega, the Benning Brothers Nursery manager, stood next to my black Lexus SUV in a Santa Claus suit, as all our Christmas tree lot managers did on their shifts.

"No problem, Matt. I was already up." I reached through my window and handed him my spare keys while Iris, my cream sable Pomeranian, lunged at him in her self-appointed role as my chief bodyguard. "My little early bird here makes sure I never sleep past seven anyway, even on Saturdays."

Matt guffawed at Iris, his breath steaming in the frosty air. "Anyway, beats me where the heck I might have left mine. The last time I remember having them was when I locked up last night. I thought maybe I left them in the gate's padlock, but if I did, they're not there now."

The padlocked gate Matt referred to was at the entrance to the tree lot. Every year we fenced off the nursery division's parking lot, converting it into our Christmas tree lot. Benning Brothers Landscape Design and Nursery was my family's business, where I worked as a landscape architect. About a year ago, I'd succeeded my late father as the company president.

I scooped up Iris, who flailed as I plopped her down in the passenger seat, holding her in place with my extended arm. "Hopefully, someone will find them. At least you can get inside the nursery offices now too."

He shuffled a bit with his head hung low.

"Something else?"

Matt tucked a stray lock of his dark brown hair inside his Santa hat. "Yeah, about that . . ." His phone pinged and he twisted his mouth to one side as he studied the screen and texted back. "Shoot. Fuji doesn't have them."

"Well, hopefully they'll turn up."

"I think it's best if I call a locksmith to rekey all the locks."

"Okay. Better safe than sorry. Could you please make sure you get a couple of extra sets for me and my uncle?" My uncle Bob and his wife, my aunt Veronica, had both come out of retirement recently to work part-time as our CFO and accountant.

"Will do."

I was ready to roll up my window, but Matt lingered. "Was there anything else?"

He blushed and avoided eye contact. "Um. Yeah. The door to the nursery office was open when I came in this morning."

"You mean unlocked?"

His gaze found mine and his head bobbed a confirmation. "Unlocked and wide open."

"Wow. That's odd. What do you think happened? Did you forget to lock it?"

"I'm almost positive I locked it last night but, I don't know, it sure seems like a strange coincidence, doesn't it?"

"Wait. You think someone found your keys and broke in?"

"I can't be sure because nothing's missing that I can tell. I don't know whether I'm just being paranoid because I can't find my keys or whether I'm imagining things because it's happened before . . ." He stopped short and his brown eyes shot me a wary glance.

We'd been down this road before. Now, whenever anything even remotely questionable popped up concerning Benning Brothers' financial security, we all experienced a bit of déjà vu. More like PTSD, to be honest.

I let out a deep breath. "At least nothing's missing."

"Again, I'm sorry—"

"Hey, don't worry about it. Let's be grateful nothing was taken. It could have been far worse. A Grinch stealing trees would be one thing. I'm just glad someone didn't cart off our computers and printers. But hopefully changing the locks will do the trick."

"Yeah."

"Anyway, glad you're on it. I'll be back later. See you in a bit."

I rolled up my window, grateful to shut out the blast of icy air that had stung my cheeks like a million tiny icicles. Had I known the way the day was about to play out, a million tiny daggers would have been more on the money. But at that moment, blissfully unaware of the macabre drama the next few hours would bring, my biggest concern was, as always, my frizz-prone hair.

I pulled down my visor mirror to assess the damage the moist marine layer had wrought on the blowout I'd just gotten yesterday. Yup. My worst fears confirmed. Gone was the sleek finish that my hairdresser, Philip, had styled. My silhouette now looked wild and out of control, a metaphor for the journey I'd taken over the past fourteen months when, within the span of a few short weeks, I'd become both an orphan and a widow, not to mention nearly losing the family business. Granted, I was a thirty-three-year-old orphan and my courtship and marriage combined lasted only four months, but I'd been devastated, nevertheless, and alternately channeled Harry Potter and Adrian Monk in an effort to cope.

My chest heaved with resignation. Ah, well. I'd pretend my frizzy curls were trendy sculpted beach waves and add it to my list of other self-delusions. At least the increased humidity would tamp down the ever-present wildfire risk in Santa Sofia, our little California coastal town tucked between Santa Barbara and San Luis Obispo.

I snapped the visor back in place and got nostalgic watching Matt Ortega jog back to the lot, the pom-pom on his Santa hat bouncing in sync to his strides. My late father was the one who'd started the tradition of having the tree lot manager on shift wear a Santa Claus costume. Over the years the idea had been expanded to include the rest of our tree lot employees, who wore reindeer antlers or elf hats.

I pulled out of the parking lot and drove up Manzanita Street. As I waited at the stoplight, Russell Fujimoto, aka Fuji, the nursery's associate manager, turned in front of me on his way to work. If it wasn't for his familiar red pickup with the signature wreath that adorned its front bumper, I might not have recognized him since his fake white beard and Santa hat provided a good disguise. Huh. Since when did our tree lot have more than one manager dressed as Santa on the same shift? Maybe he was coming in early to work on something else before working as a manager on the late shift.

I turned onto the Avenue, Santa Sofia's main drag, which was still sleepy save for a handful of boutique and gallery workers arriving to open up shop, and cruised the couple of blocks down to the closest Starbucks. I maneuvered my car into a spot in the small parking lot, grabbed Iris, and bustled up a few steps to the coffee shop's garland-decorated patio, where Ashley Payne, my BFF since grade school and former roommate for both undergrad and grad school at USC in Los Angeles, sat at a table glued to her phone.

"Hey!"

"Tory!" Ashley, ensconced in a gray cashmere jogging suit, jumped up and hugged me, smooshing Iris between us.

"Please tell me you're not on that dating app again, especially after your experience the other night."

At dinner two nights ago, Ashley had told me how she'd driven all the way to Santa Barbara last weekend to meet up with a guy she met on an app who was a no-show.

"Don't worry. Lesson learned. I'm only looking at guys from Santa Sofia now. That way I can track them down if they ghost me."

I flinched as if someone had slapped me.

Ashley was cracking up. "The look of horror on your face. Just kidding. I can take a hint. No show, no go. But there're lots of fish in the sea. Like him. Isn't he cute?" She shoved her phone in my face. On the screen was a guy who looked like a Calvin Klein model in a Santa hat.

"Cute. But you don't even know if that's a real photo or not. It might be a serial killer, for all you know. Or at the very least, spam, or a scam, or—"

Ashley tossed her head back as she let out a loud laugh.

"You can laugh, or should I say snort, but just be careful, please."

"Got it. So, what's new with you?"

I petted Iris as she started to lick me. I sighed in an exaggerated fashion. "Nothing much. Had to drop off keys at the nursery for Matt Ortega because he couldn't find his. Plus, he thinks someone might have taken them to break into the nursery office, but other than that, everything's fine."

Ashley snapped to attention. "What? Wow. Did they take anything?"

I shook my head. "Doesn't look like it, thank goodness. Could you hold Iris while I grab a nonfat latte? Do you want another one?"

Ashley sat down and Iris scrambled into her lap. "That'd be great, thanks."

I ordered and paid for our coffees and hung out at the end of the counter, where I checked out a festive twinkling Christmas tree and a gift basket display. My gaze drifted to an empty table and an abandoned newspaper lying on it. I strolled over and idly skimmed the front-page headlines. News stories about a missing student in Santa Barbara, a near-miss of a drone hitting a small private plane, and the imminent release of a man wrongfully incarcerated for murder fifteen years ago. The barista shouted out my name. I grabbed the paper and scurried over to pick up our orders, finding it difficult to contain my excitement as I rushed back to our table. Iris sat on Ashley's lap like the little princess she was, scrutinizing each new passerby who waltzed past her front-row seat with the intensity of a fox stalking its prey.

"Guess what?" I handed Ashley her drink and put mine down on the table.

Ashley cocked her head as if trying to divine my thoughts, but I was bursting with my scoop and couldn't wait for her answer.

I spread out the newspaper in front of her with a flourish. "Look! Your Innocence Project case is on the front page of the *Santa Sofia Sentinel*. It says your guy's release is pending."

Her smile lit up her whole face, from her long-lashed brown eyes and dimpled brown cheeks to her lip-glossed mouth. "You mean the Justice Program. We're like the Innocence Project but locally based."

"Right. That's what I meant."

"Actually, Lyle Bubb, the guy who was wrongfully convicted of his wife's murder and has been incarcerated for the last fifteen years is due to be released this morning. A new DNA test matched blood found on the weapon to his wife's ex-boyfriend, Dwayne Rudders, who should be turning himself in today too. If all goes well, Lyle Bubb might be free even as we speak."

"Wow. That's so awesome. And you're mentioned in the article." I leaned over and pointed to her name. "See? So proud of you."

"Thanks, Tor. It's been great working with one of my old law school professors, Barry Hayes. He heads the Justice Program and UC Santa Barbara's Institute for Justice Research."

"Impressive!"

"Yup. Saving the world, one wrongly accused at a time." Ashley winked at me. "But seriously, thanks. Bubb's still not totally free and clear quite yet. Even though the judge recommended to the high court that they vacate his conviction, we still haven't got a final ruling from them."

"But you will, right?"

She nodded. "Yep. We're hoping he'll be completely exonerated in a couple of weeks."

"That's so good. You're my hero!"

"Aw. Thanks, Tory."

Ashley picked up her cup with both hands. "Oh, that warmth feels so good. Do you mind if we relocate inside?"

"Not at all. In fact, my hair thanks you."

"Girl, tell me about it. Same here."

We found a table for two next to the window. Iris settled herself on my lap, her eyes darting back and forth, thrilled to be on a perch where she could both look out the window and keep an eye on the door.

"So, tell me more about how you got him released."

Ashley pulled out a chair and then froze. "Wait. Are dogs allowed inside?"

"Yes. If they're service dogs."

"Wait. Iris is an emotional support dog now?"

"To me she is."

"Okay, if ever there was a cue begging for me to ask you about how you're doing, that was it. Are you okay?"

I chuckled because she was right. "Maybe."

"Okay, in Tory-speak, that's a hard no. Tell Dr. Payne what's troubling you." Her eyes twinkled with mirth. "Okay, I see you're looking at me skeptically. But you can't say my tell-it-like-it-is advice hasn't helped you in the past year. And may I remind you I am a doctor."

My mouth dropped open. "Of jurisprudence. You have a JD, not a PhD." I shook my head. "I can't get over you sometimes."

She giggled. "Maybe I should change my shingle to lawyer/ therapist." She raised her outstretched hands as if framing an imaginary shingle. "Yup. I can picture that. Okay, sorry. Seriously, what's going on with you?"

"Well, I saw Ellen, my *real* therapist yesterday."

"Uh-huh, uh-huh. And . . ." She nodded in jerks.

"It was okay, I guess. It's just that sometimes I feel like I'm back to normal and other times I feel like I'm only hanging on by a thread. It's been more than a year since the wedding and . . ."

Ashley reached over and squeezed my hand.

Tears welled up in my eyes, threatening to spill over like an infinity pool. In an attempt to stop the floodgate from bursting I followed Iris's gaze to the dachshund in a snazzy plaid coat outside whose owner was tugging its leash to steer it away from the poinsettias that bordered the sidewalk. While I watched, my mind flashed back to eighteen months before when I'd first met Milo Spinelli and we fell madly in love. Our wedding took place four months later. That was the last day I'd ever seen Milo. Now I'd been his widow longer than the time I'd been his girlfriend, fiancée, bride, and wife all added together but, still, I struggled with the loss.

Ashley squeezed my hand again. "You seemed fine a couple of days ago at dinner. Did something happen since then?"

I turned to face her. "I know. No, nothing in particular other than seeing Ellen yesterday for the first time in a couple of months. I hate how I feel after therapy sometimes. Dredging everything up again feels like one step forward, two steps back. I thought I'd made enough progress and that setbacks were a thing of the past. But no. Every now and then it all hits me like a mammoth wave that knocks me down."

"Aw, sorry, Tor."

"Luckily, I haven't had enough time to think about it, let alone brood, since all the RFPs I applied for came through. Benning Brothers has never been busier. So many landscape projects. Don't get me wrong. I'm not complaining. I'm so grateful the business is doing so well. But every now and then . . ." Ugh, again with the tears. I blotted my cheeks with my hands, and when I lifted my head to look at Ashley, her eyes were glued to her phone again.

Her fingers scrolled the screen. "I'm reading about Lyle Bubb's release from prison on all the news outlets. It's even on CNN." She glanced at me. "What? I'm still listening. Multitasking is my super-power."

A reluctant chuckle escaped from me. "You always get me to laugh."

"That's another one of my superpowers." She set her phone down on the table. "Look, Tory, your heart was shattered. Not just by Milo's death but your dad's too. Anyone would be distraught over that. You've been a trooper. Holding it all in while the clues were fresh and you searched for justice. So now, as you start to process your loss more, it's only natural that you're going to have waves of sadness. See what I did there with your wave metaphor?"

Again, I was unsuccessful in stifling a slight chortle.

She resumed looking at her phone. "I think it's especially hard for someone like you who always needs to be in control of everything. And your go-to MO in any stressful situation is denial. I get that because I'm a bit like that myself. But it's that very combo of needing to always be in control and denying your negative emotions that makes for a delayed reaction. You're like the human version of an extended-release Tylenol."

"You think I'm prolonging my pain on purpose?"

She threw me a glance. "No. More like putting off dealing with it until you can handle it."

She was right. The good thing about using denial as my coping mechanism of choice was that sometimes, by the time I was ready to deal, the problem had gone away. But not this time. Their loss and the pain of that loss remained. My father and Milo were gone, and they weren't coming back.

"Thanks, Ash. You've been helping me so much through what has been the worst time of my life . . . wait, did you just call me a control freak?"

Ashley burst out in a laugh. "I was wondering if you caught that. Let's just say you have tendencies to be compulsive, about work, exercise, and your little dog too." She delivered the last phrase in her Wicked Witch of the West voice and cuffed Iris under the chin. "But you'll bounce back. You've always been a strong person. You've got this."

"Well, I don't feel very strong right now. Look at me, blubbering like a baby."

Iris started to manically lick my cheeks.

I accepted the tissue Ashley offered me. "Thanks. Sorry for losing it."

Both our phones pinged at the same time. I checked my phone. It was a text from Jake Logan, a PI I'd met last year during the series of harrowing events that occurred after my husband Milo's disappearance. *Something came up at work. Might need to take a rain check on dinner.*

Jake lived more than twelve miles away in Santa Barbara. He had planned to drive up to Santa Sofia tonight. It would have been the first time we'd seen each other since Halloween.

Ashley held up her phone. "How come you didn't tell me you were having dinner with Jake tonight?"

My face heated up. "What? How did you know?"

"No offense, but your boyfriend seems a tad technologically challenged since he just texted you on our group thread."

I checked my phone. He'd texted me on a group thread comprised of me, Ashley, and Adrian Ramirez, an old schoolmate of ours and now a cop with the Santa Sofia Police Department. The four of us had texted to discuss our Halloween plans.

"Like you've never done that. I do it all the time."

"Calm down, girl. I'm just joking with you. Not criticizing your boyfriend."

"And please stop calling Jake my boyfriend."

If I'd been ready for a relationship, I'd look no further than Jake. But I was in no way ready for a romance. Some days I wondered whether I'd ever be. But I figured a little friendly flirting was fine since it gave me something to look forward to on the days when it was hard to even get out of bed. Ellen, my therapist, called it innocent "grief relief" that was good for my mental health.

I took a deep breath, adding, "Nothing could be further from the truth."

"Oh, okay. How about this? I'll stop when you stop calling Adrian my boyfriend."

We glared at each other for all of five seconds before we both burst out laughing.

"Touché."

"Let's agree to not refer to either of them as boyfriends. Deal?"

"Deal."

My phone pinged again. I glanced at the screen. It had a calendar reminder. "Shoot, I didn't realize it was this late. I told Emma Evans I'd meet her at her food truck. It's at our tree lot today."

This was the second year we'd hired Emma to cater our Benning Brothers Christmas party. Her food was such a success last year that when Emma expanded her catering business to include a food truck over the summer, I'd jumped at the chance to book her for our tree lot this season. Emma's food truck became Mrs. Claus's kitchen for the month of December, with Mrs. Claus played by none other than Emma herself. There'd been a little bit of friction with Cynthia, our normal food trucker, but once I'd assured Cynthia she wasn't being replaced, merely augmented, peace had been restored. After we'd worked out a mutually agreed upon schedule for both vendors, all was well.

"Do you want to come?"

Ashley hesitated.

"What? Do you have somewhere else to be?"

She shook her head. "Not really."

"Then come. She's catering our Christmas party this year at the Hotel Santa Sofia. We need to discuss the menu. Tasting samples might be involved."

"When you put it that way."

"Yay! It'll be fun."

She gave me a half-hearted smile, making me wonder whether she really wanted to go or not.

"Look, if you have other stuff to do, I understand."

"No, it's not that."

"Then what?"

She paused before answering, as if choosing her words carefully, then smiled. "It's nothing."

"Okay. Great." I stood and brushed off strands of dog hair Iris had deposited on my puffer vest and black velvet leggings. "I can drive and then drop you off at your car later. Let's take these lattes to go. They'll go great with Emma's scrumptious gingerbread. And maybe a few of my fave Christmas sugar cookies with a hint of anise. And—"

Ashley gave me a fist bump. "You had me at gingerbread."

Iris rode shotgun with Ashley. We cruised over to the Benning Brothers tree lot singing along to classics on a radio station that had featured twenty-four-seven Christmas songs since the day after Thanksgiving. I'd been a longtime fan of oldies because my father always used to listen to them. He'd told me the old songs reminded him of my late mother and the happy times of their romance and early years together. It was my way of connecting to them both now.

We pulled into the parking lot for the Benning Brothers landscape architecture division, located in a one-story, designated-historical adobe building across the street from our tree lot. I opened the car door humming "Jingle Bell Rock." Other than the Christmas radio station, I hadn't really gotten into the Christmas spirit much this year. It wasn't the same last year without my father. And I'd never even gotten the chance to celebrate Christmas with Milo, since we'd met in the spring and he was gone by the fall.

As soon as I set Iris down on the pavement, she pulled at her leash raring to go. The sun was peeking through the low clouds as we all headed in the direction of the tree lot.

Ashley rubbed her hands together. "I love this cooler weather. Makes it feel more Christmassy now, doesn't it?"

Right before we crossed the street, I spotted a guy in a Santa suit smoking a cigarette at the far end of the parking lot.

"Tory. Are you listening to me?"

"Sorry. I'm just trying to figure out who that guy is in the Santa outfit. That's the third guy in a Santa outfit today. He's walking away from us so I can't get a good look at him to see who he is, but I know it's not Matt Ortega because he doesn't smoke. The only person who's supposed to wear a Santa suit is the tree lot manager on duty, and that's Matt today because I was here earlier, and he was wearing it. So, who the heck is this guy? I noticed Fuji, our associate manager, coming to the lot earlier on my way to Starbucks and he was wearing a Santa suit too. He doesn't smoke that I know of. Whoever it is, he should know better than to smoke while working, especially a manager, not to mention the fire hazard. I'll have to talk to Matt about it."

"If he has to smoke, it should be a pipe, like Santa. At least make it authentic, right?"

I chuckled. "Exactly."

Ashley tossed her cup into a sidewalk trash receptacle. "I've already had enough caffeine today. I think I'll order some of Emma's home-made eggnog to go with my gingerbread."

"Me too. It's to die for. Too bad it's so early. I like it best heated up with a shot of cream sherry in it."

Ashley nodded. "Now you're talking! And sprinkled with nutmeg."

I nodded. "Yum!"

The Benning Brothers Christmas tree lot had become a popular Santa Sofia fixture over the years. When I was a little girl, each December first my father launched the tree lot's opening day dressed as Santa Claus. We'd changed the opening date to late November and now the manager on duty donned the Santa suit every day, not just on opening day.

I breathed in the fresh pine scent bursting from the lot. As we approached Emma's food truck parked at the curb, the aroma of cinnamon, nutmeg, and sugar wafted in the air too. The truck's shutters were rolled down. Odd.

I checked my phone. It was ten fifteen. "That's weird. Emma usually opens at ten on the dot on Saturdays."

Ashley nodded in the direction of the parking lot. "She'd better hurry up. Customers are on their way. As soon as she raises her shutter it will be a madhouse."

I looked across at the parking lot and it was already filling up with cars entering in a steady stream. One of our employees in a Santa suit was directing traffic.

"Wow. That was fast. And is that a fourth Santa now?"

Ashley turned to me. "I didn't see him there a couple of minutes ago when we drove up, unless he's the guy we saw smoking. But that Santa seemed to be walking away from the parking lot. Traffic director Santa has his back turned to us so I can't tell if it's the same guy. Not that I'd be able to anyway. They all look alike to me."

As we got closer to the food truck, we could hear female voices coming from inside. They were arguing.

Ashley shot me an alarmed glance. "Welp. So much for Christmas cheer."

I gave her a weak smile. At the tree lot entrance Matt Ortega stood inches away from two employees, both also dressed in Santa Claus suits, raising his voice and gesturing emphatically.

"Oh, my goodness. Two more. Looks like every employee is wearing a Santa suit today."

Ashley whispered under her breath, "Somebody got their signals crossed."

"So far, I've seen how many? Four or five in Santa suits?"

Ashley counted on her hand. "There was the one smoking, the one directing traffic, and then Matt and the two he's talking to. One, two, three, four, five. That's enough for a SantaCon." She spread her fingers on her open hand for emphasis.

"That's crazy. Five Santas. That's assuming Fuji is one of the two talking to Matt, otherwise that's six."

Ashley pointed. "Look! There's another one in a tree aisle on his cell phone. That's six or seven. Or is that one we counted before?"

I turned my head. "Maybe that's Fuji."

"Either that or they're multiplying." She laughed heartily at her own joke. "Aren't there usually guys dressed up as elves and reindeer too?"

"Yup. I really need to talk to Matt to see what's going on."

Ashley squinted at Matt Ortega waving his arms in seeming annoyance as he spoke to the two Santas. "I don't think I've ever seen Matt so agitated before. He's usually so calm and even-tempered. He's acting more like Scrooge than Santa."

"I know. Something is definitely up."

Christmas was the most profitable time of the year for Benning Brothers Nursery. Our tree lot was *the* place for the freshest and largest selection of cut and live Christmas trees, wreaths, garlands, poinsettias, holly, and mistletoe in Santa Sofia. The last thing we needed was Santa Claus chewing out Santa wannabes and Mrs. Claus yelling at her helper. At least I'd assumed it was Rachel Downey, Emma's assistant, with whom Emma was fighting.

Suddenly, the long shutter of the silver food truck's window clanked open. Emma spotted us and waved. Her trendy version of Mrs. Claus consisted of a Santa hat she wore more like a slouchy beanie with the pointy end to the side, a fitted red jacket with white fur cuffs and, although I couldn't tell from my vantage point, I guessed the black leggings she usually favored for comfort.

14

She greeted us with a forced smile. "Good morning, ladies! What can I get you?"

Though I only had a partial view through the truck window, her assistant, Rachel, seemed to be clad in the same Santa costume she always wore, one that screamed pole dancer more than North Pole. Her V-necked minidress had an attached fur-trimmed hood that her long auburn waves peeked out from. Eight-inch fur cuffs trimmed the long narrow sleeves and the tightly belted skirt. She usually wore high-heeled black boots to complete her look. She opened the side flap of the truck without saying a word. When she turned around, she glanced at Emma with a threatening stare, her brows crossed in an angry frown. As soon as our gazes met, her expression went blank.

I decided to pretend all was well. "Hi, Emma! Hi, Rachel! How's it going?"

Rachel pouted and finally muttered a desultory "Fine."

Emma paused with pursed lips before she spoke in her normal cheery voice. "Fine, thanks. Don't mind Rachel. We had a minor miscommunication. We left the eggnog back at the kitchen. Rachel's going to retrieve it."

As if on cue, Rachel bounded out of the truck and mumbled something about meeting a car on the corner.

"Is this still a good time for us to discuss the Christmas party menu? Emma, you know my friend Ashley, right?"

Emma rested her gaze on Ashley and nodded.

Ashley extended her hand to Emma. "Hi, I've seen you at the truck before, but that was before we communicated online. Anyway, nice to meet in person and be formally introduced."

I snapped my head to look at Ashley. "You met online? Like on a dating app?"

Ashley chuckled. "No, no, no. I misspoke. We've communicated recently by email and text."

I raised my eyebrows. "Oh."

Ashley winked at Emma. "We know each other professionally."

I waited, and since neither of them volunteered any more information, I assumed that either Emma was a client of Ashley's or Ashley had inquired about ordering herself a cake for her upcoming birthday.

Eager to end the awkward silence, I went to my go-to chitchat. "Speaking of online dating—"

Ashley interrupted. "Just to be clear, we weren't."

I smiled. "Ashley's been playing around with dating apps lately. She already got stood up once."

Ashley gave me the side eye. "Thanks for sharing the details of my dating life, Tory."

Emma laughed. "Hey, I can relate. Been there, done that. Fun at first, but it gets old quick."

Ashley chuckled. "I was planning to introduce myself formally the next time we met in person so you could match my name to my face. I knew what you looked like, but I wasn't sure whether you knew my name. I come to your truck as often as possible. Oh, and I'll have a piece of gingerbread, please. I wanted an eggnog too, but I guess I'll have to wait on that."

Using waxed paper, Emma selected a hefty chunk of gingerbread and slid it into a little brown paper bag and handed it to Ashley. "Well, I'm glad you introduced yourself. Here you go."

Emma turned to me. "What could I get for you, Tory?"

"I'd like a slice of gingerbread too, please."

"Coming right up." Emma paused and frowned. "I'm sorry, Tory. I seem to have gotten off on the wrong side of the sleigh today. Can we wait until Rachel gets back to discuss your Christmas party menu since I'm the only one manning the truck right now?"

"Sure. I need to go talk to Matt anyway."

She bagged the gingerbread and handed it to me.

"Thanks." I peered into the truck. "Hey, isn't that eggnog on the back shelf?"

Emma grimaced and turned around to look. "Oh! Yes. I thought we'd forgotten to bring it."

Ashley and I stole brief bewildered looks at each other.

Emma blushed and poured us both an eggnog. "Here's a Christmas cookie for each of you, too."

Ashley reached for her wallet. "I'll get this."

"No, let me." I dug around in my purse.

Emma held up her hand. "Please. They're on the house. I'm sorry for having to make you wait to discuss your party menu. I can meet with you once Rachel gets back in about ten minutes or so."

Who didn't love free cookies! Especially anise sugar cookies!

She handed us the eggnog in paper cups. "We've done so well here at the tree lot thanks to you, Tory." She paused with a sheepish grin. "I guess you could say we have had tree-mendous success parking our food truck here."

The high-pitched titter came from me. "This is one of the many reasons why I've loved our partnership, Emma. You're so punny. And your baked goods, of course."

I set down my eggnog and cookies on the truck's counter and found a twenty-dollar bill in my wallet. I stuck it in the tip jar. "Thank you, Emma! My pleasure. Our trees and other floral department items are really moving this year thanks to the draw of your food truck. I'll circle back in about fifteen minutes."

Ashley nodded at Emma. "I'll be in touch."

Ashley and I strolled several feet away and then both of us started to speak at the same time.

I smiled. "How do you know Emma?"

"Mm. So good! That was nice of you to compliment her and leave a big tip. Is it true business is booming because of her?"

"Yes. So much so that I've heard Santa's Helpers tree lot, our main competitor two blocks north, also wanted Emma at their lot this year when they saw her popularity here. As did Yamamoto Nurseries. But she declined because she thought it would be too hectic to swing more than one location given all her catering commitments too. So, you're not going to tell me, are you?"

"What?"

"Don't act coy. About why you and Emma have an online relationship apparently."

"No online relationship. I told you already. We've exchanged emails several times."

"About what? But I can tell you're not going to tell me."

She smiled. "You are correct. If I could, I would."

"Alrighty then." I knew Emma must be Ashley's client or something related to legal stuff. Otherwise, there'd be no reason to be secretive.

We strolled over to the tree lot entrance. Matt was there greeting people but the two employees he'd been wagging his finger at were now working in the noble firs aisle. At least I thought it was them. As I looked around, two more Santas were helping customers in the Norfolk and Douglas fir aisles.

Ashley sipped her eggnog. "It's really feeling more and more like a SantaCon."

"Right? Fun for adults dressed up but confusing for little kids that come with their families to get a tree."

Ashley gasped. "I never thought of that. Way to totally confuse children."

Matt greeted me. "Ho, ho, ho!"

"Glad to see Santa's in a better mood. What was going on earlier?"

"Yeah. I was ticked off. Some bozo told everyone to wear a Santa costume today. Thought they were being funny, I guess."

"Ah. That explains the SantaCon effect, as Ashley called it."

Matt guffawed. "Good one."

Ashley nodded in thanks.

"So, who was it? Who told everyone to wear Santa outfits?"

"Well, Fuji has been doing the scheduling. He claims he was scheduled to be the manager today. He swears everyone else was designated as staff. That means they knew to wear either an elf hat or reindeer antlers. I want to believe him but . . ."

He looked behind me. I turned to see Fuji.

"Hi, Tory! I swear I don't know how everyone got an email telling them to wear a Santa suit. Someone must have hacked my account or something. Weird prank."

Ashley raised her perfectly arched brows. "So strange. How did everyone get a Santa suit anyway?"

I took a sip of my eggnog. "We issue three Christmas outfits to all tree lot employees at the beginning of each season. Only the acting manager wears the Santa suit. Keeps it fun."

Ashley cocked her head. "So theoretically, all tree lot employees can be a manager?"

I nodded. "Yup. Most of them are our regular nursery employees, and even most of our seasonal employees are regulars. Am I right, Matt?"

Matt leaned in, his Old Spice cologne reminding me of when my dad had played Santa. "Correct. The main distinction is that managers open and lock up. The costumes help create the Christmas spirit and build great morale during a busy season."

Ashley nibbled her gingerbread. "So how many managers do you have?"

Matt crossed his arms. "Six. There's me, my associate manager, Fuji, and then four assistant managers. I've spoken to Aparicio and Collins already. Haven't seen the other two, but Fuji told me they're here too. Right, Fuji?"

Fuji shifted his weight. "Yeah. They're both here."

Ashley dabbed her mouth with a napkin from the gingerbread bag. "Is it common for all the managers to be scheduled to work at the same time?"

Matt lifted his fake beard to scratch his chin. "No, not at all. That's why Fuji says he was hacked."

Fuji shifted from one foot to the other. "We have a simple rotation schedule. I email it to everyone in advance each week. I call it the SER system, for Santa, Elf, or Reindeer." He paused, as if waiting for compliments on his acronym. "Anyhow, if there are changes because someone is sick or needs to take a personal day, I send out an updated schedule to everyone."

I turned to Fuji. "So, someone hacked your email and sent out an updated email to all the managers, asking them to show up wearing their Santa suit today?"

"Yep. That's what seems to have happened."

"Do either of you have a phone on you so I can see a copy of the email?"

Matt dug into the deep pockets of his Santa pants and got his phone. He found the email and showed it to me and Ashley. "I was supposed to be off today, but this email told me the schedule had changed and I was scheduled to be manager today."

"Sorry, boss. It wasn't me who changed it. I promise." Fuji rubbed his nose. "It's someone's idea of a joke."

Matt took back his phone. "Whatever. Tell the guys to unload the new shipment of trees off the truck now and put stands on them."

Fuji shrugged his shoulders and followed Matt's orders.

I put my hands on my hips. "So, what do you think, Matt?"

"He seems to be telling the truth to me."

"Yeah, he seemed sincere to me too. Why would he make it up? By the way, why do you have someone directing traffic in the parking lot? That's never been necessary before, has it?"

"I sent Connor there to get him out of earshot when I was talking about the apparent email hack. I have a feeling he might know something about it."

Just then, Connor started to head our way. "Lot's full, boss."

Connor was the strapping grandson of Chris Kringle, the owner of our main competitor, the Santa's Helpers tree lot. I didn't know his backstory but, apparently, he was working at both lots this season for some reason related to scheduling part-timers.

Matt tipped his head. "Thanks. Hey, Connor, those fellows out back need help unloading the trucks. Can you give them a hand?"

Connor nodded to me as he passed by and continued down the aisle of trees to the rear of the lot.

After he disappeared into the greenery, I turned to Matt. "Why do you suspect Connor? He always seems helpful to me."

Matt pivoted and scanned the lot. His eyes widened at the now-crowded tree lot filling up with families on the hunt for the perfect tree. "Nothing specific. Just a hunch. Anyway, the good news is it looks like we're in for a banner day."

"Yes. Indeed, it does. I'll let you get back to work." I turned to Ashley. "Let's go back to the food truck and see if Rachel got back yet."

We went over to the food truck, where a few customers stood with puzzled faces.

I stepped up to look inside. No Emma or Rachel anywhere to be seen. "Sorry, everyone. No one is here at the moment to help you. I'm sure they'll be right back. Maybe take a look around at the trees first and come back later. I'm sure they'll be back soon and happy to serve you then."

The small group dispersed.

Ashley tipped her cup. "Hey, I need to get my tree. Did you get yours yet? Let's get ours now while we wait for Emma."

"I don't know if I'm up for a Christmas tree this year."

"Sure, you are. It'll cheer you up. You love Christmas."

"Okay. Won't hurt to look, I guess."

She knew me well. She trotted over to the cashier's hut, where we displayed our wreaths, garlands, mistletoe, and other related decorations. "OMG. I love these! Look at these cute little reindeer made out of tree boughs! Iris, they're just your size!"

"I've always loved those reindeer," I said. "I should get one for my front door. Look Iris, a friend."

Ashley roared as Iris sniffed the reindeer. "She loves it! Now you have to get one. That's my girl. Get excited!"

Ashley's enthusiasm was contagious. And who didn't like strolling through rows of tall Christmas trees. "Okay. Definitely getting one of those reindeer on my way out. Now, let's go cruise the tree aisles."

I loved our tree lot. It was like a mini forest and Benning Brothers carried the widest variety of any Santa Sofia lot. We ambled through the rows of cut and live noble, Nordmann, and Douglas firs, differentiated by their color, shape, branches, needles, and fragrance. Nobles were the most popular trees in California, noted for their strong branches good for supporting ornaments. But Nordmanns, the front-runner Christmas tree in the United Kingdom, were enjoying a U.S. boon and were popular, in addition to Douglas fir, Norwich, Scotch pines, and blue spruce, some of the other types of trees Benning Brothers carried.

Our lot was arranged according to tree type and height. Up front were the tabletops. Way in back were the super tall ones, mainly purchased by banks and people with houses from Ryder Ranch and Sycamore Canyon, two affluent Santa Sofia neighborhoods with houses large enough to accommodate a nine-foot tree. Most people shopped in the six- to seven-foot and the seven- to eight-foot tree aisles.

I was curious to see whether we had many nine-footers left. Most commercial and residential buyers of nine-footers typically bought theirs early. They were pricey and buyers wanted to get their money's worth.

Ashley and I split up. I meandered the sawdust-laden aisles lost in my winter wonderland reverie. Iris was having a ball sniffing each branch on each tree. I walked toward the rear of the lot. One of our employees in a Santa suit crossed the aisle holding a tree but I couldn't see who it was. Then, another, or was it the same one, from the opposite direction, crossed a few minutes later. Iris growled at the first Santa, but with the second Santa, Iris was having none of it and tried to charge him, jerking like a bucking bronco when she came to the end of her lead. I scooped her up to quiet her. "Don't bark at Santa or he'll leave coal in your stocking."

Ashley texted me. *I found one I like. Come and look!*

I texted her back. *In a minute. Want to see how many big trees are left.* I strolled all the way to the back of the lot, enjoying the Christmas songs we'd piped in. The first nine-footer I saw was a gorgeous, perfectly shaped noble fir with a *Sold* tag on it. Next to it, a beautiful flocked Douglas fir, also with a *Sold* tag. I started to count. One, two, three . . . up to seven big trees. Most had sold, waiting for delivery.

As I turned up the aisle to go meet Ashley, I caught a flash of red in my peripheral vision. My first thought was that one of our employees had peeled off their Santa jacket because they got too hot lugging trees. I started to walk over to pick it up and then accelerated my pace as I realized it wasn't just a jacket. It was a red-and-white Mrs. Claus jacket and black leggings. And Emma Evans was still wearing them. Emma was sprawled on the ground, faceup, her chest soaked in blood that had already colored the white trim of her costume. Her hat was on the ground.

I bent down to turn Emma over when I noticed another pool of blood starting to fan out from underneath her head. Her eyes were open but there wasn't even a flicker in them.

"No, no, no! Oh my god, no!" I screamed. "Ashley, come quick!"

Iris wrapped her paws around my forearm.

Another scream emanated from my lips, and Iris gripped me tighter. "Ashley! Help! It's Emma!"

Chapter 2

"Tory! Where are you?"

"Ashley, I'm here." I was shaking so much my voice quavered.

"Where?" Ashley's voice got louder and more frantic with each repetition.

"I'm at the back of the lot. Near the street." My gaze was frozen on Emma. I was in shock at the sight of her seemingly lifeless body on the ground.

Ashley gasped when she reached me. "Oh my god! What happened? Is she okay?"

I willed myself to tear my gaze away from Emma and look at Ashley. I shook my head. "No, I don't think so. She doesn't look good. Looks like she has a bad head injury."

Ashley let out another gasp as she shifted her gaze from me to Emma. "Oh my god, look at all the blood. She's bleeding badly."

I looked down in horror at the growing pool of blood flowing from her head. "I don't think she's breathing."

Ashley reached for Emma's wrist. "I can't feel a pulse, can you?"

I leaned over to make a weak attempt to take Emma's pulse. I shook my head. "No. I don't know though. Call nine-one-one. I don't want to set Iris down on the ground."

Iris had been unusually docile during all this time. I was trembling and Iris sensed my fear, wrapping her paws around my forearm like a little koala bear.

Ashley's hands were shaking as she dialed nine-one-one on her phone. "I need an ambulance right away. Someone here is unconscious and bleeding badly. Looks like she's been attacked with some kind of weapon. She's not breathing."

I struggled to control the tremor in my voice. "Head injury. Tell them she has a head injury."

"She has a bad head injury, among other injuries. Her eyes are open, but she's not blinking." Ashley paused, reluctant to confirm the obvious. "I think she might be dead. We're at the Benning Brothers Christmas tree lot on Manzanita Street."

"Give them the address."

"That's right, on Manzanita Street." Ashley looked at me. "She said they have it. They said to stay on the line. I'll put it on speaker."

Iris still gripped me tightly and I kissed her head.

Ashley petted Iris and Iris reciprocated by licking Ashley's hand. "I think we should stick together until the ambulance gets here. Did you see anyone?"

I shifted my gaze from side to side and turned around to check my surroundings. "All I saw were Santas. But that's all we've been seeing all morning."

Ashley shuddered as she hooked her arm around my free arm. Normally, this might have made Iris growl, but she seemed to sense it was a gesture of solidarity. Nor did Iris flail to get down, for which I was grateful since there was no way I was going to let her muck around in what was clearly a crime scene.

Matt Ortega came running up. "What's going on? Some customers said someone was sick?"

"Someone attacked Emma."

Matt's eyes popped open and instantaneously brimmed with tears. "No, Emma! No, no." He bent down over Emma's chest to listen for a heartbeat. After about fifteen seconds he turned to us. "I don't hear a heartbeat."

A screeching siren and the loud rumbling of a fire truck came to an abrupt stop, followed by the sound of other fire trucks.

Ashley squeezed my arm. "I'll go meet the EMTs so I can show them where we are."

A small group of customers peered from the aisles of trees. Fuji appeared and kept them at bay, telling the growing cluster of people to clear the main aisle for the EMTs. The next minute two EMTs ran to Emma. Behind them were a couple of other firefighters, who told people to clear the area.

I hovered over the EMTs. "Is she?"

An EMT bent over Emma and took her pulse. After a minute that felt like an eternity he stood and shook his head. "I'm afraid she's gone."

My gut felt like someone was punching and kneading it like bread dough. An overwhelming sense of fear came over me as I realized the power of the violence that had been wreaked on Emma. A person angry and violent enough to kill her. A person who was on the loose. As I tried to process what had happened, I realized that I'd probably seen the murderer as I'd made my way to the back of the lot. Suddenly, my stomach felt even queasier.

A fireman whistled as he turned Emma's body over. If there had been any doubt she was dead, the deep gash at the back of her head confirmed it. My knees felt weak and buckled slightly. More sirens pierced the air and then suddenly ceased. The next minute several members of the SSPD trotted through the tree lot, led by Adrian Ramirez, our childhood friend who'd recently been promoted to lieutenant in the detective division. He and Ashley had struck up a closer relationship in the past two years that was on-again, off-again, mainly because of Adrian's driving ambition to work his way up in the SSPD and Ashley's reaction to the time he spent working so much.

Adrian nodded to us. His solemn expression briefly softened when he recognized the victim. "I know her. The food truck lady, right? Did anyone see what happened or who did this?"

I edged closer. "I found her. I didn't see anyone. Just . . ."

"What?"

"I saw two Santas in the aisles right before I found her."

Adrian stood up and instantly directed his gaze to Matt and Fuji, both of whom were wearing Santa suits.

Matt answered Adrian's unspoken question first. "I'm the manager today, even though I hadn't planned to be."

Adrian knitted his brows together and glanced at Fuji.

Fuji shuffled his feet. "I was out back organizing today's scheduled deliveries and making sure last night's shipment was unloaded. There were several guys there with me when we heard the commotion."

Adrian's gaze roamed the small gathering of customers and employees, lingering for a few seconds on two of our managers, Aparicio and Collins, who were both wearing Santa outfits, before moving on and landing on me.

Iris wiggled, fed up with being held in my arms for such a long time.

I adjusted her position and stepped closer to Adrian. "Ashley and I first talked to Emma about twenty minutes ago, before we talked to Matt and looked at trees. Emma and I had planned to discuss the menu for our Christmas party she was going to cater but she told us she couldn't step away until Rachel returned to the food truck, so she said to come back in about ten minutes."

Rachel slipped through the small crowd that had gathered. She shrieked and the horror animating her eyes was almost palpable. When Matt Ortega spotted Rachel, he strode over and encased her in his arms.

I turned to Ashley to see her reaction. She had a glassy stare and swayed beside me. The next second she leaned on me heavily.

"Ashley, are you okay?"

She clearly wasn't.

"Can someone help me, please? My friend looks faint. Can someone help her?"

Fuji took a step forward to help.

An EMT was a step ahead of him and grabbed Ashley around the waist and stabilized her by propping her up against him. "Take a deep breath. That's great. Let it out slowly. Another breath. Slowly. Let it out slowly."

Fuji disappeared and returned quickly with a folding chair for her to sit on. The firefighter steered her over to it and sat her down. He told her to put her head down. Fuji rushed away and came back with a water bottle. After several minutes Ashley looked better and seemed fully revived. Although the jury was out on whether it was the deep breathing, the water, or the cute firefighter that did the trick.

Ashley stood up shakily, steadying herself by gripping the back of the chair. Once she gained her balance, she gazed into the firefighter's eyes. "You look so familiar. Don't I know you?"

My concern for her immediately intensified. What was she blabbering about?

Ashley managed a weak smile. "Didn't we meet at the Firefighters Benefit about a year ago? At the Hotel Santa Sofia? You're—"

"Trey. That's right." The firefighter nodded.

Now I remembered him, too, because he'd fixed my shoe's broken heel on that fateful night. Ashley had been obsessed with him as soon as she laid eyes on him.

Trey smiled. "Yes, we did. I was wondering if you'd remember me. Your memory seems fine. That's always a good sign. How are you feeling?"

"Much better now, thanks." Ashley straightened out her cashmere hoodie. Her purred response sounded like my cat Otis when he rubbed against my legs after being fed.

I whispered to Trey, "She's always been squeamish around blood."

Trey nodded. "She's not alone on that. But she looks like she'll survive. She's a strong lady."

It was difficult to discern whether Ashley's half grin was due to her wooziness or if she'd swooned in response to Trey's description of her. Probably both.

Adrian's gaze surveyed the small crowd of employees and customers. "Okay, everyone. This is a crime scene. Can everyone please take a couple steps back? Thank you."

Other cops started to put up yellow crime scene tape.

Adrian turned to Ashley and me. "I'd like both of you to stay here, please, while I ask you some questions. Everyone else please stay on the lot. We'll be talking to each of you at the front of the lot while we check out the area. After you've completed an interview with us, you'll be free to leave. Now, please follow the officer to the front of the lot for interviews. Thank you for your cooperation."

Ashley leaned over and whispered to me, "This is creepily familiar."

"I know. Finding murder victims among the greenery is not a habit I want to form." I squeezed her upper arm. "Are you sure you're okay?"

"I'm fine now, thanks. I think it's the initial shock that stresses my system."

"Good. You had me and Iris worried."

"Aw, thanks, Iris." Ashley held out her hand for Iris to lick.

It never failed to amaze me how our lives can change in a second. One minute everything is fine, the next minute disaster, and vice versa. We never knew what was around the next corner.

I stared at the nearby trees, lost in their dark density, thinking how their beauty was one of the last things Emma had seen before she died. I tried to imagine how it could have possibly happened. Emma lured from the food truck somehow, walking through the tree lot, possibly ambushed. Or had she arranged an urgent meeting with someone among the forest of trees looking for an out-of-earshot place to talk, her assailant getting agitated and grabbing something to hit her with? I looked around. There was nothing around the lot normally that I could think of that could be used as a weapon. I had to surmise the killer had brought a weapon and kept it. Or tossed it somewhere nearby. In either case it struck me as premeditated.

"Tory?"

"Huh? Oh, sorry. What did I miss?"

Adrian raised his black eyebrows. "Um, nothing. I was waiting for you to tell me how Emma seemed to you today. Was she her normal self? Or did she seem frightened?"

"Oh, sorry. I was just thinking about her and her last moments and zoned out for a moment. She seemed normal. Definitely not frightened. If anything, she was in a kick-ass mood. She was unhappy with Rachel for . . ." I stopped myself and glanced over at Rachel, who, along with Matt, still lingered at the crime scene. I didn't want to incriminate Rachel.

"That's okay, Tory." Rachel turned to Adrian. "Emma and I quarreled this morning. It wasn't a big deal."

"What did you quarrel about?" Adrian jotted in his notebook.

"Nothing important really."

Adrian stared at Rachel for a few seconds. "Care to elaborate?"

"Oh, it was about eggnog. We forgot the eggnog."

I must have failed to suppress my feelings of surprise because Adrian turned to me and said, "What? Something wrong?"

I felt as if Rachel's laser-like gaze would burn a hole in my face if I didn't turn away. "Um, no, just that they had eggnog. I saw it."

At this, Ashley nodded her head to back me up, her bouncy curls emphasizing her agreement. "Yup. Emma even gave us some eggnog on the house after Tory spotted it."

"When I pointed out the eggnog on the shelf to Emma, I just got the feeling that she was using the eggnog as an excuse for what they were really arguing about."

"Sorry, Rachel, that's how I interpreted it too." Ashley shot Rachel an exaggerated pout.

Rachel glowered at us. "Maybe try not to stick your nose into other people's business. Look where that has led us."

Adrian stepped in between us. "Whoa. Hold up. Are you saying you know who killed Emma?"

"Isn't it obvious? It's me. I argued with her therefore according to Sherlock and Watson here, I must be the killer."

"Wait, Rachel. I don't know where you got the idea that I think you murdered Emma. I just wanted to be perfectly honest with Adrian. He needs to know everything so he can nab the right person." Although even as my self-righteous words were rolling off my tongue, I felt like biting my tongue, because clearly whatever they'd been arguing about made them both huffy.

Adrian's gaze fell on Ashley for a second before he scanned the small group of onlookers who lingered around us. The corners of his mouth turned down ever so slightly. "Okay, thank you all for helping us and sticking around, but we must clear this area now as it's a crime scene. We'd greatly appreciate it if you could all move to the front of the lot, where you can give your formal statements to one of our officers. If for some reason you can't stick around for another hour or so, please speak to me first about scheduling an appointment to give your formal statement at the police station. That being said, it is of the utmost importance that you give your formal statements as soon as possible while everything is still fresh in your minds."

Most everyone seemed to appreciate the need to stick around and give their statements to him. After Adrian thanked them, they trickled toward the front of the lot.

Adrian stepped closer to us. "Sorry, Tory, but we'll need to close the tree lot to protect the integrity of our investigation."

"You can use the nursery offices if you want for interviews."

"Thanks. That would be great."

"How long will the lot be closed for?"

"Minimum, a couple of hours, but possibly until tomorrow. Sorry, I know this is an important time of year. We'll do the best we can to open it as soon as we can."

My knees got wobbly.

Adrian grabbed my arm. "Are you okay?"

"Yeah. I'm fine. I think my body is having a delayed reaction to the shock of it all. Emma's murder is just starting to sink in. And now with the lot closed. I know you're just doing your job, and finding her killer is the number-one priority, but it's just . . ."

Another murder was bad enough, not to mention all that it triggered for me. But another trigger was gunning for me on a different level. Clearly not as tragic or profound as a murder, but still powerful, nevertheless. It was difficult for me to admit to myself, let alone Adrian, but it wasn't just Emma's murder that got me weak-kneed. Closing the lot for a whole day during our most profitable time of year would result in a big chunk of lost revenue, which triggered my anxiety related to when Benning Brothers had financial difficulties not too long ago. And I was just getting over that. I couldn't bear to go through it all again. I certainly didn't want to relive it. Coupled with the thought of another murderer running around, this was a lot of déjà vu to process.

Ashley stood taller and adjusted her cashmere outfit. "It's not just an important time of the year, it's the most important. December is the most profitable month for Benning Brothers' nursery business and its Christmas profits support the company throughout its leaner months. It affects everyone, all her employees and vendors, not just Tory."

"Yeah. Our seasonal employees depend on us too. Some have been coming back here to supplement their income at Christmas for years."

Adrian acknowledged us with a nod. He asked Matt and Rachel to follow one of the officers to the nursery offices. I turned to watch them walk away just as SSPD Sergeant Ernesto Gomez, aka Ernie, showed up coming from the opposite direction. Like Adrian, Ernie was a childhood acquaintance with whom I'd recently been reacquainted. But unlike my reconnection with Adrian, which had been a pleasure, reconnecting with Ernie had all the charm of finding a moldy piece of cheese in your refrigerator. Like the cheese, Ernie had been a little stinker when I'd first met him in middle school, but when I met him again as an adult, I'd found he'd gotten even worse, not only stinky, but slimy too. What's more, he'd morphed into something even more distasteful, a cop on a power trip who threw his weight around. The type of cop who arrested first and asked questions later. I knew from firsthand experience. Last year he'd tried to pin a couple of murders on me. That, in a nutshell, was Ernie. I hadn't run into him since then.

Ernie nodded in our direction, oddly civil for him, given his general lack of empathy. Even in distressing situations where there'd been a loss of life, he could be a real jerk.

I turned slightly and whispered to Ashley, "What's up with Ernie? Weirdly restrained for him."

Ashley pretended to cough and raised her hand to cover her mouth. "I don't know. Maybe he's sick?"

"Maybe. Something's definitely up. No snide remarks or ogling."

Adrian grabbed his phone from his pocket. "Tory, Ashley, I have to take this. Be with you guys in a minute." He turned and moved away several yards as he took a call.

As soon as Adrian was out of earshot, Ernie sidled closer. "When I heard over the radio there was a possible homicide incident at the Benning Brothers lot, I just shook my head. How is it that you've discovered yet another murder, Tory? Oh, I know. You attract trouble like a magnet. Why is that?"

Iris growled.

Ashley whispered under her breath, "And there it is—he's back." Anticipating my lunge for Ernie's throat, Ashley grabbed my arm.

Ernie took great delight in taunting and harassing me. Had it not been for Adrian, one of the good cops, running interference for me, Ernie would have been happy to see me behind bars last year and let a real killer get away with murder. Despite the fact that Adrian was the one who had been promoted to lieutenant last year, Ernie's tendency to jump the gun before conducting a thorough and unbiased investigation seemed to be alive and well. He was also notorious for leering and making inappropriate remarks to females. But so far today, there was no evidence of that particular peccadillo of his, making me wonder if he'd been warned to clean up his act in that regard at least. Or maybe his usual lascivious manner was absent because Adrian was around. Given that Emma was killed on my property, I figured Ernie would love another opportunity to pin another murder on me or someone dear to me again, just to make my life miserable.

Adrian was off his phone call and he beckoned Ernie to join him out of our earshot.

I mouthed "thank you" to Adrian and he winked at me. He appeared to give Ernie some task, because Ernie trotted off and Adrian returned to talk to us.

Adrian's expression softened momentarily as he regarded Ashley. "I hear you about closing the lot. I totally understand. We will work hard to get the lot open as soon as possible. Now, Tory, think carefully, was there anything striking about the two Santas you saw right before you found Emma?"

"Well, actually . . ."

"What?"

"It could have just been one. I'm not really sure whether I saw two different Santas or if it was the same Santa going back and forth." The thought occurred to me I might have seen the murderer going to meet Emma and then after he killed her. I shivered at the realization. "It could have been the same person. I don't know. I'm so confused because so many of our employees were dressed in Santa suits today."

"Is that normal?"

"For one of our employees to be in a Santa suit, yes. Usually the manager. But not for everyone. Today someone apparently hacked into the email system and told every employee working today to come dressed as Santa."

"Convenient to create confusion on the day of the murder. Do you have any idea who would do that or why?"

"I have no idea who. As to why, other than to aggravate people in charge, like Matt Ortega, I haven't a clue. Someone emailed him to come in, too, even though it was his day off. And it wasn't Fuji, the associate manager in charge of scheduling. He swears he didn't do it. I'm assuming it was someone pranking Matt for some reason."

Adrian listened intently and seemed to be processing everything I said. "Your associate manager, Russell Fujimoto, or Fuji, as you call him, told me he saw Emma walking with someone dressed as Santa in the lot. But when I pressed him for details, he said he couldn't tell who it was, all he knows for sure was that whoever it was wore a Santa suit."

Ashley counted on her fingers. "There were so many Santas. There must have been at least six. The one with the cigarette, the one directing cars, Matt, Fuji, and a couple of others in the lot. Although we don't know if we might have counted any of them more than once."

I leaned closer to Adrian. "I think you're right. I bet it wasn't just a coincidence that everyone dressed as Santa on the day Emma was murdered. I'm beginning to think maybe that was exactly the point—to confuse us. Brilliant, really. Wearing a Santa suit when everyone else is wearing one is the best disguise ever."

Ashley turned to Adrian. "Agree."

Adrian nodded. "Yup. It's early in the investigation, but I bet the email hack telling everyone to dress like Santa was definitely meant to make it impossible to ID the killer with certainty."

I exhaled loudly. "Very clever, very evil. Clearly premeditated."

"Yes. It's becoming clearer by the minute the hacker believed he or she would create enough cover to get away with this. So, Tory, please think hard now. Was there anything about either of the Santas you saw that was different or similar to the other Santas you saw today?"

I closed my eyes, trying to recreate the scene as I walked between the aisles. It wasn't too hard to remember some parts since I was still at the tree lot experiencing them—the softness of the ground cover of sawdust and wood chips, the fresh fragrance of pine with a hint of cinnamon. I remembered talking to Matt at the entrance of the lot. Directly behind the entrance was what I referred to as the staging area. This is where our workers dragged the trees that were piled at the back and cut off the twine wrapped around the limbs to protect them from breakage. Here they'd propped the trees on wooden sawhorses and sawed a slice off the bottom of the tree trunk before they attached a stand. In addition to the metal stands we sold we also offered the option of a free wooden stand that consisted of two pieces of crossed wood that our guys nailed directly into the bottom of the trunk. After the stands were attached, we'd move the trees to the main part of the lot. Moving the new trees to the aisles for display would account for one reason our workers walked to and fro among the aisles. The other reason workers traveled the aisles was to show customers where certain types and heights of trees were.

I tried to remember every detail of each Santa. Wearing Santa outfits made them all more or less look alike. All their outfits appeared to be standard-issue Santa—red plush hat, jacket and pants, snowy fur trim, black belt and boots. The only difference had been their height, weight and any visible characteristics the beard didn't cover up. Fuji had tan skin, was medium height, and had a wiry build. Some of the other Santas were huskier and taller, and at least one seemed on the shorter side. Some had ruddier complexions, but even skin color had been mostly hidden from view now that I thought about it. Some Santas might have even worn gloves.

When I opened my eyes, both Adrian and Ashley were looking at me expectantly. Ashley's mouth was creased in a slight smile and Adrian tipped his head encouragingly.

"Nope. I got nothing. I think one or two might have been wearing gloves. But other than that, I got nothing. But sometimes things come back to me when I'm not trying to remember. I'll let you know if that happens."

A middle-aged woman in a leather jacket and jeans came up to Adrian. "Officer, I was picking out a tree in the aisles near where the victim was found and just remembered a detail that might be helpful. I passed a Santa about five minutes before the screaming started. He smelled like cinnamon or pine or a combo of the two."

Adrian bent his head toward the woman. "Did you know the person in the Santa suit? Had you seen them before? Could you identify them if you saw them again?"

She shook her head. "No, his face was covered in his beard and the fur trim of his hat. But I do remember his scent. Like I said, he smelled a bit like cinnamon and some other spice, nutmeg, maybe? Cloves? And maybe pine. Although perhaps the pine smell came from the trees."

"Okay. That's helpful. Thank you, ma'am. Could you please go to the nursery offices to give your name and statement? Thank you."

Adrian straightened up to his full six feet. "Well, hopefully, you and others will start to remember other details like that."

A cop I didn't know approached Adrian. "Sir, we have a few people, customers, who claim to have seen two Santas in the aisles around the time of the murder. One of them said the Santa she passed smelled like Old Spice."

It didn't take me long to remember when I'd last breathed in that scent. It'd been earlier this morning here at the tree lot. It'd been when I was talking to Matt Ortega.

I listened to my voice as if I was having an out-of-body experience. "A lot of guys wear Old Spice. My father used to."

Again, all eyes turned to me.

Ashley cocked her head at me and then her eyes enlarged in comprehension. She breathed in deeply. Her look of astonishment told me she remembered too that Matt Ortega had reeked of Old Spice.

Adrian studied me and Ashley with a quizzical expression, as if waiting for us to explain the silent communication going on between us. "Everything okay with you two?"

We both nodded.

"Okay, then. The police will stay at the lot to protect the integrity of the crime scene for at least several hours. Hopefully, you'll be back in business sometime tomorrow."

"As if anyone will come to our lot now."

Ashley fidgeted with her Uggs. "I know. Especially until we find out who the murderer is and whether Emma knew the killer or whether it was some rando. What's your initial take, Adrian? Emma was probably targeted, right? Since it looks like the purpose of the hacked emails was to cause confusion by having everyone show up in Santa suits. So probably not random, which would be better for business, right?"

Before Adrian could say a word, and I had serious doubts he'd let us in on his thinking about the crime, especially in public, Ernie strolled up. "I guess this is your lucky day because I think I've already solved the crime."

Iris, who'd been docile since Ernie had left, growled a warning at him.

Adrian stood up straighter. "Really. Please do us the honor of filling us in then."

"Clearly it was someone who worked here at Benning Brothers." Ernie drilled his gaze my way, his tight smirk giving away his smug delight in wielding his authority as he so liked to do.

I riveted my gaze on him. "Why would you say that?"

"The weapon."

Adrian's mouth fell open. "You found the weapon?"

Ernie's smirk disappeared. "No. But clearly, judging by the loss of blood, I'd guess the victim was either stabbed with one of the knives the employees use to cut the rope the trees are tied in or maybe bludgeoned with a tool like a hammer or mallet like the ones they use at the lot."

"Ernie's right. The guys use knives to cut the rope and hammers to attach the wooden stands to the bottom of the trees." I couldn't believe the words that came out of my own mouth. I'd never have thought there'd be anything that I'd agree with Ernie about, let alone marvel at what he said, but I was impressed with his deductive skills.

Adrian leaned in. "My guys are already on it. Assuming a tool was the weapon. We don't know for sure. But definitely we're looking for anything heavy enough to have inflicted a fatal blow and sharp enough to cause so much blood loss."

Ashley scrunched up her face. "Ew. So, the killer used more than one weapon? And probably with blood all over them."

Adrian pursed his lips and nodded solemnly. "Sometimes we can find traces of blood on alleged weapons even when the perp might have wiped off the blood and put the tool, if it was a tool, back in its normal place. We'll check all the tools used at the lot."

I threw in my two cents on the matter. "Well then, maybe we should be looking for a bloodstained cloth or whatever could be used to wipe off blood."

Adrian held up a hand as he took a call on his phone and moved out of earshot.

Ashley checked her phone and had a weird expression on her face I couldn't read.

"What's the matter? You look like you've seen a ghost."

"Remember that Calvin Klein model look-alike with the Santa hat?"

"Uh-huh."

"He just texted me. That's seven times now."

"Wow! That's a bit much. And you don't even know whether that's his real photo! Just block him. Don't answer. He'll get the message eventually."

Ashley cocked her head. "You mean ghost him?"

"What? Yeah, whatever you want to call it. Why do you look like you're scared? Or is that look related to Emma's murder? Sorry, but I'm still stunned so my facial expression processing is probably a bit off."

"No. You're dead right, although scared might be too strong a word, more like nervous. It's just that I'm not totally sure about the nature of his interest in me. I don't know whether I should be flattered or whether I'm being stalked. He's contacted me way too many times."

"Seems a bit bizarre to me. I'd just ignore him."

Ashley was busy scrolling and counting aloud. "Seven times. That's bordering on obsession. Crap. Make it eight times. In an hour. That's out-and-out stalking, isn't it?" She looked up at me, biting her lip.

The moment when Emma commented on using dating apps flashed in my head. What was it she'd said? *"Been there, done that,"* or something to that effect. I paused for a few seconds to collect my thoughts because I didn't want to scare Ashley and let on how freaked out I felt about the juxtaposition of Emma's murder, only minutes ago, our brief discussion with Emma about dating apps, and now Ashley's apparent harassment on a dating app. But I got a grip and assured myself I was just being paranoid, especially because the last minutes had triggered the trauma caused by last year's incidents.

"Yeah. That seems excessive. Some guys don't seem to understand that less is more, especially when you don't know each other that well and your impressions are still forming. Is he being weird?"

"You mean other than repeatedly texting me?"

"I don't know, maybe he's an extrovert. What is he texting about? Anyway, if it's just awkward flirting, your overzealous admirer is the least of our worries."

"Sorry, not sorry. A client of mine just got murdered. Forgive me if I'm feeling a little vulnerable."

"Wait a minute! Emma was your client? I knew it! As soon as you guys talked about how you knew each other through emails and texting, I figured she must be one of your clients. So, what type of case?"

Ashley put her hand to her mouth. "Gosh, sorry I let that slip. She really wasn't a client per se."

"What does that mean? She was a potential client?"

"Not exactly. Can we just put the nature of our relationship on hold until I double-check on the legal propriety of discussing it?"

"Well, now you really have my interest. Are you going to tell Adrian?"

"I think I have to. I mean it is a murder investigation with the murderer still loose."

"Yeah."

"Also, I'm trying to distract myself from reality right now."

"What's this about an admirer?" Adrian held out his hand to Iris and she licked it.

Note to self. Adrian had really good hearing, especially since he'd been on a phone call while Ashley and I had chatted.

Ashley shook her head. "Nothing. Nothing's important now except Emma."

Adrian raised an eyebrow. Then he quickly put his cop face on again and turned to me. "Okay, before I let you two go, other than the one or two people in Santa suits you saw just before you found Emma, is there anything else? Did you hear anything?"

Fuji had drifted back into our circle. "I heard a woman's voice coming from the aisles when I was walking through the lot, not long before I heard Tory's screams."

Adrian perked up. "You did? Did you recognize the voice?"

Fuji shook his head. "No. Just that it was loud. She sounded real mad."

"Did you hear what she was saying or who she was talking to?"

"I only heard one voice."

"You're positive it was only one female voice? Not two arguing?" Adrian looked at Fuji expectantly.

Fuji's eyes widened and he paused before answering. "Pretty sure."

Adrian's shoulders slumped slightly. "Okay. If you remember anything else, let me know." Adrian handed Fuji one of his cards. "Tory, I'm assuming the lot has security cameras, correct?"

"Yes. Matt can help you with everything you need to know about our security cameras."

"Great. Let's go talk to him now."

"I think he went with Ernie to the entrance."

"After you." Adrian gestured with his hand for Ashley and me to lead the way.

Ashley walked next to me. "Did you see Fuji's face when Adrian asked him if he was positive it was only one woman? He for sure doesn't know. Let's hope the videos will clear this mystery up right away."

"Yes. Like that hadn't occurred to him before. It shook him up for a second."

The lot was teaming with crime scene investigators and Adrian stopped to talk to two on our way to find Matt. "Make sure you talk to all the workers. Check all the tools in the area where they hammer on the tree stands."

One of the cops nodded. "We're in the process of doing that right now, sir."

"Good. Let me know when you're done."

When we reached the front of the lot, Matt and Rachel were huddled together deep in conversation.

Adrian hailed Matt. "Tory told me you're the person to talk to about the security cameras."

"Certainly. Right this way."

We all followed Matt to the nursery and garden center, where his office was located. Matt sat down at his desktop computer on his oversized desk and Adrian, Ashley and I gathered around to view the security camera videos.

Matt fiddled with his computer. "That's funny. I can't access the footage for some reason. Haven't needed to replay any footage in a while. I'll figure it out in a minute."

After a few minutes it was clear Matt wasn't going to be able to access the security footage any time soon.

I felt helpless but I'd never familiarized myself with our security cameras. That had been Matt's job. "Sorry, Adrian. I can contact the security company to find out what the problem is."

Adrian put his hand on my shoulder. "No need. I can let you know what we find once we get it straightened out. If Matt can't figure it out, our tech person, Sarah Ng, will work her magic."

My phone pinged. Iris squirmed in my arms, definitely tired of being held this long. It was Jake Logan. *Hey. Work plans changed. If you haven't already made other plans, I'm now available for dinner again.*

Ashley held her hand over her mouth and whispered in my ear, "Someone sending you sexy pictures on the dating app?"

I furrowed my brow and hissed back. "No! Why on earth would you ever think that?"

"Because you're blushing."

"Am I? I didn't realize I was. I'm fair-skinned. Maybe it's from the sun." Suddenly I felt so hot I must have been the color of Santa's hat. "No . . ."

Ashley chuckled. "Right. That must be it, the sun. Must be good at piercing through this misty marine layer to find you."

"It's practically all burned off."

"Mmhmm." Ashley's phone pinged and she foraged in her mini cross-body bag and plucked it out. "My cell service clearly isn't as strong as yours. It's Jakey, still unclear on the concept of group versus individual text threads apparently, saying he's now free for dinner. Where shall we go?"

"What!" I checked his text, and sure enough he'd sent it on the wrong thread again. I chuckled. "Let me tell him to pay more attention to threads."

She motioned me to move closer to the hallway outside Matt's office so as not to be overheard. "Let me revise my comment, where are you two going for dinner?"

"I don't know whether I should go. Earlier he canceled because of work. Now it's on again. Does that sound weird to you?"

"Canceling dinner plans for work? Are you kidding? That's Adrian's main move. Rescheduling dinner after work plans change, also a favorite move of Adrian's. But why should it matter either way? You guys are just friends, right? Or that's what you keep telling me anyway. What's the problem?"

"Yeah, you're right. I don't know why I got so flustered. It must be Emma's murder. I'm super anxious right now. Actually, Jake is the ideal person to decompress with, can't beat a PI for a good convo about possible suspects, right?"

"Wait, wait, wait! You're not even thinking of getting involved in another murder investigation, are you?"

"Shh!" I spun my head around to make sure no one had heard. I spoke slowly but firmly. "Ashley, a popular local caterer and food truck owner was brutally murdered in the Benning Brothers tree lot. No murder suspect has been identified, let alone caught. We don't know for sure yet whether she was targeted or if it was random. The police have closed down our tree lot, a big moneymaker for Benning Brothers nursery each year. Ernie already is insinuating that the perp might be one of our employees. How many is that, four?" I paused to count. "More like five or six reasons why I must get involved."

She patted my shoulder. "I hear you, hun, but—"

Adrian walked toward us and patted my other shoulder. "Don't worry, Tory. Leave the investigation to us. Like I said, we'll get the lot open as quickly as humanly possible after we go over the crime scene with a fine-tooth comb. We'll collect evidence, interview everyone who was on the lot at the time, and her friends, and investigate her life to see if she had any enemies. We're on it."

I was at a loss for words, stunned that Adrian had heard our conversation. He had phenomenal hearing.

Ashley leaned in closer to Adrian. "She's having dinner with Jake tonight. He'll walk her back off the ledge, hopefully."

The light lines around Adrian's brown eyes crinkled in merriment. "Make sure you tell him hi from me. By the way, you two are free to go now. I'll walk out with you. Remember to call me if you think of anything else and keep in touch."

He said the "keep in touch" part while locking gazes with Ashley. I told him I would.

Adrian accompanied us as we walked through the tree lot to the entrance, where a couple of officers were taking statements from customers.

Ashley gave my sleeve a slight tug. "Tory, I understand your frustration and need to get this behind you. I truly do. But we all also want you to be safe. You don't need any more risk or danger. The last year or so should be your life quota."

Ashley was referring to my involvement in the showdown with Milo's murderer. She was a hundred percent correct. That dangerous incident will be etched into my memory for life. I certainly wasn't looking to put myself in any danger again. But that being said, I considered myself smart and cautious. I've never been a risk-taker who foolishly puts herself in the path of danger needlessly.

"Ashley, I know my limitations. I'm not a ninja or a superwoman. I'm always careful and plan for almost every eventuality."

"I know. It's that unexpected random event you haven't planned for that I worry about. With all the time you spend working out, you probably could be a ninja."

I laughed. "No, Ash, you're the one with superpowers."

Her eyes danced with glee. "We make a great team—ninja and super-woman."

"That's right. So maybe you can use your superpowers to help me figure out something that's been bothering me. After we found Emma, Matt and Fuji showed up right away. I noticed our other managers, Aparicio and Collins, shortly thereafter. Why is it that earlier you counted at least five or six Santas, when after Emma was murdered we only saw four?"

Adrian perked up. "Who's missing?"

Chapter 3

Ashley chuckled. "That's not a superpower. That's just plain math."

I nodded. "Math sometimes seems like a superpower to me. So maybe a Santa or two ditched their outfits."

Ashley had a weird look on her face. I followed her gaze to the group of people in Santa costumes standing at the tree lot entrance. "Oh, look. A cluster of Santas."

A bunch of guys in Santa suits were in front of us. As we got close to them I recognized Matt Ortega, Fuji, and two of our assistant managers, Rodney Collins and Joe Aparicio. The fifth guy dressed as Santa was Connor, our part-time seasonal worker.

"Oh, okay. Never mind. So much for that theory. There's the fifth Santa. Problem partially solved, at least. Maybe there were only five."

Ashley scrunched her face up. "Hmm. Fuji claimed all four assistant managers showed up for work. Plus himself, Matt, and Connor. That's seven. I don't know if we can really say for sure how many different Santas we saw earlier."

I pursed my lips. "Agree. I don't think we'll ever have an accurate count since we never knew whether we were looking at different Santas or ones we'd seen before. Gives new meaning to the name Santa Sofia."

Ashley rolled her eyes. Adrian shook his head and made an entry in his notebook. "Okay, we'll be with you five gentlemen in a few minutes to get your statements."

As we turned to head out of the tree lot Adrian had one last thought. "Tory, I know how hard on you this must be, having spoken to Emma earlier and then finding her body minutes later. Thank you for filling me in. You gave me a lot of information and now we have to scour the property. Same goes for you, Ashley. Maybe you can both go grab a late lunch and decompress some. I'm sure Iris is long overdue for a nap right now too." He tousled Iris's fluff. "Then come down to the station tomorrow and we can talk to each of you again and get a formal statement."

Ashley and I both exhaled deeply. I was still shaking a bit and Ashley looked wobbly as we walked to my car.

"I'll drive back to Starbucks first so you can get your car."

"Okay, thanks."

On the short ride back to the Starbucks Ashley looked at her phone while holding Iris on her lap.

At a stop sign I glanced over and saw she was looking at a dating app again. "I can't get over you. Give it a rest with texting random strangers, please, can you?"

"Not random strangers. I prefer to refer to them as potential suitors."

"Ashley!" I bit my tongue for a second so I wouldn't blurt out what I was really thinking, that they were more like potential murderers than suitors.

"What?"

It didn't work. "I'm sorry but I can't hold it in any longer. Are you crazy or do you just have a death wish?"

"Okay, calm down and ratchet the pending doom predictions down a few notches. I'm trying to distract myself, like a certain someone I know does all the time. I'm just glad I didn't pass out at the crime scene. I'm still trembling. That's scary stuff. One minute she's giving us free cookies and the next minute . . ."

I was trying to hold it together by not thinking about it, but that wasn't working either. Seeing Emma lying on the ground was an image I couldn't un-see.

A few minutes later we turned into the Starbucks parking lot. There was a free space next to Ashley's BMW. I parked and shut off the engine. We both sat in silence for a few minutes.

Ashley turned to me. "I can't believe we're dealing with another murder again. It's surreal."

"I can't believe it either. What are the odds?"

"I know, right?"

A few moments of silence followed again. I think we were both still in shock. I reached for a water bottle I had earlier. I poured the last remaining water into a plastic cup I kept in my car and Iris lapped it up.

"You started to tell me about your therapy session with Ellen, but then you got distracted because you were running late to meet Emma. What else did Ellen have to say? Any insights? Hearing what a professional had to say about dealing with drama trauma right now would be great."

I thought back on my appointment yesterday. It seemed like eons ago. "I think I told you everything. Just that I'm still not back to normal. I feel okay most of the time and then every now and then a wave of sadness overcomes me. But the good thing is they've been occurring a little less frequently. But now, after Emma . . ."

"Yeah. That's not going to help at all."

I gave Iris a little squeeze, prompting her to lick my hand. "But at least I have this little nugget to thank for always being such a loyal little dog, comforting me and guarding me and scaring away all the bad guys. And you've been my rock through all of this too, Ash. I couldn't imagine a better best friend. I'm very grateful to both of you. You and Iris always have my back. So enough about me. What else is going on with you?"

"Well, speaking of finding love online—"

"Were we though?"

She gave me a saucy wink. "Anyway, what I'd been planning to suggest to you, before Emma was killed, obviously, was that it was about time you had a dating app profile. I was going to help you set it up."

"Oh, okay. Let me take a better look and see what all the hoopla's about." I grabbed her pink sparkle-covered phone and pinched the screen to zoom in to get a better look at "David," the supposed name of the shirtless guy posing like a Calvin Klein underwear model, inspecting his photo as if he were an adoptable dog on a rescue site. He had luminous green eyes like my cat Otis. He was wearing nothing but a Santa hat and low-slung jeans, with abs as chiseled as the faces on Mount Rushmore. No Santa beard, only a five o'clock shadow on his square jaw so perfect it must have been Photoshopped. Maybe his abs had been Photoshopped too. I tapped his profile. "Does David have a last name?"

"I'm sure he does but you don't share that info at first."

"Handy for murderers so you can't Google them and see their criminal record." I passed her phone back to her. "Well, at least he doesn't seem to be a political fanatic or in a cult."

"That's what I thought. The only weird thing is the obsessive texting, but maybe he's technologically challenged." She laughed. "Okay then." She reached over and swiped right to accept the match.

"I thought you already swiped right. How else did you exchange phone numbers?"

"Huh. You're right. I must have already swiped right and given it to him. I can't remember the order of what happened when. The murder has me in a state of shock. I'm lucky I can work the app. Hope I can drive home okay."

"I know. I feel stunned too. Just make sure you do a thorough Google search once you find out his last name. You never know."

She jutted her jaw. "Please. Have I ever *not* done a Google search? He says he's twenty-five. Is that too young?"

"Too young for what? You're the lawyer. You tell me."

We both laughed. We were both thirty-four. Well, technically, Ashley wouldn't turn thirty-four until her birthday next week.

"I still don't know why either of us need to be on a dating app. You have Adrian and I'm not looking for, nor am I ready for, a relationship."

"First of all, Tory, I don't 'have Adrian.'" Ashley gestured with air quotes. "I don't even know what our relationship is. We haven't hung out together since before Thanksgiving—"

"You're basically boyfriend and girlfriend. That's what it seems like to me."

Ashley sighed, drooping her shoulders. "Sometimes it feels like we are. Other times, not so much. And certainly not lately. Plus, he hasn't said the 'L' word—"

"Yet."

"Well, to be fair, he does say he loves spending time with me and—"

"There you go. He's building up his courage to say it. It's a big commitment and Adrian takes things seriously."

Ashley continued to scroll through photos and then stopped at one profile.

"Huh. This guy looks so familiar. I feel like I know him from somewhere else."

Iris growled at a passing pedestrian outside.

"No, Iris, not him. Auntie Ashley's looking at her phone, see?" I winked at Ashley.

Ashley handed me her phone. "Here. See if he looks familiar to you. I'm parched. I'm going to go inside and get some tea. Do you want anything?"

"Tea sounds great. Maybe another water, too, and a Puppuccino for Iris. Thanks." My gaze fixed on the photo of a brown-eyed, brown-haired guy who looked to be fortyish. "He looks angry."

"I know. I'm sure he's trying to portray a brooding bad boy vibe, but that's a hard swipe left for me."

Ashley cracked open the car door but stayed seated.

I pinched the screen to enlarge the photo. "He does look familiar."

"Right? Hold that thought. I'll be back in a minute." Ashley jumped out and shut the door, then trotted up the steps to the Starbucks entrance.

I wracked my brain trying to remember where I'd seen this guy on the app before. Was it at the tree lot maybe?

Ashley was back in a jiffy juggling a cardboard tray with two teas and two water bottles and the Puppuccino. She had stuck one water bottle under her arm, one on the tray, and held the little paper cup with whipped cream for Iris. Iris lunged at the Puppuccino before Ashley had even shut her door and devoured it while I held the paper cup.

"Wow. Iris loves Puppuccinos, doesn't she?" She took back her phone from me and handed me a bottle of water. "Here. Let's trade."

"Thanks."

"Look, Tory. I'm just playing around. Don't worry."

"But I do worry. He has your phone number. What if he's a weirdo and somehow finds your address online in a reverse phonebook? He could not only figure out who you are but also where you live. This is so uncharacteristic for you."

"Relax, Tory. I'll be fine. He doesn't have my phone number. We're messaging through the app."

"I thought you said you were texting with your cell phone number."

"Did I? I guess I must have given him my number then. I can't remember all the details now, Tory, because, hello, someone I know just got murdered. Remember, I knew Emma both professionally and personally so, forgive me, if I'm a little flustered and getting mixed up. I'm trying to keep it all together."

"Sorry. I forgot you knew her professionally too. I'll try to back off, but no guarantees. I will not stand by silently if I think you're engaging in risky behaviors."

"Okay, Mom." Her impish grin told me she had moved on already. "Give me your phone. I'll set a basic profile up for you and add you on my profile as a matchmaker. That way you can follow me, and you'll at least see how it works. Then, if you're ever so inclined to look for your own matches, you're all set to go."

I was too tired to resist. Plus, Ashley was smart. She probably was correct about it being safe. Wouldn't hurt to check it out myself though and keep my eye on her at the same time. "Oh, okay. Here. Have at it. But if I start getting stalked—"

"You won't. And you can always delete the app if you want. Consider it dating prep for now. Plus, it'll take your mind off murder."

"Actually, it'll make me think of murder more. Didn't Emma say she had been on a dating app? Maybe she met the murderer on the app."

She handed me my phone back. "Doubt it. But if that's what you need to tell yourself to justify being on it, go with it. But I bet a lot more people who use dating apps get married than murdered.

My phone pinged. Someone responding to a rental ad I'd placed for

MURDER *in the* CHRISTMAS TREE LOT

Milo's condo and asking when it was possible to see it. I texted back and, immediately, my phone pinged again. It was Jake. *I was thinking around seven at Sadie's Seafood? Meet you there?*

"Jake wants to meet me at Sadie's."

"Good! Let me know what he thinks about Emma's murder. He might have some insider information since he has a lot of law enforcement contacts."

She fiddled with my phone for a few minutes and then handed it back to me. "There. You're all set. Peruse it at your leisure." She gave me a cheeky wink as she opened the door to leave. "And try to have fun tonight."

Chapter 4

I'd agreed to meet Jake at Sadie's Seafood on the pier, a restaurant we both loved. I'd been fantasizing about their lobster rolls ever since we'd agreed on the time and place. I might have even checked out their website and stared longingly at pictures of their lobster rolls, as you do before going out to eat.

The Santa Sofia pier was bustling with cars and diners and I had to circle the street around the Promenade for about ten minutes before a parking spot opened up fairly near to the pier. I entered the boardwalk area watching my step so that my heeled booties wouldn't get caught in between the planks. The clickety-clack of cars driving on the pier planks brought back memories, mostly good, but some were darker, like the ones of my father's death. I shook my head to shake away dark thoughts and focused on the festive multicolored Christmas lights that adorned the pier.

I was soon at the entrance of Sadie's. They'd decorated their front door with what looked like a big Benning Brothers wreath. I recognized the short sturdy branches of noble red fir accented with the soft swags of western red cedar. I stuck my nose close and took a deep breath of the intoxicating scent that made me feel I'd been transported to the middle of an evergreen forest. I stepped back and admired the embellishments the restaurant had added to our wreath, a few starfish and tiny sand dollars, gilded grasses, and an oversized glittery gold ribbon.

A small living Norfolk Island pine Christmas tree with white twinkle lights graced the cramped entrance of the restaurant. I was pretty sure it was one of ours since none of the other tree lots in Santa Sofia that I knew of sold living trees in tin bucket planters. I looked around the restaurant's wooden tables lit with red votive candles for Jake. He'd snagged a window table where we could view the pier's Christmas lights and the decorated boats twinkling out in the water from inside the cozy restaurant, protected from the chill and evening marine layer's frizz-inducing mist. We waved to each other and hugged briefly before I sat down.

Once seated we each ordered a glass of house Chardonnay to go along with the lobster rolls and coleslaw we'd come for. We changed things up by ordering cups of Rhode Island clam chowder as starters.

I delighted in Sadie's Christmas décor. To match their tree near the entrance, each table had a tiny Italian cypress in a mini tin planter. Each tree was adorned with a handful of silver glitter that sparkled in the candlelight.

After a few sips of wine and me oohing and aahing over the festive decorations, I started to relax. "So, Jake. What's going on with work that it's on one minute and off another? You said first you had to work tonight, then you didn't. What happened?"

Jake popped a couple of tiny oyster crackers that accompanied the chowder into his mouth and gazed at me with his riveting blue eyes.

I sipped my wine.

"Can you keep a secret?"

"Of course. I rarely have secrets myself, but I'm pretty good at keeping secrets others have entrusted me with."

He took a gulp of wine. "You know the job I mentioned that got canceled?"

"Yeah."

"It was here in Santa Sofia."

I leaned back in my chair hard. "What? Who hired you?"

"That I can't tell you." His eyes squinted with amusement.

"Tease."

Jake raised one eyebrow slightly in response.

"Why even tell me then. Can I guess?"

"I'm telling you all I can right now." Then he mumbled, "In the wake of Emma's murder."

I leaned toward him over the table. "It's related to her murder? How?"

He held a finger to his lips and lowered his voice. "That's what I'm trying to figure out right now. I'm in a tricky position. I have a confidentiality agreement with my client. But obviously, I don't want to impede a police investigation. Quite the opposite. I have both a civic and moral duty to help out Adrian in his investigation."

I whispered back, "Are you positive it's related to Emma?"

"I didn't say it was related."

"Don't be coy. Then what does 'in the wake of Emma's murder' mean?"

He chuckled. "Well, I guess I gave that impression. More like it might be related to something related to her murder at this point. That's what I intend to figure out."

"Related to something related to her murder? That sounds like friend of a friend."

"Actually, you're not far off."

I squinted in puzzlement. "Huh. I'll have to think about that another time, when I haven't had an exhausting day and a glass of wine."

"His facial muscles relaxed into a less intense expression. "What's the latest in your real estate dealings? Any bites?"

After the deaths of Milo and my father, I found myself the owner of three homes, mine, my father's, and Milo's. My father's house, the one he moved to when I went to college, was located in the eastern foothills of the Santa Ynez Mountains, in the southern portion of Santa Sofia known as Sycamore Canyon. Milo's condo was on the coast a bit north from the pier, about five minutes away from my Spanish-styled white stucco, red-tiled-roof bungalow. I was in the process of renting them both. The tenants for the condo were leaving at the end of the month.

"I've had a few bites. More for Milo's condo than my dad's house in the hills. But the house won't be ready for another month. I'm having some work done before it's ready for tenants."

"Living near the beach is everyone's dream."

"Yes. Luckily, it's a great place too. Hopefully it won't be too hard to rent. I have two appointments with prospective tenants scheduled to look at it tomorrow. And a couple inquiries for my dad's who said they'd get back to me to set up a time to see it. So, who knows?"

"Well, good luck!"

"Thanks. I need it more than ever now with the lot closed temporarily. My dad's house is paid off, thank goodness, but there are still a lot of associated monthly expenses. Same with the condo. It has homeowner association fees too. I'd love to get the condo rented as soon as possible. But it's December, with the holidays and people traveling, not the best time to find good tenants."

Our food was delivered and we both dug in, pausing only to share rave reviews of the lobster rolls.

I blotted my mouth with my red napkin. "So good."

"I know. The lobster is succulent."

"I'm not talking about the food. I'm talking about your skill in changing the subject away from Emma's murder."

He gave me a quick smile. "How's work?"

"There you go doing it again."

He laughed. "Where are you with the Hotel Santa Sofia condo project now?"

I leaned back in my chair. "I'm finalizing the landscaping plans now that the building is under construction. Nice try to deflect again."

Jake responded with a deep chuckle. "Guilty as charged. I cannot break my confidentiality agreement. With a layperson, at least."

I needed to get Ashley on the case to figure out what Jake was investigating somehow. Or Adrian. Or both of them. My thoughts drifted to how I could play matchmaker for Ashley and Adrian by getting them both to try and find out who Jake's Santa Sofia client was. A win all around.

Jake tapped my arm. "Hey. What are you cooking up now?"

"Who, me? Nothing. Nothing at all."

"You're not thinking about murder?"

"Well, to be honest, I guess I am, sort of. I was just thinking about lobsters. I'm conflicted. I adore lobster rolls, but hate how lobsters are killed in boiling water."

"You're worried about lobster murders. Not thinking at all about Emma. Ri-ght."

"What? You don't believe me?"

Again, the deep chuckle. His blue eyes. Our gazes locked.

My heart fluttered. "Look, Jake. I'm not being a busybody or a reckless risk-taker. I've got a stake in all of this. Emma was murdered on my property, she was a contractor with whom I had a business relationship to sell her wares out of her food truck parked on my property, and—"

I caught myself before I said anything about Matt Ortega. Ashley and I were the only ones, so far, who'd made the connection between the customer who'd said she'd encountered a Santa who smelled like Old Spice near the crime scene and Matt.

"And? What is it? Something to do with her murder?"

For a few seconds I tried to assess Jake's ability to separate his professional PI identity from his personal side and our friendship. Who was I kidding? I'd trusted Jake ever since he'd been the self-appointed captain of "Team Tory," as he coined it, when I was a suspect and we both were investigating Milo's murder. "There was one witness who said she ran into someone in a Santa suit that smelled like pine and cinnamon moments before I found Emma."

He gave me an encouraging nod. "Mhmm."

"I know which Santa that was. It was Matt Ortega. I feel it's only a matter of time before Ernie connects the dots and decides that Matt is the murderer."

"How do you know?"

"Because Matt was wearing Old Spice today. Ashley and I both noticed it. And another witness said she passed a Santa who smelled like Old Spice too."

"You don't think Matt did it?"

"No, of course I don't. But the problem is he once dated Emma."

"Oh." He let out a long breath. "Jilted lovers do weird stuff sometimes."

"Matt wouldn't hurt a ladybug."

Jake looked at me with a quizzical twinkle in his eyes. "Ladybug? Isn't it a fly?"

"Yeah, well. We sell flytraps at the nursery. So technically, he does hurt flies, or enables others to. I guess he's sort of an accomplice."

Jake's lips creased into a slight smile. "Wouldn't he be more of an accessory to the crime?"

"Anyway, I know Ernie. He always goes the path of least resistance. In no time Ernie will be calling Matt his prime suspect, enjoying it all the more because of his long-standing resentment toward people in general, me in particular."

"But even if Matt is innocent as you believe, it's not looking good for Benning Brothers anyway right now since the only people spotted near the crime scene appear to be your employees. They were the ones wearing Santa suits, right?"

I pouted. "Yes, but . . ."

Raised eyebrows arched over the baby blues told me he was skeptical.

"But anyone could have gotten a Santa suit. Besides, that's only circumstantial evidence. That doesn't necessarily link it to one of our employees."

I brooded for a minute.

He tapped his long fingers absently on the table as he stared out the window, seemingly deep in thought. His tapping stopped. "Why was Emma at the back of the lot?"

"Excellent question. She'd been working the truck. And since Rachel had apparently left the lot to meet her eggnog hookup, that means Emma abandoned an unmanned truck. So, whatever it was, it must have been pretty important for her to do that."

"I agree."

"I can't imagine her leaving her truck unattended under any circumstances unless it was a life-or-death . . ." I stopped as what I'd said sunk in and locked my gaze with Jake's.

"So, it looks like she was the intended victim. Highly unlikely she'd be randomly walking around the lot and ran into a killer."

"Yep. I think she was targeted. Someone must have lured her to the back of the lot somehow. Otherwise, why else would she have been there? Obvious now that we're parsing it. Adrian said as much when we were talking with him."

"What I've learned from working as a PI is that often what's obvious to an objective observer isn't at all obvious to a person involved or experiencing a crime. For you, Emma was a friend and colleague."

"Yes. All I could think about when I found her was helping her and then I was in shock that she was dead." I covered my mouth with my hands, recalling the horror of finding her.

"Exactly. You didn't think of why she was back there or who was watching the truck then."

"I wonder if she was texting or talking on the phone to the murderer. Maybe that's how she was lured to the back of the lot. I didn't notice a phone near the body. Maybe the killer took it."

"Possibly."

"I can't get over that I didn't worry about the possible danger of her killer lurking nearby." That triggered another thought. "Our security cameras! Adrian is looking at that right now. Hopefully, that will give us some answers."

The phone rang. It was Adrian. "Hi, Tory, I've got some bad news."

Chapter 5

My heart pounded. I didn't know whether or not I could handle any more bad news. I took a deep breath. "Okay. What now?"

"Your security cameras were disabled."

"You're kidding me. All of them?"

"All? Matt told me both were disabled. You have other cameras?"

"Yes, at least four. Which ones were disabled?"

"Really? I wonder why Matt didn't mention that. I think he said the front and rear entrance cameras were down."

"I can't be positive as to actual number, but I'm pretty sure there's one camera for each corner of the lot. Because, normally, that's the nursery's parking lot. Matt should know for sure. He's the one who handled their installation several years ago." I couldn't imagine why Matt hadn't told Adrian about the other cameras. Odd.

"Interesting. Okay." Adrian spoke faster, like a hunting dog raring to pursue a new scent. "Thanks, Tory. We'll check it out and get back to you."

Shoot. Had I just added another reason to suspect Matt, as if they didn't already have enough?

Jake studied my face. "I take it the security cameras were disabled? Don't despair. Yet."

"I'm trying not to. Hopefully, the ones they haven't checked yet weren't disabled too."

My phone pinged. It was a dating app notification. I clicked on it. Someone had liked my profile. My face heated. I thought Ashley had said it wasn't activated.

"What's the matter? You're flushed."

For a moment I debated the pros and cons of sharing our lark with dating apps. "Promise you won't judge?"

He chuckled. "Wow. Now I'm really intrigued."

"Ashley and I set up dating app profiles as a joke." I paused to gauge his reaction.

His mouth creased in a hint of a smile, but it didn't reach his eyes. "Were they real or decoy profiles?"

"What do you mean? Real. But we only use our first names. What are decoy profiles?"

"Something I came across recently in a case I was working on. The group I encountered was called Valentine Vigilantes, self-described anonymous hunters of online dating app predators. They conduct sting operations to catch bad guys on dating apps."

"Wow. I never heard of them. But good that someone's out there trying to track down the bad guys."

He could no longer suppress a full smile.

"What? Is that so preposterous? Do you think we won't get any likes?"

He shook his head. "Quite the opposite. First of all, it amazes me that two women that have everything going for them like you and Ashley would even think that, but it's refreshingly humble. And second, I would have thought you'd have been bombarded by likes."

"Thanks. That's nice of you to say. But we picked an app where the guys can't contact the girls until the girls swipe right. At least I thought that was the way it worked. I don't know why I'd get a like if I hadn't swiped right first. Hmm. Anyway, Ashley had set up my profile so I could follow hers. Mine wasn't supposed to be live, or so I thought." I looked more closely at the notification. "I'm a bit puzzled. That little devil. She must have activated my profile when she took my phone. Maybe she swiped right on some profiles too. Oh, also, before I forget, make sure you check the text thread when you text me. You were texting me about dinner on the thread we had shared with Ashley and Adrian."

Jake's eyebrows lifted briefly in an expression of surprise. "I did? I'm usually so careful to make sure I'm on the right thread. Sorry. Luckily it wasn't anything bad, right?"

"Bad? Like what? Gossip about Ashley? As if."

Jake sipped his wine before responding. "Bad was the wrong word. I meant more private or personal."

Now Jake was the one turning red. I tried to pretend I hadn't noticed to prevent him further embarrassment.

"Anyway, we were just playing around. I'm texting her right now to scold her for activating my profile."

"Ah. I won't even try to pretend I get it. I thought Ashley and Adrian liked each other."

"They do. Only they don't really know it yet. He likes her but he's also at a stressful point in his career, so he's kind of distracted with getting a good review since it's a year since he's been promoted. And Ashley is a tad gun-shy because of a few previous relationships where she was cheated on. She's still a bit shell-shocked and wary. She doesn't want it to happen again."

"That's totally understandable. I can certainly relate."

This was one of the first times Jake had revealed anything about himself in terms of his previous relationships.

"Oh? Do tell."

"You know I'm divorced, right?"

I sat up straighter. "I know now. You never mentioned that before. Why?"

"It never seemed like a good time to bring it up. You were grieving and in shock with everything changing in your life. It seemed irrelevant. You needed a friend, not a boyfriend."

"You are correct." An awkward silence followed. "Yeah, I can see that. We didn't talk about anything other than finding the killer pretty much. With all the other commotion since we'd met, it's not at all surprising it'd never come up before. Sorry to be so self-involved that I never asked."

The blush returned to his face. "Yeah, somehow my high school sweetheart who I'd adored morphed into a person who found me boring. I don't want to get into it but suffice it to say my puppy love blinded me to who she really was."

I leaned in a little. "I'm sorry."

"She was into organic living, nature—we even planted an olive tree at our wedding to symbolize peace and harmony and wanted to watch it grow along with our love. The tree only lasted two years. Like our marriage."

"Oh, no. Foreshadowing. That sucks when that happens. But you have to realize, when one door closes, another opens up."

His gaze lingered on mine. "Exactly."

"Can I bring you anything else?" The waiter's interruption abruptly ended our conversation.

We both shook our heads. The moment of connection we had was lost.

I shot Jake a quick smile. "Getting back to Emma's murder, I'm upset not just because of the lot closing for a day. It's not just about losing the day's revenues, it's about our reputation and future business too. I'm not overstating it when I say that the livelihoods of dozens of our employees and their families are at stake, not just mine. The ripple effect carries far, especially in a small town like Santa Sofia."

Jake sat up straighter. "I hear you. The sooner the SSPD can come up with a theory of what happened, the better. Until we know for sure whether Emma was targeted or not, I'm afraid you're right. People will be freaked out that there's a potential random killer loose, roaming the local tree lot." He finished the last of his wine and his fingers tapped the glass while he seemed to be deep in thought.

I finished the last swig of wine in my glass and folded my napkin and placed it on the table. "You know, I was thinking."

"Uh-oh, what have you been cooking up now?" His eyes were twinkling playfully.

"Just that it's highly unlikely it was a coincidence that two of our cameras somehow became disabled. Sure, one might have been disabled accidentally. But two of them? And somehow both at the same time?"

Jake scratched his chin. "Yeah, totally agree. It really makes the case that her murder was premeditated."

"Which would be better for Benning Brothers because it implies it wasn't random, right? If it turns out it wasn't random, then hopefully people can come to the lot without fearing the killer will strike again."

Jake pointed at me. "But there's still a problem."

"What's that?"

"The disabled cameras suggest an inside job, perhaps implicating a Benning Brothers employee. Who else would know about the cameras and have access to them?"

I saw where this was headed. In the process of proving it was premeditated, it might implicate someone I knew and trusted. "Our regular employees knew for sure. I don't know about our seasonal ones though. And maybe our regular customers noticed them too? Or a crook? That's part of a crook's job description, I would think."

"I don't think you can necessarily exclude anyone if they're relatively visible. An argument could be made that it was common knowledge."

I thought for a minute. "I guess. Most of our cameras are fairly visible."

"Some prosecutors base their whole case on circumstantial evidence."

"Hey! Whose side are you on?"

He raised his hand as if taking an oath. "Team Tory. Forever. I promise."

After an overly enthusiastic chortle that I was sure did not make me sound very attractive, I got my wits about me and gave him a high five. "All right! That's what I'm talking about." Good god, who was I? Slow your locker room roll, girl.

The waiter brought the check and we agreed to split it, as always.

"Anyway, that's why I need to expedite things. We both know from past experience that the SSPD can hastily come to a theory based on circumstantial evidence yet at the same time be super slow when it comes to integrating new evidence that might cause them to alter their theory. It could take weeks before—"

My phone pinged with a text from Adrian. I shook my head. "One of the other two security cameras was also disabled."

"And the other?"

"Not disabled! Want to come with me tomorrow to the police station to view it?"

"Wouldn't miss it for the world!"

Chapter 6

Early the next morning I drove to the SSPD to view the video. I checked in at the front counter, taking note of SSPD's own version of Charlie Brown's Christmas tree, a skinny tinsel tabletop model perched on one corner of the front counter, and the silver menorah on the other corner. I waited in the foil-garland-decorated lobby wondering how, with all this tinsel and foil, the police station's metal detectors hadn't gone into overdrive and self-destructed.

After a few minutes I was buzzed through to the inner sanctum of cubicles and offices and a female officer led me to Adrian. Jake and Adrian were chatting at Adrian's desk when I walked into Adrian's office.

"You got upgraded from a cubicle."

Adrian smiled. "Yep. One of the perks of my promotion." He yawned, then pointed me to a fancy coffee maker. "Help yourself to some coffee."

"Thanks. Another perk?"

"Actually, Ashley got it for me when I got the promotion."

I snapped my head. "She did?" I wondered why she hadn't mentioned it to me. But maybe she had. I'd been in a state of shock last December. "Okay, so what did you find on the surveillance video?"

Adrian sipped his coffee from a huge mug. "I haven't viewed it yet."

"What! How could you stand the suspense? I would have checked the video the moment I got it. I tossed and turned last night in anticipation."

Adrian's full lips turned up slightly.

Jake patted my shoulder. "What Adrian means, Tory, is—"

I nodded vigorously. "Sorry. Sorry. Of course, you know what's on it already. You just haven't viewed it personally yet."

Jake winked at Adrian. "Other officers have checked it and reported its content to Adrian."

"Yes, of course they did. It's a murder case, for goodness sakes. I blame the early hour. I haven't had enough coffee yet, clearly. I assume it didn't show who did it then?"

Adrian set down his mug. "Yes and no. Let's watch it and we can see for ourselves. But first let me warn you. My staff said it's disturbing due to the graphic violence. It shows Emma getting attacked."

I grabbed Jake's arm. I don't know what I thought I'd be viewing, maybe people coming and going, but I wasn't at all prepared for one of the cameras to actually catch the killer in the act. Overwhelmed with the prospect of seeing Emma murdered, my knees wobbled.

Jake bent his head toward me. "You're trembling. Are you sure you're up to seeing this?"

I nodded. "I'm okay."

"If by okay you mean you're shaking like Jell-O."

"Really, I'm fine." But I leaned against Jake in the hope of abating my tremors. I figured if my body heard me say out loud that I was fine and felt Jake's steadiness, it would quit reacting like I was trying to walk during a six-point-five earthquake.

Jake patted my hand wrapped around his arm. "You sure you're all right? All the color has drained from your face."

Adrian narrowed his eyes. "Tory, you don't have to view it. It's difficult to watch."

"I know. But she was a friend and business colleague. And it did happen on our property. I feel like I owe it to her. The least I can do."

"Ready?"

"I am."

We all gathered around Adrian's computer.

Adrian started the video. "Okay, this is from the camera that's mounted on the light standard at the back corner of the lot."

"Right. The one behind where we have our tallest trees, the nine-footers. It would be camouflaged a bit by all the tall trees. Normally, it's much more noticeable. But in December the parking lot is filled with trees."

Adrian supplied a narrative. "The camera is positioned as if you were in the far west corner of the tree lot, near the street."

I chuckled. "And you're ten feet tall."

"Right. It's aimed toward the front of the lot." Adrian leaned on the corner of his desk. "We see customers making their way down the center aisle toward the back of the lot and employees in Santa outfits milling about. And Emma. Here she is walking toward us. She's talking to someone dressed in a Santa suit. They stop and have an animated conversation. Then Emma turns and starts to head back to the front of the lot. But the Santa grabs her arm. She shrugs off the hold and they can be seen once again having an animated conversation. Emma gesticulates wildly. The Santa heads toward the other corner at the rear of the lot and off camera. Another Santa is seen heading toward the back of the lot. Emma turns toward the front of the lot and then looks at her phone. And texts someone. Then changes direction and heads to the back of the lot again. Then out of nowhere comes a Santa from an aisle and hits Emma from behind with something. Hard to tell. A hammer maybe. And the person drags her into an aisle out of sight. A few minutes later a person dressed as Santa then runs across the main aisle until he's out of view. Then after a few minutes more it looks like a third Santa crosses the aisle, and back again, or the same one, and then there's Tory."

"Oh, my goodness. I was so close to the killer." I tightened my grip on Jake and he patted my hand again.

Adrian paused the video and looked at me. "Are you sure you want to see the rest?"

I nodded.

He resumed the video and his narration. "Okay, that's Tory strolling through the aisles heading toward the back, then she disappears from view. Then after several minutes she comes back into sight, turns into the aisle and disappears from view. Presumably, that's when she finds Emma on the ground. The next minute she appears again."

"Yes. I started to scream for help. And then Ashley came running over to me and I think we both tried to see if Emma had a pulse."

Adrian shut off the tape after we saw Ashley on her phone.

"That was Ashley calling nine-one-one."

Jake whistled. "Great. The good news: Santa did it. The bad news: Which Santa?"

Adrian. "Exactly. It appears it was no accident that everyone was told to wear a Santa suit. The killer knew it would be a great way to muddy the waters."

It seemed obvious to me. "I'd venture to say whoever hacked the emails telling all our employees to wear the Santa suit yesterday is the murderer."

Jake cocked his head. "Hold on. Not necessarily. They could have been an accomplice to murder, not the actual murderer."

Adrian chimed in. "Or even an unwitting accomplice. Maybe whoever did the Santa thing did it as a prank and the killer saw it as a perfect cover."

I shook my head. "No, that seems like too much of a stretch. Too much of a coincidence. How would the killer know that . . . unless they knew each other, and the killer knew about the prank?"

Jake twisted his head from side to side. "I'd say the killer hacked the emails or got someone to do it for them makes more sense. Too much of a coincidence otherwise."

Adrian stood up. "I tend to agree. But I'll add that doesn't mean the hacker knew they were a part of a murder plot. In any case, once they get wind that they aided the cover-up of the killer's identity, the hacker is going to go through some heavy reckoning with what to do."

"You mean whether to fess up to the hacking?"

"Yeah."

"Assuming that's the correct scenario."

"Half of our investigations are based on assumptions."

"I wonder who Emma was texting? I didn't notice a phone when I found her."

"We're looking for it. I suspect the killer took it. They probably ditched it or hid it somewhere so they wouldn't be caught with it. We're working on obtaining a search warrant to investigate Emma's phone records right now. Once we send the warrant to the phone company we're hoping they'll comply quickly. They usually do in murder cases. But for all we know, the killer used a burner phone to make it more difficult to trace him."

I sighed and unwrapped my arm from Jake's. "So, the whole thing was premeditated because of the Santa suits? Well, that's a little better than the thought of a random attacker, isn't it?"

"Not much. Right now, the killer is hoping not to be detected. So far, they've done a good job covering their tracks with the Santa suits. But as we get closer to discovering the killer's identity, they will get increasingly more desperate to stay undiscovered." Adrian squinted at me. "I'm looking at you, Tory."

"I know, but it did happen on my lot and if my employees are suspected—"

Adrian stood up straighter as if to enforce his authority. "Look. Let me be perfectly clear. This is not your job. It's my job and we'll find the killer. We actually have some leads already."

My ears pricked up. "You do? What."

Jake turned to me. "Tory, Adrian's right. Desperate people are dangerous."

I shook my head at both of them. "How dumb do you think I am? I know that. All I wanted to do was ask some questions. See if I could figure out if Emma had any enemies."

Jake spoke softly. "Well, obviously she had at least one."

"Okay. I get you don't want me to interfere in your investigation. Don't worry. I don't want to get killed. And you both know I'm cautious. I let people know whenever I go anyplace I feel unsure about."

I gathered Adrian did not like my response one bit based on his agitated pacing.

Jake nudged me toward the door. "Thanks, Adrian. Please keep us posted. Understandably, we're all still in shock over Emma's death."

Adrian stood by his door. "We'll have our tech team examine the video more carefully. They're good at picking up minute details we don't see at first glance."

Jake and I exited Adrian's office. We wound through the sea of cubicles and out the locked door to the lobby.

As soon as we were outside the station, I relaxed a little bit. "Hey, want to grab a coffee? I have an appointment to show Milo's condo in just over an hour. But I need caffeine."

"Sure, that sounds good."

We walked down the Avenue toward Clementine's, a locally owned café.

"Mind if we take the long way past the tree lot? I want to see whether the cops are still there."

"And what it looks like decorated with yellow crime scene tape instead of Christmas garlands?"

"Right. Please, don't remind me. Nothing conveys a holly jolly Christmas like yellow crime scene tape."

"Did Adrian say when you'll be allowed to open again?"

"He said whenever they're done working the crime scene."

"Okay. So probably today sometime."

"Hopefully."

Three police cars and a news truck from a Santa Barbara NBC affiliate were parked on the street in front of the lot. As we neared the lot, I noticed a familiar face. Simon, my wedding photographer, was taking photos of the tree lot.

"Simon!"

"Hi, Tory. I haven't seen you since . . ."

Awkward pause. "The wedding. What are you doing here?"

"I freelance for the *Sentinel*. They asked me to come out and take a few pics of the lot. The police have been hush-hush about the victim and the whole case, actually, not that we have that many murders in Santa Sofia to compare it to." He stopped. "Sorry, Tory. I wasn't thinking."

"No problem, Simon."

"Anyway, there were a couple of news trucks here last night, broadcasting live for the ten o'clock news. They didn't seem to know much or have any details either. It's almost as if a gag order's been issued for the case. At least I don't have to worry about being scooped with the police being so tight-lipped."

It wasn't that hard to scoop the *Sentinel* since it only came out once a week. But the other news trucks were what concerned me. I hadn't watched any TV coverage of Emma's murder yet, but even though the police were being discreet, the detail that had been made public was that it happened at our tree lot. My fears about negative publicity hurting business just became worse.

A loud voice called out, "Tory!"

I turned. It was Ernie Gomez. He ducked under the yellow tape and sauntered toward us.

"Hi, Ernie."

"Returning to the scene of the crime, huh?" He smirked.

"I own the lot, Ernie. I kind of have an interest in seeing how the investigation is going." I ignored his poor attempt at what I guessed was his idea of cop humor. "I wanted to find out how much longer before we can open the lot."

"We're nearly done."

"Have you found anything interesting?"

"Wouldn't you like to know."

"I would. That's why I asked." Jake tilted his head as if to warn me to reign it in. "Sorry, I'm just concerned. This is the peak week when people buy trees. We need to reopen ASAP."

"Understood. We're nearly done. We should be wrapped up in the next ten minutes or so."

I was surprised at his civility. "Oh. That's great. Thanks."

"Believe it or not, the department has some bigger issues on the table at the moment."

I wondered what could possibly be bigger than Emma's murder.

"Funny how everything points to the killer being one of your employees."

And there it was. His snark was still in good shape. "Oh, have you found evidence indicating the killer was a Benning Brothers employee?"

"He was wearing a Santa suit."

"Lots of people do this time of year. It's Christmas."

Jake put his hand on my shoulder.

I gave him a glance to acknowledge his warning to stay calm. "Anything other than that? Have you found the weapon yet?"

"Well, the email telling all employees to wear Santa suits must have come from an employee. That is, unless anyone can use your Benning Brothers email under the scheduler's name."

"Of course not. But that doesn't prove anything other than someone other than the scheduler accessed the account. It could be a friend or a friend of a friend who accessed it."

"Or a hacker," Jake added.

Ernie nodded. "A possibility. I'm looking at opportunity. That's all. I start with the most obvious first."

"The low-hanging fruit."

"Sometimes crimes aren't that complicated, Tory. I can see where you're coming from, given the past. But the truth is, it often is as simple as who had the opportunity and a motive."

"Agree." When someone is right, even if it's someone like Ernie, I liked to give credit where credit was due.

"Speaking of motive, I hear that your manager, Matt Ortega, and Emma were in a relationship."

"Emphasis on the 'were.' It's my understanding they broke up."

"Exactly. We could characterize him as a jilted lover, definitely a motive, and someone who had access to the email system, correct?"

"Yes, but, that's all circumstantial evidence. Surely, you need to delve further to see who else might have had a motive."

"Like I said. Sometimes it isn't that complicated."

Chapter 7

True to Ernie's word, five minutes later the police started to pack up. Soon they would lift the crime scene status on our tree lot.

I beckoned to Jake. "Come on. Let's poke around to see if we can find anything that seems like a clue before they remove the yellow tape and Matt opens the lot."

Jake nodded. "You think we'll see something the cops might have missed? Okay, I guess there's no harm in that. Let's split up. It'll be faster that way and we can focus."

"Good idea. I really need to talk to Matt ASAP, but this is our last chance to scour the area before people are let in again."

"I'll take this side and you take the other."

Jake turned and headed down the main aisle of trees. I stuck to the edge of the lot that was next to the nursery building. A couple of sawhorses and a stack of wooden tree stands punctuated the clearing that was usually stirring with activity. Slices of tree trunks riddled the sawdust. The hut where our cashier accepted payments and scheduled deliveries was empty.

Then I remembered our delivery truck. We'd have a backlog from last night. I'd have to check with Matt on that too. I wondered whether Adrian and Ernie had examined the pickup we used to deliver trees. I continued circling the perimeter. All of the tools, the saws used to cut the bottoms off the trees to refresh them before attaching the stands and the hammers and mallets to pound on the wooden stands were all missing. I assumed they'd been confiscated as evidence so they could be tested for prints. Good luck. Probably every employee's prints were on them. But I still wondered if they'd examined the truck.

I poked my head in the nursery office and knocked on the doorjamb.

Matt turned toward me from poring over the computer screen. "Hi, Tory. I'm going over today's deliveries, making sure the customers who we couldn't deliver to yesterday are first on today's delivery list. What can I do for you?"

"I was just coming to ask you about the truck. Who was scheduled to deliver yesterday?"

"One of our temps, Connor, was supposed to do deliveries. You remember him, right? Chris Kringle's grandson."

"Yes, I saw him yesterday when we were talking to you. I knew he was Chris Kringle's grandson. I haven't been formally introduced to him though."

"He's a hard worker."

"I never got the full story. Why does he work here and at the Santa's Helpers lot? Seems odd that he'd work at his grandfather's main competition."

"He appealed to me mainly because he has his own truck and is willing to use it for deliveries. Delivery people usually make good tips. So, what he lacks in hours he can make up in tips. And working at both lots combined gives him a decent income."

"Oh. I didn't know he used his own truck. I'm assuming we pay him mileage then too?"

Matt nodded. "Correct."

"Where is the Benning Brothers delivery truck now? I'd like to take a look at it before you start loading it. Where's it parked? I don't see it around anywhere."

"It's on Benning Lane, near the back entrance. Connor used it yesterday to make our early deliveries because his truck was in the shop and then he parked it back there. He should be there now waiting for a new shipment of trees."

Jake appeared at the door of Matt's office as I was leaving. "Hi. I finally caught up with you. Where're you going now?"

"To look at the delivery truck. Want to join me?"

"Sure. I thought you had a condo showing."

"Not for another half hour."

We walked along the sidewalk that encircled the lot on two sides to the back side of the lot on Benning Lane, a short, private cul de sac solely used by Benning Brothers personnel. It led to a loading area for the nursery. No one was there and the rear entrance gate was ajar.

"I guess we could have just come through the lot. I didn't know the gate would be open. Doesn't look like the new shipment of trees has arrived yet. This looks like it does at the end of most days."

Jake wandered around and disappeared around a bend in the road. "Hey, Tory! Is this the delivery truck you were talking about?"

I rounded the corner. "Yes." I jogged over to the delivery truck Jake was pointing to. The windows were open. The truck bed was empty.

Jake caught up with me and moved to the other side of the truck. We faced each other through the truck's open windows.

His gaze traveled the inside of the truck. "See anything of interest at your end?"

I opened the door of the cab and looked around. I climbed into the driver's seat. The keys were in the ignition. I jiggled them. "That's odd."

"What?"

"I think these are Matt's missing keys."

"Matt lost his keys? When?"

"Yeah. Yesterday. I had to drop off an extra set for him yesterday morning. I guess he found them and forgot to mention it."

Jake climbed in the passenger side and whistled.

I snapped my head in his direction. "What's wrong?"

Jake already had his camera poised and took several shots of the floor. I followed the camera's aim. It was a hammer. A bloodied hammer.

"Is that—"

"The murder weapon. Yes, that would be my guess."

"Ernie was right." Wow. Again, never thought I'd hear myself say that.

"About what?"

"He said it would be a hammer or mallet that we used to hammer the tree stands."

"I'll call Adrian."

"Thanks. Hope we get him and not Ernie. I don't know whether I'm up for him lording this over all of us."

Jake and I both took photos of the hammer and I took pics of the keys too. Adrian arrived in less than five minutes with two crime scene investigators.

I smiled at Adrian. "Well, Ernie will be thrilled. He was right about the weapon."

"Let's not jump the gun. It's highly likely it's the weapon but we have to make sure the blood matches Emma's before we can call it the murder weapon."

"Of course. But it probably is, right?"

Adrian nodded. "And you won't have to worry about Ernie for a while."

"Why? Has he been reprimanded for not behaving? He's actually seemed a tiny bit better than usual to me."

"No. But that's good to hear. He just requested a personal leave right before I got Jake's call."

"He did? For what?"

Adrian grimaced and clicked his tongue.

"What does that mean? Is he ill?"

Adrian leaned in conspiratorially. "He didn't specify. But I think his father is on another bender. At least that's been the buzz around the department. He apparently told one of the other officers."

I leaned back as if a ghost had given me a shove. My feelings were a hodgepodge of shock, surprise, compassion, and, yes, guilt. I tried to live my life by several mantras, and one was to be kind to everyone, especially because we never really knew what others might be dealing with. I hated to admit it, but I knew nothing of Ernie's family situation and really had never given it much thought. I knew he wasn't married. But in junior high when I'd had the most interaction with him, it had never occurred to me that I knew nothing about his family. I didn't know whether he had siblings. I assumed if he had they'd have been far apart in age since I never saw him hanging with siblings, or with anyone, for that matter.

"Oh, no. His father's an alcoholic?"

"Appears to be."

"So that might be why Ernie is so messed up. Poor Ernie. I had no idea. How did we not know this before? His mother always seemed fine. I don't ever remember seeing his dad."

Adrian heaved a sigh. "Yep. I'm assuming it must be an awful situation if it forced him to take time off."

Somehow none of this jibed with what I knew of Ernie. He didn't strike me as the self-sacrificing type at all. "Are you sure he's telling the truth? Do you think that's the real reason he's taking off?"

Adrian raised his eyebrows. "Why on earth would anyone lie about that? For sympathy? I doubt it. Even Ernie isn't that hard up."

Which led me to my second mantra, to always remember that sometimes things aren't what they appear to be. Story of my life, apparently. Except for Milo. I was right about him. I still couldn't believe he was gone. And that someone so great had been mine, for however short that time was. Although his love would live forever in my heart. Leading me to my third mantra: always be grateful, because things could always be worse.

"Tory, you okay?"

"What, yeah. Just daydreaming. Going down memory lane." I turned to Adrian. "So how long will it take to see if the blood matches Emma's?"

"Not too long. A couple of days at most. Also, we'll want to see what prints we might be able to pick up, if any, and run them against those in our system."

"Got it. Okay, so I guess we just sit tight."

Matt Ortega jogged up to the truck. "What's going on? Why is everyone around the truck? Where's Connor?"

Adrian stepped toward Matt. "We found a possible murder weapon inside."

"Murder weapon?" Matt's mouth fell open in shock.

"We found a hammer with blood on it in the cab. Sticking out from under the passenger seat. Well, Jake found it."

"Matt, you didn't tell me you found your keys."

Matt wiped his brow. "What do you mean? I didn't."

"Aren't those your keys? They have the little tape measure on them like yours."

Adrian's phone pinged. "I need to take this." He walked away toward the lot.

"So, Matt, I'm still unclear. Those were your keys in the truck—"

Matt stuck his head in the truck window to take a look. "Those are my truck keys. But those aren't the ones I lost. I gave these to Connor yesterday. He was our delivery driver this weekend. I didn't keep my truck keys with all the nursery keys that are missing. Well, actually, now that I think of it, there was an extra truck key on the lost set of keys. But I never used that truck key because it would have been awkward with all the other keys on the ring clanging around. It was there as a spare for an emergency."

My phone pinged. It was a text from Ashley.

I sighed. "Great."

Jake cocked his head. "Something wrong?"

"Ashley said the guy they ID'd as the real killer in her Justice Program case has disappeared. He didn't show up at the police station as agreed this morning, and when they went to his house he wasn't there. Looks like he skipped town."

Jake twisted his mouth to the side. "Skipped town? More likely he probably freaked out and is in hiding in town somewhere. His lawyer will remind him that if he doesn't turn himself in, he can say bye-bye to any plea-bargaining option. That's usually enough to get some of them to follow through with the original plan."

My phone pinged again with another text from Ashley. "Ashley says Dwayne Rudders, the alleged murderer, had told Barry—Barry's the professor who headed the case—that he was a changed man. He had claimed to have led a good life for the past fifteen years and had hoped that would influence the judge to be lenient."

Jake smirked. "Well, he can kiss that goodbye if he doesn't turn himself in soon."

"To be fair, I don't think that's Ashley's take. I don't think she's actually ever met him. That's just her impression from what Barry told her."

Jake sighed. "Got it. Well, hopefully he'll come to his senses and surrender. He's just making it worse."

I nodded. "I know but I'm sure the thought of losing his freedom gave him cold feet."

Adrian returned from his phone call with his brow furrowed and looking slightly flushed. "My day just got super complicated. I've got to get back to the station. The CSI crew are wrapping things up and you can use the truck again then."

"Okay, thanks. Does your complicated day have anything to do with Ashley's Justice Program case by any chance?"

Adrian's face registered surprise. "What? No. She told you about that? Yeah. No. Different case."

"Ashley told me Dwayne Rudders never turned himself in."

Adrian looked at his phone. "I think technically he had all weekend to turn himself in, even though they'd agreed he'd turn himself in at noon yesterday, so she shouldn't panic yet. And I heard that Lyle Bubb, the guy who was exonerated, was released without a hitch. So, one step forward, at least, despite some other setbacks. Anyway, I'm probably going to have to take a trip down to Santa Barbara for this other matter."

Jake gave Adrian's arm a soft punch. "Sorry, man. Been there with the setbacks. Hey, I'm going back to Santa Barbara tonight. If you need a place to stay, you're more than welcome to stay at my place."

"Thanks, bro. I just might take you up on that unless they assign someone to tag along with me. Let me make sure I've got your number."

Jake and Adrian both verified each other's info on their phones.

Adrian turned to leave and addressed Jake. "Thanks again. I'll let you know either way once I get more details."

"Sounds good. I plan to be in Santa Barbara around six. Depends on how long my meeting here lasts."

Adrian got another text. "Looks like I'll be flying solo. Text me your address."

"Will do. See you there." Jake looked at his phone. "I have some missed work calls and then a meeting that was moved up. I better respond. Catch up with you later?"

I checked the time on my phone. "Yikes. Look at the time! I'm going to be late for my condo appointment." I had a missed call and voice mail. "My three o'clock appointment just canceled. They found another place. My next appointment isn't until five."

Jake squeezed my shoulder. "I need to take off now."

I smiled. "Good luck on your meeting or whatever. See you around."

See you around, right. He lived twelve miles away in Santa Barbara, the only way I'd see him around is if I went there or he visited Santa Sofia again. To be honest, it wasn't the distance so much as what living in two different towns symbolized. It was like we were living in two different worlds. I was a landscape architect with a family business to run, and still grieving the loss of my father and husband. Jake was a private investigator who worked alone for the most part. Santa Barbara really wasn't that far away, and with super light traffic was only a half hour away. It just felt like more than physical distance was working against us. Plus, I didn't know how I felt about this new BFF chumminess between Jake and Adrian. It was nice but I had to admit I was a bit chagrinned that Adrian would visit Jake's place before I did. Or if I ever would, was more accurate.

"Thanks. I'll let you know how it goes. If this turns out to become a new client, then I might be coming to Santa Sofia more often."

"Cool. See you."

He gave me a hug and off he went, passing Matt Ortega on his way.

One CSI guy was left still taking photographs of the truck.

Matt and I moved away from the truck.

"Any updates on our computer hacking and the scheduling of all the Santas?"

Matt scratched his head. "I've been thinking about that. You know, in connection to Emma's death . . ."

"I know. It puts a whole new twist on it, doesn't it? Like not just a prank, but maybe part of an intentional ploy to make it impossible to ID a murderer."

"Yep. Can't be just a coincidence. Everyone dressed alike."

I put my hands on my hips. "Making it hard to tell who's who. I think the cops think that too. At first it seemed like a stretch to think it was intentionally orchestrated to mask a murder. But the more I think about it, I think that's exactly what it was."

"Scary if that was the case."

"Also, Matt, related to the hacking, it might not be a great idea for Connor or other delivery guys to leave your keys in the truck. Someone can steal it or . . ."

Awkward silence. He nodded. "Or plant evidence. I know it looks bad, Tory. But I swear I would never hurt Emma. I had zero motivation."

"I was thinking more of getting in a wreck or hitting someone, but since you brought it up, I did know you two dated for a bit. Didn't she break up with you? I can see how Ernie, and maybe even Adrian, would focus on questioning people who might have a grudge with Emma."

"I don't know where you're getting your information, but I broke up with Emma. She's, or was, a nice person but she had a—"

"Control problem. Yeah, I picked that up just in my business dealings with her."

"No, I was going to say needy."

"Emma? Needy? I never saw that side of her, personally."

"Yeah, it came out of left field. She wasn't that way at all before I ever asked her out. But once we started seeing each other she just got too clingy for what I was looking for. Abandonment issues, I guess."

"Hmm. So how did she react when you broke it off with her?"

"Not great. She accused me of cheating on her. Which I did not. Under her confident façade she was actually pretty insecure."

"Wow. I'd never have guessed that."

"Yeah, then when I started dating Rachel . . ."

"Oh, I wasn't aware you and Rachel were officially dating. I noticed you seemed close."

"Well, it's more than dating. We've been in a relationship for about two months now. And that didn't sit well with Emma one bit."

I wondered if that was what Emma and Rachel had been arguing about yesterday morning.

"Rachel was in a tough spot. She adored working for Emma. Said she was a great boss. But Rachel was considering quitting because Emma just couldn't move forward. Stuck on Rachel and me in a relationship."

"You told all of this to Adrian I hope, right?"

"Yep. Explained it in detail with a timeline."

"Good."

The last CSI guy had packed up his equipment and told us he was done with the truck.

"Okay then. I must head out. I have an appointment to show Milo's condo to a potential renter. I know you'll be busy with deliveries and getting the lot back to normal."

We walked through the lot to the front entrance. "Looks like you'll have plenty of time to set up. Very light for the Sunday three weeks before Christmas. I guess people heard about the murder."

Matt nodded somberly. "News travels fast in Santa Sofia. It was the main story on the local news last night."

"Well, hopefully it'll die down soon, er, sorry, poor choice of words. Oh, one last thing, Matt. Can I have Rachel's phone number please?"

He gave me a wary look and hesitated.

"I want to talk to her about a job. I think Cynthia's food truck might want to hire her. I'd certainly recommend her. Now with Emma gone, I'm not sure what arrangements she made. Will her business fold now or did she have a silent partner or investors, do you know?"

"I don't, but I know Rachel would really appreciate any recommendations you could give. Thanks so much, Tory."

I crossed Manzanita Street over to the Benning Brothers landscape architecture offices parking lot. As soon as I got into my car, I called Rachel.

She picked up after three rings. "Hi, Rachel. How are you doing?"

"As well as can be expected, I guess. My boss is dead, and I think the police suspect my boyfriend as her killer. But other than that, things are awesome."

"I'm sorry. I have a bit of experience with my world collapsing from all sides, so please know I'm here if you need someone to talk to. We just found a possible murder weapon, so I'm sure any suspicion the cops have about Matt will be quickly cleared up once they find someone else's prints on the weapon."

"Yeah, Matt just texted me."

"Are you up for grabbing a snack or a coffee? I have an appointment in about an hour and a half, but I have a possible lead for a job you might be interested in. I'd like to share it with you if you have time."

"Um, okay. I'm not hungry but coffee sounds good."

"Okay. How about Clementine's bakery?" Since Jake and I had gotten detoured from going there, I'd had Clementine's on my mind. "They have great goodies. I can use some comfort food today. How long will it take you to get there?"

"I can be there in ten to fifteen minutes."

"Great. See you then."

Chapter 8

On my way over to meet Rachel, I decided to swing by the Santa's Helpers tree lot to see how business was doing for Benning Brothers tree lot's main competitor. I turned right on the Avenue and headed toward the foothills, the majestic backdrop for Santa Sofia, as the sun was setting over the Pacific and the marine layer returned. Twinkle lights were everywhere, strung across the Avenue, wrapped around the trunks of palm trees, and netted over storefront topiaries. Cedar garlands and evergreen wreaths with red bows adorned almost every door and window. My phone rang. It was Ashley.

"Whatcha doin'?"

"I'm on my way to meet Rachel at Clementine's. What about you?"

"Just wrapping up the paperwork on the Justice Program case. Our client was released. Finally. After fifteen years."

"That's great. Adrian had mentioned that. Wow. That's a long time. What's he going to do now?"

"I don't really know. I know what I'd do. I'd go to Shake Shack and order a cheeseburger, fries, and a milkshake. Then I'd take a long nap. Then I'd go to Sadie's Seafood for dinner."

"You're getting me hungry. Now I feel like making a detour and cruising by Shake Shack for a burger." I laughed. "So, what happens to the guy that you think is the real killer, Rudders? He has to have a trial now, right?"

Ashley cleared her throat. "Theoretically. But the DA will try to negotiate a plea deal first."

"By the way, have you talked to Adrian lately?"

"No, why? All I got from him recently was a cryptic text that said he'd be laying low for a while because of a new case. And not to take it personally."

"What! He actually said not to take it personally?"

"Well, I think his exact words were that his performance review is in two weeks and he wants to finish strong."

A chuckle escaped my lips. "Oh. A little different. But anyway, guess where he's spending the night tonight?"

"Oh my god, where? I knew it! He's seeing someone else, isn't he? And how did you find out?"

"Slow down. No, no one else that I know of, unless you call Jake someone. I was there when Jake made him the offer." I giggled.

"What? I don't understand."

"Adrian has to go to Santa Barbara for a case and Jake offered to let him stay with him."

"Aw, that was nice of Jake. Two cute BFFs."

I stopped at a light and stared at an adorable lighted twig reindeer in a clothing store window. "I know. Nice they've become buddies."

"Did Adrian say what the case was? I wonder if it has to do with Emma."

"Not really. Just that there was an unexpected development in an ongoing investigation."

"Hmm. An ongoing case in Santa Barbara. I wonder why Adrian would be involved. The only crime news I've heard about that happened in Santa Barbara was that woman who went missing. Did you hear about that? About a week ago?"

I inhaled deeply and exhaled to calm myself. I'd heard, all right. And tried to repress it. "Yeah, I did. Her roommate said she went to meet someone she met on a dating app."

Ashley gasped. "Get out! I hadn't heard that part. And you still let me make a profile for both of us! What were you thinking?"

"Ashley. I've never liked the idea of dating apps. You know that. You told me the app you were using was different because women controlled the process more. And I only saw the part about the dating app this morning in a news update."

Ashley sighed. "Fine. But when were you going to tell me?"

"I think I just did."

"Well, no need to worry. I'm very careful and now I'll be even more careful, just for you. You have access to my profile. But, to be honest, this has made it a little less appealing now."

"A *little* less appealing? Props to you for not living in fear though."

"Tory, I wouldn't be a lawyer if I was afraid of bad guys."

"Good point. You're a badass. Got it. Anyway, the cops haven't let out any details about her identity or the actual circumstances, which is weird. Until they do, we really won't know what's going on. And thank you. I'm glad you're going to be more prudent from now on."

"Anyway, the reason I called was to know if you want to have dinner tonight."

"That sounds great. Where were you thinking?"

"Sadie's?"

"I'd love to. I haven't been there since yesterday." I laughed.

"We can go somewhere else if you want."

"No. Sadie's is fine. Maybe I'll try something new on the menu this time."

Ashley chuckled. "Bold move. Okay. I'll make a reservation for around six. Is that okay? I have a big day at work tomorrow, so I don't want to stay out too late. In fact, I should get off the phone right now. I have to wrap up some loose ends on our Justice Program case now too."

"Perfect. Okay, I'm at my destination now too. See you then. Thanks."

I cruised past the front of the Santa's Helpers tree lot. Strings of lights with big white bulbs lit up the crowded corner location. I caught a glimpse of the owner, Chris Kringle, easy to pick out in his Santa outfit as I passed by. He was talking to a couple of elves, hence the Santa's Helpers moniker. As my late father told it, though both lots were institutions in Santa Sofia, Benning Brothers was the first lot where employees wore any type of costume. I circled around the block to where Cynthia's food truck was parked and, judging by the throng around it, business was thriving. I wondered if Cynthia had been quite that busy before Emma's murder. I made an impulsive move and parked a few spaces away from her truck.

Cynthia saw me, waved me over, and greeted me warmly. "Hey, Tory, how are you?" Her face dimpled in various places, having the overall effect of watching a cookie pucker in the oven while baking. "What can I get you, doll?"

Cynthia's blond hair was tucked under an elf's hat and she was dressed in a black long-sleeved turtleneck top and a red apron with an appliquéd Christmas tree with little jingle bells stitched on it. She motioned me closer while one of her employees tended to customers. "I heard about Emma. Please tell me it was someone she knew and not someone who had a grudge against food truck owners."

In spite of myself I smiled. "Of all the many scenarios of possible motives that have swirled around in my head, a food truck serial killer was not one of them . . . until now. Although, the police leave everything on the table until they have a theory based on evidence, so you never know."

She blessed herself. "Oh, lordy. Hope they catch whoever did it soon. But can you imagine my shock? We're a tight little community, us food truck owners. Of course, we're all friendly competitors, but first and foremost we like to help each other."

That seemed like the opposite of my impression. I'd found the food truck owners who I'd dealt with to be very competitive and grudgingly helpful toward each other, Exhibit A being my experience negotiating a schedule that Emma and Cynthia both agreed to for our tree lot this year. Alternate days were what we ended up with.

I cocked my head. "I wanted to find out if you'll be able to come to our tree lot more frequently now and fill in the gaps Emma's truck had covered?"

For a moment her eyes glinted with what looked like gloat, but only for a nanosecond. "Of course. I'll call Matt Ortega to work out a schedule. Her employees aren't going to continue without her?"

"I don't really know. I'm on my way to meet with her assistant, Rachel, right now. I have no idea what their arrangement was or if they had a succession plan in place if something happened to Emma. Do you know?"

"I heard Emma recently had a silent partner buy into the business.

So, I'm assuming their identity will be made public soon." A smirk lit her face briefly. She knew who the silent partner was. I was sure of it.

"You don't know who that silent partner might be?"

"I might have heard rumors but—"

Her gaze fixed on something behind me. I felt someone standing close behind me off to one side. When I turned around it was Chris Kringle in his Santa suit.

He towered over me. "I thought that was you, Tory. How are you? Heard about the horrible incident at the lot. Awful business. And, awful for business. Have the cops caught the culprit yet?"

"Hi, Chris. They're working on it." I almost mentioned the hammer found in our delivery truck but caught myself. "Looks like your lot is doing well, as usual."

He looked ready to launch into one of his long monologues, which were actually endearing, but before he could an elf tapped him on the shoulder. I recognized Connor in the jaunty red-and-green-striped hat with pointy ears. He made eye contact and nodded. "Excuse me, Gramps, but the new delivery just arrived, and we need you."

"What? Oh, okay." His gaze followed his grandson. "Duty calls. Nice seeing you, Tory. Hope you can reopen soon."

Before I had the chance to inform him that we already had, he'd trotted away in the same direction as his grandson. I turned back to Cynthia. "We actually are already reopened."

"Oh, that's great news." Her voice made the right intonation to express joy, but her eyes blinked rapidly. I couldn't tell whether her fidgeting resulted from the news of our reopening or her distraction as she eyed the growing line of customers waiting to be served. "I'd love to talk more, Tory, but I better get back to work."

"Okay. One last thing, I'm on my way to see Emma's assistant, Rachel. Obviously, she's upset. But if she's up to it, would you be in the position to hire her for the rest of the holiday season? I'm sure she'd be grateful, and it might be good for her to have the structure of work to help her cope."

"Sure. We can always use good help. Have her call me." She dipped into her apron pocket and pulled out a business card.

"Thanks. Don't know if she'll take you up on it, but I'm sure the gesture will be much appreciated."

I hopped back into my car and headed to Clementine's, fretting over the loss of business we might experience if Emma's killer wasn't arrested. I found a space right out front. Rachel was walking along the sidewalk as I got out of my car.

I waved. "Perfect timing."

Rachel wore fashionably ripped jeans and a navy sweatshirt. Her auburn hair was swept up into a high ponytail. We hugged briefly and entered Clementine's. A small round table next to a window beckoned and we settled ourselves on the bentwood cane chairs while exchanging accolades for one of Santa Sofia's favorite bakeries and cafés.

"So. How are you doing?"

Her gaze flitted from the floor to the ceiling and skimmed the shiny glass cases of baked goods across the room before she gave me very brief eye contact. "Hanging in there, thanks. I think I'm still in shock."

"Me too. I can't believe it." I paused for several seconds. "Ashley and I heard you and Emma yesterday in the truck. Your voices were raised. Can you tell me what you were arguing about? She told me it was about you forgetting the eggnog. But we saw the eggnog on the counter. It wasn't about eggnog, was it?"

Rachel squirmed in her seat. Her eyelids fluttered as she looked at the table. Finally, she looked me in the eye. "Yes and no."

"How so?"

"Well, Emma wanted to have extra eggnog because we've been selling out on weekends. And I'd forgotten to bring the extras."

I waited for her to continue. "And the 'no' part?"

More fidgeting with her hair and wiggling around in her chair before she took a deep breath. "She was upset about me and Matt. She accused me of stealing him away from her, which wasn't true at all. But she wouldn't believe me."

"How did you end it?"

"We didn't really . . . that's why I feel so badly. We had customers to serve and I needed to fetch the eggnog, so we just left it hanging."

Ashley and I were the customers to whom she referred. I was lost in my thoughts for a moment, wondering if their fight would have ended more amicably had Ashley and I not shown up, and marveling how one variable could affect subsequent outcomes and change the course of events.

"You went and got the eggnog?"

She nodded sullenly. Dressed down and with no makeup, she reminded me of a forlorn child who'd gotten separated from her mother in a crowded store—scared and on the verge of tears.

"So that was the last time you saw her."

Tears trickled down her cheeks. "If only I'd insisted on making up then and there and to not end on an angry note. Maybe she'd be alive right now."

Her statement triggered my own feelings I felt after Milo disappeared. What if I'd done something differently, would he still be alive? What if I'd insisted that he waited with me while our photographer, Simon, took photos of me? The circumstances were different, true. Milo went missing without a trace at first. Emma was found right away. But still. I shook my head. "Wait, why exactly do you think Emma might be alive had you not argued?"

"Because of the text she got. She said this must be her day to confront all her enemies."

I gulped. "Do you know who the text was from?"

She sniffled. "I think so."

"Who?"

"Matt." Now the floodgates opened.

Had Matt lied to me? I was under the impression he no longer communicated with Emma, given that he'd dumped her. Why on earth would he have texted Emma and not mentioned it? Rachel's sobs snapped me out of my reverie.

I got up and gave her a hug. "I'm sorry, Rachel. I didn't mean to make you cry." I had to remind myself that not everyone processed grief like me. She was letting it all hang out, something I hardly ever did.

She emitted a snorting noise that sounded like a cross between a sniffle and a sob. "No, I'm the one who should be sorry, Tory. I've got to get control of myself. I don't want to get Matt in trouble. But I'm not going to lie either."

"But you're not positive the text was from him though, right? That's just your guess."

"Who else would it be? She was mad at both of us."

I got up and went to the counter and ordered two chocolate chip cookies and tea for both of us. While I completed my transaction, my thoughts drifted to different theories of the case. Crimes of passion often occurred between quarreling lovers or ex-lovers. And usually, by definition, were spontaneous. Yet the hacked email instructing all our employees to dress as Santa suggested premeditation, not a crime of passion, assuming the hacking was related to the murder, which seemed to be the consensus. A clerk with a cheery bandana on his head gave me the cookies in a small paper bag and said he'd bring the tea to us at our table. I waited a few minutes without speaking while Rachel pulled herself together. Our tea arrived and we both took a bite of the melt-in-your-mouth cookies.

"Hey, I saw Cynthia at the Santa's Helpers lot and she mentioned that Emma had recently acquired a silent business partner. Do you know anything about that?"

She swigged her tea in the mug and shook her head. Her gaze then flitted around the room and out the window, which I took to indicate she very well did know who the partner was and for some reason didn't want to reveal the identity and/or didn't want to let on that she knew who it was.

I tried a different tack. "Cynthia also told me she might need extra help. So, if you're interested, you should give her a call." I reached into my pocket, where I'd dropped Cynthia's business card, and handed it to Rachel.

"Aw, thanks, Tory." She smiled for the first time, reminding me that when your world implodes sometimes it's the little gestures that help you through it all.

"I hate to bring it up again, but I want to make sure I understand before we go. You think it was Matt who texted Emma because that's what you and Emma were fighting about, but can you think of anyone else she might be fighting with? Like her silent partner or other business acquaintances? A family member? Was she dating anyone new?"

"Not that I know of. She was on a dating app. I think she was doing it just for fun. I don't know whether or not she actually went on a date with anyone. I kind of doubt it actually. She worked a lot. We didn't get much time off. The time we weren't working at the truck was spent ordering and keeping track of inventory, and of course, baking."

I looked at my phone. "Oh my gosh! I didn't realize how late it was already. I have an appointment to get to in less than fifteen minutes. I better get going. Thanks for taking the time to meet with me."

"Thank you, Tory. The pleasure was mine. It felt good to let it out actually. Sorry to break down like that."

"Hey, I know it's tough. Trust me, even though it might be hard to believe right now, time is the big healer. And do follow up with Cynthia if you feel like working. It's a great way to get your mind off your problems, at least for me it is. Let me know if you remember anything else about anything Emma said or anything you overheard."

I took the Avenue down to the Promenade and drove north along the coast. The road hardly had any traffic and I made good time as I raced to Milo's condo. I couldn't bear to sell his condo, so I'd rented it out. The current tenant was moving at the end of the month and I'd advertised on a real estate website that listed local rentals. I'd only gotten a few bites and was mad at myself for running late, possibly jeopardizing the prospect that had seemed the most promising based on our phone call. I called to let her know I was running late but her voice-mail box was full. I was hoping she'd notice my call and contact me. I'd already met with one couple who were looking for something larger, or so they claimed, and I had another appointment set up with a different couple for tomorrow.

It was getting dark and Miramar Lane, where his modern white stucco townhouse was located, was deserted. His townhouse and the one next to his were dark except for the Christmas lights that decorated them. I pulled into the small parking lot next to his unit and noticed all of the three guest parking spaces were vacant. Great. My prospective tenant hadn't arrived yet. I parked in Milo's designated spot since the current tenants had driven to visit their family for the holidays and hustled to the door.

When I got inside the condo, I turned on all the inside lights and the porch and balcony lights to make it seem inviting. I'd rented it out furnished, another reason why it was a little harder to rent. Most people wanted unfurnished. But I couldn't let go of Milo's furnishings quite yet either. Looking around his living room, it didn't look that different from when Milo had lived here. The current tenants hadn't started to pack up yet, but despite their own touches, a decorative pillow here, a large plant there, Milo's presence still came through. Milo had had the same minimalist taste that most architects I knew preferred. The tenants' attempts to warm up the stark interior design with Santa dish towels and decorative pillows would not have gone over big with him, although he might have approved of the chartreuse tinsel tree sitting on a glittery skirted table.

My phone buzzed. It was a text from Ashley. *Hi. Just wanted to let you know I'm on my way to Sadie's. See you in a bit.*

I texted Ashley back that I was still waiting for my prospective tenant. I checked the time—five twenty-five—and double-checked to make sure I hadn't missed a message. Nope. I assumed the prospective tenant must be on her way. I wondered if I hadn't been clear about the time or whether I'd failed to confirm our appointment. Sometimes I was guilty of thinking I'd responded to a text, only to find the unsent text later. But nope. When I checked our texts the meeting details were clear and confirmed. I sighed. Maybe she'd found another place and had forgotten to let me know. As I reflected on our texts it made me think of Emma. Who had she been texting prior to her murder? Did the murderer text her or was it someone else she was meeting at the back of the lot? Did Emma double-check her texts like I'd just done? Did someone cancel on her? Why did she change directions in the lot? The answers must lie in her phone. I wondered whether the police had found her phone yet.

After ten minutes had passed, I figured my prospective tenant wasn't coming. Ah, well. I started to turn off the lights all over, retracing my steps. The phone on the kitchen counter rang three times and then there was a shrill whistle signaling someone was about to leave a message. A loud click sounded. They'd hung up without leaving a message. That was weird. Why wait for the tone and then hang up? I shuddered and then decided it was probably a robocall.

The ride to Sadie's Seafood on the pier was short. I turned onto the pier and drove along the weathered wooden planks that clicked and clacked under me and spotted someone pulling out from a space in the wharf parking lot and parked right on the pier. I jogged to the restaurant, where Ashley was waiting for me, her head bent down scrutinizing the menu.

My face had warmed from my mini workout. "Felt good to get some exercise."

Ashley stood up and we hugged. "Every little bit counts. I went grocery shopping this afternoon and got some exercise in by parking farther away in the lot and returning my basket to the rack."

"I do that too. I haven't had a chance to exercise all weekend."

Ashley scooted her chair closer to the table and went back to studying the menu. "Says the woman who's married to Gym. I already ordered wine and I'm now in a quandary about whether I should order the lobster roll or branch out and try something new. The grilled salmon with lemon and herbs sounds particularly good."

I perused the long narrow menu for a couple of minutes. "I'm going to branch out. Salmon and a side of sautéed spinach sound divine."

"Hmm. Good choice. Okay. I'll take the plunge too. But it attests to the excellence of their lobster rolls that choosing something else presents such a dilemma."

We both tittered as the waiter brought two glasses of white wine and asked whether we were ready to order.

Ashley had her head down over the menu. "You go ahead."

I chuckled. "Afraid I'll bail on the salmon and order the lobster roll at the last minute?" I ordered the salmon.

Ashley giggled. "No. I trust you. I was making extra sure I was happy with my decision."

"Shall we get an appetizer too? Clams on the half shell sound so good."

"Do it. I'll have the salmon and spinach too please. And for an appetizer I'll have a cup of the Rhode Island clam chowder. Thanks!"

Ashley raised her glass. "How about an early toast for the new year?"

"Yes!" I clinked my glass against hers. "Here's hoping we have a new year without a murder. That would be refreshing."

"Speaking of which, how'd your meeting with Rachel go? I bet she's devastated about Emma, huh?"

"Yeah, she seemed pretty upset. She's also upset about Matt being a possible suspect. Seems like there'd been no love lost between Emma and Rachel recently. Rachel told me she felt guilty that their last interaction had been a negative one."

"Did she tell you what they were fighting about?"

"Matt and eggnog, apparently."

"Well, I don't think eggnog would ever be a motive for murder—a means perhaps, but not a motive."

I sipped my wine. "Agree. But a love triangle certainly has been the root of many murders. She swears she didn't date Matt until after he dumped Emma. But Emma didn't like the idea of Rachel dating him. Branded it disloyal."

"I could see that. But still, seems like Emma would be the one looking to murder, not the other way around."

"Right? Usually it's the odd man or woman out who wants revenge.

95

The old 'if I can't have them then nobody can.' Doesn't make sense for Matt to have a motive."

"Unless he's lying about their breakup. Maybe it was Emma who broke up with Matt."

I shook my head. "Eh. It doesn't look that way. Rachel made a big deal about Emma being mad at her for dating Matt. Why would Emma be mad if she was the one who dumped Matt? I'd say good riddance. And happy he was occupied with someone new and no longer bugging me to get back together."

"True. Unless of course Rachel's lying too. Maybe both of them wanted Emma out of the picture."

"What on earth for? What picture? She was Rachel's boss. No Emma, no job."

Ashley swigged her wine. "I'm just throwing stuff out there. Brainstorming theories of the case. Reminds me of when we were trying to figure out what happened to Milo. The only good thing to come out of that was how well we worked together in solving that mystery. Like Holmes and Watson. Nick and Nora Charles."

I laughed. "More like Lucy and Ethel in the maze."

Ashley chuckled.

The waiter brought our appetizers and we dug in. My phone pinged. "Oh, no. Did you set my phone to get notifications every time you get a match on that dating app?"

She lowered her head and then snuck a peek at me. "Maybe. Look, Tory, don't get mad. But think of it as an added precaution, a safeguard, especially after that girl went missing. You can keep your eye on me. If it really bothers you, just deactivate your account. I just wanted you to get a feel for how it works."

"Says the girl who's been on it for one whole week." I clicked on the app. "Hey, I got another match. I thought I was just supposed to be following you." I had to admit I was a little excited to see who had expressed interest in me. "Let me see who my match is." I clicked on the friend request and it revealed my match. I couldn't suppress a guffaw.

"It's that same guy you matched with, the Calvin Klein model Santa. What should I do? Wasn't he the one who was twenty-five?"

"Well, he said he was twenty-five. Whether or not he really is is anybody's guess. Why would a good-looking guy that young even resort to a dating app anyway? I think it must be a fake account."

"Oh, I get it. When he shows an interest in me it's a fake account. Is that how it goes? You were swooning when he matched with you."

"Did he leave a message?"

"Let me see. No, I don't think so."

"You have to click to get a message and then—"

The waiter had our food and the transition from appetizers to entrées demanded our full attention. Our arms entangled with the waiter's as we exchanged plates and juggled bowls with him as if we were playing a game of Twister.

"So glad we ordered this." Ashley closed her eyes fleetingly as she savored her first bite of salmon. "Oh, so good."

I quickly followed suit. "Delicious. The salmon is so succulent. The spinach is perfection too."

We ate quietly, both of us in food heaven in between sips of wine, for a minute or two.

My phone rang. I set down my fork and grabbed my phone. "It's Rachel."

Ashley raised her eyebrows. "Hope she's okay."

"Hi, Rachel. What's up?"

"They've arrested Matt!"

My body went from light wine and food buzz to high alert in a second as I flipped it to speakerphone and set it on the table. "What? Who?"

"The police. We were having dinner and now they're taking him away. What should I do?"

Ashley leaned closer to the phone. "Hey, Rachel, it's Ashley. I'm a lawyer. Don't worry. They'll take him to the station to book him. We'll meet you there."

Chapter 9

Ashley waved her hand to get our waiter's attention. "Let's get doggy bags for our spinach and salmon."

"Wait. Is that a good idea? Who knows how long we'll be at the police station."

"You're right. Fish is super perishable. I'll just ask him for the check."

Ashley and I locked gazes and we both smiled, knowing what we had to do. We both gulped down the last chunks of our salmon and sautéed spinach like we were in a pie-eating contest while we waited for our check.

"Now I really feel like Lucy and Ethel."

I laughed.

After feeling like I'd just won the chocolate bonbon conveyor belt race, we dashed out of the restaurant.

"I'm parked right over there." I pointed to my prime spot on the pier. "Where are you?"

"On a side street off the Promenade."

"Hop in. I'll drive you to your car."

I dropped Ashley off at her BMW. "See you there."

As soon as we entered the police station's garland-decorated lobby, Rachel jumped up from her chair in the otherwise empty waiting area. "Thanks so much for being here. I couldn't get any information out of them other than what I told you on the phone."

Ashley patted Rachel's shoulder. "Don't worry. Everything they do is predictable if they go by procedure, and we have no indication that Matt's case will be any different.

"Right now, it appears they just brought him in for questioning. Based on how that goes, they will either release him or ask the district attorney to charge him. If they decide to book him, then they will set a bail. Meanwhile, as long as they have him in custody, they'll interrogate him."

"Yes, that's what the public defender's office told me already."

"Good. Now, let me see if I can find out what led them to make him their prime suspect."

Ashley explained to the cop at the front desk that she was representing Matt and he made a call. A few minutes later he buzzed open the locked door. As it opened, I saw Ernie come to escort her. Hmm. I thought he had taken personal leave. Clearly, he was back. With Adrian away, Ernie would love to take over.

Rachel and I sat down on the plastic molded chairs bolted down to the floor.

I unzipped my faux leather jacket and made myself more comfortable. I felt a tad uncomfortable after chugging my salmon so quickly and popped a breath mint in my mouth, hoping fresh breath might brighten my mood. "Do you have any more ideas, Rachel, about who Emma might have been arguing with?"

"Well, there was this guy on a dating app I told you about."

"You mentioned she was on an app. I don't recall that you told me she argued with someone." It seemed as if Rachel suddenly remembered a possible suspect now that Matt had been arrested.

"Yeah. Also, Connor got her mad because he wouldn't take no for an answer from either me or Emma."

I raised my eyebrows. "Connor? You mean Chris Kringle's grandson Connor?"

She nodded. "Yes, that Connor."

"He works at both the Benning Brothers and the Santa's Helpers tree lots as a part-time temp, right?"

"Not by choice. Neither lot wanted to hire him permanently was my understanding. I for one was glad because whenever there was a lull in activity, he'd start flirting with me. Emma got mad at him the night before. Apparently, he even had started hanging around the bakery and her house, too, in a menacing manner. She said she'd say something to Matt if he didn't quit it."

Hmm. This didn't jibe with what Matt had told me about Connor. Matt had made it sound like the arrangement was satisfactory for all.

"I saw him at the Santa's Helpers lot yesterday. He didn't strike me as having a menacing bone in his body, but that might have been because he was dressed in an elf costume. And on Saturday at our lot he was in a Santa outfit so, it's hard for me to see him in a menacing light." Although all evidence pointed to the murderer most likely wearing a Santa suit. It seemed like everything having to do with Emma's murder was a case of things not being what they appeared to be. "Hmm. Anyone else Emma had issues with you can recall?"

"Other than Connor, the only other one was the dating app guy."

Both of whom she only remembered after Matt had been arrested. And another strike against dating apps for me, like I needed any more. I was still an old romantic after Milo, and organic meetings were the best. Although, when I think back on how I basically cyber-stalked him to find out his relationship status, maybe it was all relative.

Ashley came out of the enclosure. Her mouth was set as it often was when she was lawyering, I called it her resting lawyer face, and her confident stride told me she had worked her magic. "The DA is still reviewing the so-called evidence and hasn't made a decision yet. If and when they charge him, there's a standard bail schedule they'll use to set bail. I'd have to double-check, but I think if he's charged with murder the bail will be around two million dollars. But so far, they haven't yet charged him with anything. Ernie has acknowledged the evidence they've assembled is all circumstantial and inconclusive at this point."

"Two million dollars!" I swallowed hard. "I'd like to post bail for him if I can. I'll discuss it with Uncle Bob, but Matt is probably his favorite of all our employees and I'm sure he'll agree."

Rachel sighed with relief. "Thanks, Tory. So sweet of you." She turned to Ashley. "What's the timeline?"

Ashley's mouth turned down. "Sorry, but I'm afraid Matt will have to be here overnight. We'll have to wait until tomorrow morning to find out whether or not they end up charging him with anything at this point. But Ernie promised to expedite matters, so hopefully we will know what's what fairly early."

"That's great if they don't charge him."

Ashley crossed her fingers. "Fingers crossed they won't."

I walked out to the parking lot with Rachel and Ashley. We all were drained and promised to text each other when we all got home.

Iris started barking when my car pulled up in the driveway. I stared at my little stucco bungalow, bereft of any Christmas decorations, and promised myself to pick up a wreath and a couple of poinsettias for the front doorstep at the nursery. Baby steps. And yes, Iris barked loud enough for me to hear her from the driveway.

The minute I opened the door and snapped on the lights both Iris and Otis commenced to give me the best welcome, as if I'd been away for months, not hours. I bent down and pet both of them before heading to the kitchen to feed them, what they really wanted more than my affection at the moment. I texted Ashley and Rachel to let them know I'd made it home okay, and within the next couple of minutes I'd heard back the same from both of them. I texted Uncle Bob, who I'd spoken to on my drive home, to thank him once again for his help with regard to Matt's bail if needed. I changed into my pajamas, charcoal gray lounging joggers and a light gray slouch-shouldered T-shirt with *If you can be anything, be kind* written on it, my latest favorite saying.

"Okay, guys, who wants a story before bedtime? How about *Pickle Things?*"

My father used to read me *Pickle Things* by Marc Brown before I could read. He had told me I'd memorized it and then pretended to read it myself. With no kids of my own to carry on our family tradition, Iris and Otis were it. All three of us cuddled on the bed while I read.

The singsong of my narration had succeeded in lulling both pets asleep. I grabbed my laptop off the bedside table and Googled Connor Kringle to see what I could find out about him.

A text from Jake interrupted my search. I couldn't get over that, once again, he was texting on the thread that included Ashley, even after I'd told him to watch it. I let out an exasperated sigh and Iris opened her eyes. *As it turns out, I need to come up to Santa Sofia again unexpectedly tomorrow. Hope we can meet up at some point.*

Immediately, Ashley texted me on a separate thread, obviously having received Jake's text too. *No mention of Adrian or their sleepover. Press for details please.*

I asked Jake how Adrian was doing.

Jake texted me right back on the group thread. *Good. We had pizza and a beer for dinner. He's already hit the hay. His case down here blew up and he's got a busy day tomorrow.*

Ashley texted me on our separate thread again. *Thanks. I wonder what case took him down there in the first place? Must have something to do with a Santa Sofia case or resident, right? Why else would he be in Santa Barbara?*

Why, indeed. I wondered whether it had to do with Emma's murder, reflecting on the timing. Now with Matt in jeopardy and Ernie once again looking for the easiest path to an arrest and conviction, I had to admit that, oddly, I felt better emotionally than I had lately. When I thought about why, I concluded it was mainly because I wasn't focusing on my own loss of my father and husband anymore. I wanted to help Emma's friends, like Matt and Rachel, to get through theirs. Sure, I was impacted and so was my business and employees. But the brunt of the stress fell on Matt because he was a suspect and Rachel because he was her boyfriend.

And then I had an epiphany: This is exactly what I needed, to help someone else instead of focusing on my own problems, which paled in comparison. Taking action helped me heal. With this revelation, I hunkered down under the covers in a temporary state of ignorant bliss. Thoughts about Jake, Adrian's mysterious case, and illustrations of personified pickles faded away as I drifted off to sleep, unaware of the turn of events that was about to come.

Chapter 10

Early the next morning on my way to the office, my uncle called me as he headed to the courthouse to post bail.

"I spoke to a bail bondsman about arranging bail already. I also talked to Ashley. She told me Matt wasn't technically arrested yet, but an arrest might be pending. They just brought him in for questioning. She doesn't know whether or not the DA will proceed to the next step. But if they do decide to arrest him on suspicion of murder, she confirmed that bail will be two million dollars."

I whistled. "I'd hoped she'd been wrong about the amount."

"Yep. But Ashley seems confident it won't come to that."

"Okay, good. That's kind of what she thought last night. Love Ashley's confidence. Please let me know if there's anything I can do and keep me in the loop."

"Will do."

Work on most of my projects was caught up for the year. Our landscape architecture division, like the architecture firms we partnered with, was starting to pack up for the holidays. I sent some emails and responded to others. I started to peruse my projects list with due dates for the new year but my mind kept wandering, preoccupied with worrying about what was going to happen to Matt. I wondered who really had killed Emma and why, since there was no doubt in my mind that Matt was innocent. He'd always been even-tempered and solid since I'd known him. I had to admit I'd have felt a lot less scattered if there had been some solid evidence to back up my belief Matt was innocent rather than relying on gut feeling. I got up, stretched, and walked around my office a few times.

I decided to take a walk to a nearby coffee shop. When I stepped outside, I saw Cynthia's food truck at our tree lot. I strolled over and was pleasantly surprised to see Rachel manning the window.

"Rachel! You got the job!"

She beamed back at me. "Yes! Thanks so much for your help, Tory."

Cynthia popped her head around the door. "I'm lucky to have her. My chef, Crystal, typically has this shift but she called me this morning. Not feeling well. Rachel had emailed me her résumé yesterday, I called her, and the rest is history." She held her hand to her mouth conspiratorially and winked. "Already love her work ethic."

Rachel blushed. "I'm happy to get my mind back to work."

I ordered a Christmas coffee, as Cynthia called it, a mix of espresso, chocolate, milk, and cinnamon by the taste of it. I started to leave when I caught sight of Connor staring at Rachel from afar. I strolled over. "Hi, there. I'm Tory Benning. We haven't been formally introduced. I've seen you around the lot. And the Santa's Helpers lot. You're Chris Kringle's grandson, aren't you?"

He gave me a quick smile. "That's me. You know my gramps, right?"

"Yes. Not very well, but my father and he were good friends for years. I see you're working at both lots this year. You were an elf at the Santa's Helpers lot. And you get to wear reindeer antlers here. That's fun."

"It's okay. It pretty much adds up to a full-time job, so that part is good."

"But? You'd rather only work at one place?"

"Yeah, kinda. Especially after . . ."

"After Emma."

He nodded. "Yeah."

"Did you know her?"

He stuck his hands in his pockets. His head inclined downward. "Yeah. Not that well though."

I was at a loss to know how to follow up on his response given what Rachel had told me without sounding like a weirdo interested in his love life.

"Well, I guess we both should get back to work."

I started to head back to my office and Rachel motioned me over to the truck. She'd dialed back her racy outfit and traded it in for an apron with a candy cane pattern worn over her ripped jeans and long-sleeved T-shirt. Her auburn curls peeked out of a Santa's hat.

"I just wanted to thank you again for recommending me to Cynthia."

"Oh, no problem."

"And to thank you for your help with Matt. Ashley's optimistic he won't be charged."

"Fingers crossed."

"And to warn you about Connor."

"Warn me? Why?"

"If you show him any interest whatsoever, he starts hitting on you."

I laughed. "I'm about ten years older than him, I doubt it."

"He's thirty. He looks younger than he really is."

"Thirty? Really?" And still working temp jobs. I wondered what his story was.

"Yeah, he's hit on me and Emma both."

"Yeah. You mentioned that last night at the station."

She nodded emphatically.

I wondered whether Rachel had been in shock last night and didn't remember telling me about Connor. Also, I questioned her judgment since she was dissing Connor when he was most assuredly within ear-shot. As proof, when I glanced over at him, his eyes were riveted on us.

I turned my back toward him and spoke as softly as I could. "Did either of you go out with him?"

"Um, no. He asked us both out like a week apart. Did he think we didn't talk to each other? So lame. Neither of us felt like we'd encouraged him at all."

"Hmm. Well, some guys just aren't good at taking hints."

"There's more. When each of us declined his suggestion to get together, he got all pissed off. When I texted him back 'no thanks' because I had plans, he made some rude comment back, like, 'I didn't really think you were my type.' And when he asked Emma in person and she said no, he threw his drink and cake in the trash."

"Wow." I was doubly shocked. Not only for his anger toward Emma but for throwing the food away. "How could he do that? Her cake was to die for." I grimaced, instantly aware of my unfortunate word choice. "When was this?"

She thought for a minute. "Last Wednesday or Thursday, maybe."

"Did you mention this to the police?"

"No, should I have?"

"Don't you think it's coincidental that a guy gets so angry at Emma only days before she was violently attacked?"

Her face transformed. Her eyes grew wide and her mouth formed into the shape of an O. "What are you saying? You think Connor killed Emma? Over not going out on a date with him? No, I didn't mean to imply that."

Her overly dramatic response made me think she wanted to imply exactly that.

"I didn't mention it to the police because that seems unrelated to me."

And yet she purposely waved me over to tell me all this. Strange.

"Well, you know what the police always say, tell them everything you know and let them decide what information is relevant to their investigation."

"Oh, okay. When you put it like that. I didn't know. Who should I tell? The main cop gave me his card the other day when we found Emma."

"Adrian Ramirez. Yes, call him. Leave a detailed message if you don't reach him. I'm sure he'll get back to you. I think he's working a case in Santa Barbara right now but I'm sure he checks his messages."

"Okay. I'll do it on my break."

"Good."

I wandered back to my office. Connor had left to deal with customers. I wondered why Rachel hadn't mentioned anything about Connor when we met at Clementine's. I'd have to figure out a way to talk to Connor again to get a better feel for him, because his reaction when I mentioned Emma earlier hadn't suggested someone who was guilty or that still harbored anger toward her. He looked genuinely upset. Uncomfortable, definitely. But not agitated like in a dangerous way.

My phone pinged. It was Uncle Bob.

"I wanted to let you know Matt is now officially released. Ashley was right. But he's not off the hook yet. As I told you earlier, he'd been brought in for questioning and an arrest was pending. Well, they've decided to go ahead and arrest him on suspicion of murder based on circumstantial evidence. She told me they'll arraign Matt within seventy-two hours of his arrest. It's at the arraignment where Ashley can argue for a lower bail. But she seems confident the original charges won't hold and will be dismissed before it gets to the arraignment stage."

"Oh my gosh. I hope she's right and the charges will be dismissed. Spending the night in jail must have been awful. Thanks so much, Uncle Bob."

"Don't thank me. I didn't do anything."

"Look at you. So modest. That's a big chunk of change you put up for him."

"No, you misunderstood me. I didn't have all the details worked out with the bondsman yet, to be honest. When I got to the courthouse though, someone else did."

"Who?"

"Chris Kringle."

"Chris Kringle?"

"Yep."

I was blown away. Why on earth would Chris Kringle be willing to post bail for Matt? I didn't even know they were friends. I was so confused. Chris must have really believed in Matt. Or maybe Chris knew something that could help me find the real murderer. But the thought of unexpected help also brought the feeling of pressure. Not only must I find the real murderer to clear Matt, but also to redeem Chris's bail money. I still couldn't believe Chris had done that for Matt, especially since I was under the impression Chris wasn't particularly wealthy. Where did he get the money for bail?

When I got back to my desk, I got a call from Ashley. "Chris Kringle posted bail for Matt."

"I heard. Just talked to my uncle. Do you know why?"

"Do you really want to know?"

"Yes, of course. I really want to know. Why are you acting so coy?"

"I just don't want you to get upset. Or any more upset. I know stuff triggers you lately."

"For goodness sakes, Ashley. My imagination is worse than any scenario. Trust me. I can handle it."

"Okay. He did it because of your father."

Immediately I felt like I couldn't handle it. More secrets about my family? I'd thought that had all ended fourteen months ago.

"But it's all good."

I released a deep breath. "Next time, can you lead with the good part, please. For goodness sakes, tell me. How on earth does my father figure into Chris Kringle posting Matt's bail?"

"Because your father helped save Chris Kringle's life decades ago. Well, that's more dramatic than it was. Let me try again. Their nursery businesses were competitors and despite that, your father started a fund to help Chris Kringle when his wife and daughter were in a car accident because—"

"Stop right there. I know why now. Because my mother was in a car accident with me. My mother died and I survived with scrapes and bruises. Empathy." I had a sudden welling of emotion in my chest. Boy, did I ever miss my dad. And my mother. But I had their memories. Two more loving and self-sacrificing people you couldn't find. Tears came next, clouding my vision.

"He said he felt so badly for you and your family and the whole Benning Brothers crew last year but felt helpless to ease your pain. And now this. This, and I quote him, was an action he hopes speaks louder than words."

Now I was bawling. I hadn't cried this much since about three months after Milo and my dad had died.

"Tory, are you okay."

I snorted into the phone like a pig sniffing out truffles and responded with a shaky voice. "Yeah. Wow."

"Phew, because for a minute there it sounded like a herd of wild boars were on the phone and I wanted to know what they had done with Tory."

I snorted again, but this time it was a snort of laughter. "Sorry. That just took me by surprise. I need to go thank Chris. Do you want to come with? Then I have an appointment to show Milo's condo again with different prospective tenants. A couple of lawyers actually. Then we can go out to eat. On me." I grabbed a Kleenex from a cube on my file cabinet and dabbed my tears.

"Now there's an offer I can't refuse. I can come to your office and then we can go to the Santa's Helpers lot together."

I went out to my car to wait for Ashley. The employee-designated section of our parking lot was full. The customer section only had a few cars, meaning only a few customers were at our lot buying trees. Monday noon wasn't necessarily our peak period, but Christmas was only three weeks away. We should be busier. I feared this might be the status quo until Matt was exonerated.

Ashley zipped into the parking lot in her black BMW. I had a theory about BMW drivers, that all of them were impatient, judging by the way so many cut in and out of lanes around our local streets and highways. Ashley's tendency to push the speed limit had made her leader of the pack.

"Wow, you got here quick."

She held up her hand as she got out of her car. "Save it. I drove well within the speed limit the whole way, as I always do. I'm a lawyer and well aware of the laws, thank you very much."

"Okay. I just don't want you getting hurt in an accident."

She rested her hands on my shoulders. "Tory, calm down. I appreciate your concern, but you know you start getting overly protective when you're stressed. Sorry to dredge up all the emotions when I told you about Chris Kringle and what he said about your father. I knew it'd upset you. Now I feel guilty for telling you."

"No, no. You know me. I detest being kept in the dark. I'd rather power through the emotions and I'm in a better place now to handle it." I hoped.

"You sure you want to go talk to Chris now?"

I nodded. "I have to. Time is of the essence."

"Okay, then. I'm assuming Ms. Control Freak wants to drive?"

"Yes, I do. Thanks."

We hopped in my car. Ten minutes later we pulled up to the Santa's Helpers lot.

I parked in the first available space. "Look, there's Connor. I'd like to ask him some follow-up questions."

"About what?"

"About his angry outburst after Emma refused to date him."

"Just off the top of my head, given he's a possible suspect, do you really think it's a good idea to confront a possible killer?"

I twisted my mouth to the side and realized she was right. "Well, I wasn't going to say it exactly like that. Just come at it from a different angle and see if what he says jibes with what Rachel says."

"You mean you don't believe Rachel?"

"I don't know. She was very upset about Emma until Matt got arrested. Then once he got arrested, she seemed to forget about Emma and started to come up with other possible suspects. Didn't skip a beat."

"Maybe that's just the way she handles grief." Ashley gave me the side eye.

"Got it. Who am I to call her out? Point taken. Yeah. Maybe she's trying to deflect suspicion away from Matt. And for whatever reason, Connor seems like a likely suspect to her."

Ashley turned up the collar of her faux suede jacket. "I guess anything is possible. How well do you know Rachel? I hardly know her. I've only seen her at the truck the times I've been with you."

I pulled my hair into a ponytail and held it for a few seconds, hoping to tame it before I got out of the car. "I'd classify her as a friendly acquaintance. Like a pre-friend. The more I get to know her, the more comfortable I feel with her. Plus, she is Matt's girlfriend. And I trust his judgment a lot."

Ashley slammed her door shut. "Yeah, but judgment in the nursery business does not necessarily mean he has good judgment in life. In relationships."

We walked toward the entrance of the Santa's Helpers lot.

"True. But I've seen him in life situations. And under duress. I trust him. That's why I know he couldn't have killed Emma. He just doesn't have the temperament, nor the worldview of a killer."

"So, Hercule, tell me. What's the worldview of a killer?"

I flashed her a smile of appreciation since we were both Agatha Christie fans. I paused for a couple of minutes before I responded. "Someone who is blinded by their obsession with self. Someone who takes everything personally. Someone who can't keep things in perspective."

"So selfish, with paranoid tendencies."

"Pretty much."

"So then, if not Matt, who?"

"That's exactly what I'm hoping to find out right now."

Chapter 11

As soon as I laid my eyes on Christopher Kringle in his Santa suit at the front of the Santa's Helpers lot, I felt like running up and throwing my arms around him. But since I didn't know him all that well, instead I trotted up to him with my hand eagerly extended. "I can't thank you enough for posting Matt's bail. I'm so touched. Not only by the gesture but also I know it must be hard financially too."

Ashley caught up to us. "Hi, I'm Ashley Payne. I'm Matt Ortega's attorney. Yes, thank you so much, Mr. Kringle. That was so generous of you."

His eyes twinkled, not unlike St. Nick's. "My pleasure. Glad to pay it forward. And please, call me Chris." Then he opened his arms and we hugged. It was a strong hug that reminded me of my father's.

I gave his hand a squeeze. "That was so nice of you. I know business is booming in your lot right now, but I think that might be partly due to Matt's arrest, because our lot is pretty dead right now . . . I know, just heard it, empty, empty I should say, our lot is pretty empty."

He blinked, amused at my awkward word choice. "What's that got to do with wanting to pay it forward? Especially in this holiday season, a season of giving and love."

I wiggled around uncomfortably, searching for the right words to express my gratitude without chastising him for possibly putting himself at risk financially.

Ashley chimed in. "I think what Tory is trying to say is can you really afford to bail out Matt? Without jeopardizing your own finances, especially around Christmas?"

The smile broadened on Chris's face and froze, like he didn't know what to say in response to Ashley's questions. Ashley and I glanced at each other. I narrowed my brows and shook my head slightly. We'd clearly overstepped. We needed to back down.

I turned back to Chris, whose eyes still twinkled at us, but I detected a hint of bemusement now. "Well, thanks again. I'm sure Matt appreciates it more than any of us."

"He was very appreciative and effusive in expressing his gratitude. He's a good guy and I'm glad he's out."

Ashley's phone pinged and she drifted away to check it.

I turned to Chris. "He's probably so relieved to get out of jail. Now to find the real killer so we can clear Matt." And not live in fear of a mad killer on the loose, not to mention our nursery taking a financial hit. I gave Chris a little wave and headed over to Ashley.

Ashley caught my eye and gestured for me to step closer. "That was Adrian."

"What did he want? Is something wrong? You look like you've just seen a ghost."

We walked to a corner of the lot where there were fewer people.

"Adrian wanted Barry's cell phone number. And he wanted to know if I knew where he was, whether I've heard from him."

"Barry? You mean Professor Hayes? Why?"

She nodded. "He said Dwayne Rudders still hasn't turned himself in. Adrian couldn't reach Rudders's attorney. Apparently, some officers went to Rudders's home and he wasn't there."

"Wow. I wonder where he is and why he didn't show up?"

"I don't know. He's not answering his messages either. Adrian wants to get a hold of Rudders and explain to him the repercussions of not honoring the deal they had made about when to turn himself in."

I patted her shoulder. "Why do you think he's not turning himself in?"

"I don't know. But this won't end well if he takes off."

I grimaced. "Maybe he just had cold feet. Or had second thoughts and is just dragging his feet?"

"Any more feet metaphors?"

"No."

"Anyway, Adrian is trying to get a hold of Barry to see whether he's heard from Rudders. If so, he wants Barry to talk some sense into him, but Adrian was having a hard time reaching him. Adrian has left several messages on Barry's office number at school. That's when Adrian thought I probably had his cell phone number."

"Good idea. The longer Rudders waits to turn himself in, the more annoyed the cops will get. And cops are persistent. I know from personal experience. Ernie, for one, will not give up. The man's got a lot of flaws, but lack of persistence isn't one of them."

Ashley touched a tree bough. "These seem nice and fresh. We still need to get our trees." She turned her attention back to me. "Yeah, my hope is that Barry is trying to persuade Rudders to turn himself in and is purposely not responding to Adrian until he can provide a specific time when Rudders will do it. But Barry hasn't returned my texts either lately. So, I don't know what's going on." Ashley's eyes widened slightly.

I absently flexed a branch and smelled it. "Mm. These are fresh. Our trees are fresh too. Anyway, I hope Barry's not in trouble."

"I can't imagine him doing anything wrong. He's the poster child for a decent human being."

"When's Adrian coming back to Santa Sofia?"

"I don't know. He didn't say. Once I gave him Barry's phone number, he said he had to go."

"Hmm. When did you hear from your professor last?"

"Yesterday. When he told me Rudders had disappeared."

"Hmm."

"I'm going to give him a heads-up that Adrian is losing patience." Ashley texted him.

"Good idea."

She continued to text. "I should let the other Justice Program peeps know too. Also, I need to contact the public defender to see what she knows."

"He has a public defender?"

"Yes, the one that is officially assigned to him as a matter of course. Our project lawyers have done the majority of the legwork and paperwork pro bono."

We strolled around the lot in the direction of Cynthia's food truck again.

"Hear back from anyone yet?" As I spoke her phone buzzed.

"It's one of the Justice Program lawyers. He hasn't heard from Rudders or Barry, and he's been trying to reach them both too."

"At least they're all on it. I'm sure Rudders will come to his senses."

"Hope so. Because otherwise his plea bargain just bit the dust. The DA was ready to deal, given Rudders's lack of previous offenses in the past five years. He's been gainfully employed for the last five years too."

"That's a good sign then that he'll turn himself in, right? Where'd he work?"

Ashley nodded. "Carpenter's . . ." She paused, her eyes shifting to the right. "Assistant—" Her eyes widened. "Look, there's Connor."

I snapped my head in the direction of her gaze. "Oh, good. I'd love to talk to him again to find out more about his relationship with Emma."

"I thought we agreed to be very careful when talking to a possible suspect. Don't poke a hornet's nest."

"That's assuming what Rachel said was true. I'm not so sure of that."

"Just be diplomatic, please."

We both waved at Connor. He was dressed in his total elf getup, from pointy ears to bells on his booties.

I quickened my pace to get ahead of Ashley. "Hi, Connor. Wow. Your costume puts Benning Brothers to shame. All our elves only wear hats, as you know."

He gave me a weak smile. He seemed embarrassed to be in full elf regalia. Or was his hesitancy to engage based on something else?

"Hi, Ms. Benning. Yeah, thanks. Gramps always says go big or go home."

"So, I wanted to follow up on some of the stuff we talked about earlier. About Emma. That you once asked her out?"

He blushed, matching the red stripes of his outfit.

"Who told you that?"

"Is it true?"

"Yeah."

"And did you go out together?"

He shook his head.

"Why was that?"

"She said I was too young. Said she was flattered. But she didn't date guys my age."

"And that was the only reason?"

"That's what she said."

I tried to not reveal my surprise at his answer. He didn't seem at all touchy about it, just self-conscious. Why was he lying?

Ashley edged in. "How did you feel when she told you that."

He shrugged his shoulders. "I don't know. Almost kinda expected an answer like that. But it was worth a try." He shot us a sly smile.

"Emma was an attractive person. I can see why you'd want to ask her out. But I've heard she could have a temper."

"Really? If she did, I never saw that side of her. She was always nice to me. Even when she turned me down."

"What about Rachel?"

He got agitated. Ashley and I locked our gazes for a nanosecond, acknowledging his agitation.

"You seem upset. Do you and Rachel not get along?"

"We did."

"What does that mean?"

"We used to go out?"

"You mean date."

"Yeah."

"And it didn't end well?"

"Not really."

"Care to elaborate?"

"I just wanted to keep it casual. She wanted something different."

"Was this before or after you asked out Emma?"

"Before. I just asked Emma out around Thanksgiving, right when the Benning Brothers tree lot opened, and her truck was there all the time. Rachel and I dated . . ." He paused briefly. "Around Halloween. I remember because we went to a costume party together. We stopped seeing each other about a week after that."

"Got it. Anyway, it must be hard to work both jobs, huh?"

"Yeah. But fun. People are usually in good moods and most are nice. Speaking of which, I need to make a delivery."

"Oh, yes, go. Sorry to keep you from your deliveries. Don't want those good moods turning sour."

He laughed and jogged toward a truck.

Ashley let out a soft whistle. "What do you make of that? Do you think he was telling the truth?"

"About what, Emma? I don't know. He didn't really seem agitated when he spoke about her. Only when Rachel came up."

"Do you think Rachel lied to you?"

"I don't know. Sometimes she seemed to be telling the truth. But so did Connor. I just don't know. What do you think?"

Ashley brushed sawdust off of her boot. "He seemed a bit awkward when talking about Emma, but that could have been because he was embarrassed that she turned him down."

"Totally. But now that I think of it, I don't really know much about Emma, Rachel, or Connor, for that matter, other than pleasant work-related stuff. They could all be serial murderers for all I know."

"And now we're spiraling." She laughed. "What time are you showing the condo again?"

"At four." I checked my phone. "You're right. We better get going."

We arrived at Milo's condo a few minutes after four. Twinkle lights were already turned on outside the complex.

Ashley slammed the car door. "Ooh. It looks so Christmassy."

"I know. Very festive."

We walked up to Milo's unit and unlocked the door. I flipped on all the lights, including the tree.

Ashley browsed around the condo. "So pretty. This is a great condo. I'm glad you decided to rent it out instead of sell it."

"Me too. I just hope I can get a new tenant and not have to worry about showing it anymore."

The doorbell chimed.

"Make sure it's the person coming to look at it. Text them."

"Okay, Columbo." I texted. "They're at the door. Happy?"

"So far. Did you do any kind of prescreening?"

"Now you ask me? A little late for that. I told them the rent and they said no problem."

"So basically, no."

I opened the door and an attractive couple wearing luxury branded activewear who seemed to be around my age stood before me. We all introduced ourselves. The female looked Hispanic. She had brown skin and wore her long black hair in a power ponytail. The Black male was about five foot nine and wore tortoiseshell glasses. They seemed nice. Both were lawyers. As it turned out after chatting with Ashley, they had friends in common with her. They said they loved the condo. Exactly what they were looking for while they built a house nearby since they'd just sold their home. I told them I'd run a credit check and if everything came back fine, we had a winner.

After they left Ashley and I ordered takeout. "Done. Our Tender Greens order will be ready for pickup in twenty minutes. We can go pick it up, then I'll drop you off at your car."

"Good thinking. Then we can celebrate the condo rental over dinner and a glass of wine with Iris and Otis at your place."

I picked up my purse and admired the twinkling Christmas tree once more before shutting off the lights to head out the door, when the phone rang. "Odd. It rang the other night when I was here too."

"Aren't you going to answer it?"

"No. The tenants are still living here. It'll flip to voice mail like the other night."

"When are your tenants moving out?"

"Right after Christmas, I think. They've paid through the thirty-first. So definitely sometime before New Year's. And these people want to move in ASAP, so I'll be busy making sure we get the cleaning crew lined up to get it ready for them on—"

The shrill tone of the phone pierced my sentence, signaling someone was leaving a message. A raspy male voice sounded: "Mind your own business. Stop asking questions about Emma's murder. You just bailed out the real murderer."

Ashley grabbed my wrist and our gazes froze in unison. "What the . . ."

"Who was that?"

All of a sudden, the whole condo went dark.

Ashley tightened her grip on my wrist. "Did you do that?"

"No, of course not. How could I when you have my wrist in a death grip?"

"Oh, sorry about that. But good thing I do. At least we're together."

I peered out the front window. "Looks like the whole complex has a problem. The outdoor lights on the property are out too. Man, it's pitch dark." The only light outside was from the streetlight and the full moon.

Ashley tightened her grip. "Let's go back to the car. At least we'll be able to see each other then."

Just then we heard someone at the front door. It sounded like they were trying to open the door.

Ashley gasped. "Call nine-one-one."

I retrieved my phone from my shoulder bag and punched a favorite contact. "I'm calling the building security. They're right here."

After one ring the security guard picked up.

"Hi. This is Tory Benning in unit ten."

"Sorry, ma'am. We're aware of the power outage. We're working on it."

"No, someone is trying to break into my unit."

We heard them try the door again.

"I'll be right there."

Ashley's voice was shaky. "Maybe we should try to get out the back door?"

"But what if there's more than one?"

"Well, we know one's at the front door. What other choice do we have?"

"Um, to sit tight."

The sound of tinkling glass coming from the direction of the front door told me they were smashing the frosted glass panels that bordered the front door.

Now it was my turn to have a tremulous voice. "Okay. I'm convinced. Let's go."

Still gripping on to one another, we headed toward the back door. We heard more glass breaking, chiming louder this time, as if larger shards of the panel fell to the ground. We reached the back door, opened it, and ran around the back of the complex to the front of the building. The complex had ten units altogether arranged in a row, all with ocean views. In back of the townhouses was a swimming pool, which was now more like a black lagoon.

"Be careful. We don't want to fall in the pool." A flashlight swung back and forth ahead. "That's the security guard heading to my unit."

"Thank goodness."

"Let's make a sprint for my car now."

We galloped to my car like we were running a three-legged race since Ashley was still glued to my wrist as I groped around in my shoulder bag for my keys. I found my fob and unlocked my car with a beep. Ashley and I piled into the vehicle and I automatically locked the doors.

Ashley was breathing hard. "Lock the doors."

"I just did."

"Yikes. Shut off the damn lights. We're like sitting ducks here with the light on." She fumbled around trying to shut off the interior lights.

I started up the car.

Just then a figure in dark clothing zipped in front of us, illuminated by my headlights.

"Oh my god. That must be who was trying to break in."

"Should I follow him?"

"I don't know. What if he has a weapon?"

"Good point."

Someone tapped my window and I flinched so hard my heart nearly stopped. It was the security guard.

I rolled down the window. "Hi. I'm the one who called you from unit ten."

He held a walkie-talkie and spoke into it. Shrill static followed by a garbled voice emanated from the walkie-talkie and he told them his location. "I called our security company. They're on their way."

"Someone just ran by us. They went in that direction." I pointed east along the beach.

Ashley grumbled, "They'll never find them now."

"You never know. Not that many people walking along the beach at night."

"Walking, no, but running, yes. Lots of joggers out."

"Darn. You're right."

The security guard conveyed the info into his walkie-talkie. "I called the cops too. They should be here soon."

Two security company cars pulled up. The guard pointed to the beach and they took off.

He turned back to us. "Did you get a look at the suspect? Could you describe them?"

"Only now when they ran by the car. They were dressed all in black and we probably wouldn't have even seen them if I hadn't just turned on my headlights."

"Okay. Can you stick around till the police come?"

"Sure." I thought of our Tender Greens order.

Ashley read my mind. "I'll call Tender Greens and tell them to push our order back an hour."

"Thanks."

Two SSPD cars sped into the parking lot and shrieked to a stop just as the power was restored and the building and grounds all lit up again. The security guard ran over to the cars and spoke to the cops for a few minutes.

Ernie emerged from one of the patrol cars and jogged over to us. "Hi, ladies. What's up? I hear you had a little excitement here tonight."

Ashley and I shot glances at each other. Why was Ernie being civil?

We told Ernie the whole story, including the menacing voice mail.

"Can I listen to it? I'd like to record it."

We trudged back to the condo. The security team had already boarded up the broken glass panels.

The guard with the walkie-talkie smiled. "I'll get the glass company out first thing tomorrow. Shouldn't take long at all to fix."

"Thanks." I started to tremble when I realized our close call. I played back the message for Ernie.

He listened intently and then replayed it to record it on his phone. "Okay. Do you recognize the voice?"

"Nope. I don't think I've ever heard it before."

Ashley shook her head. "Me neither. Except maybe in a *Scream* movie. But they could be using one of those apps that disguises your voice."

"Are there security cameras?"

"Yes. One at each door and two on each floor."

"Good. Let's take a look."

We marched to the security guard office and he pulled up the footage for Milo's condo. Luckily, the security cameras had backup batteries that had guarded against any lapse in the surveillance video. We played back the tapes. The intruder's face was well hidden.

Ernie scratched his chin. "Okay. I'll let our tech department listen to the voice mail and take a closer look at the security tape."

We turned to go.

"Tory, I don't know who you've been talking to regarding Emma's murder, but obviously you've annoyed someone. Remember one suspect is out on bail."

I took a deep breath.

He shifted his position. "Look. Before you get all pushed out of shape, calm down. I'm not saying Matt Ortega is the correct suspect. All I'm saying is the actual suspect is still out there somewhere, whoever it may be. And it might be someone you've been talking to, it might be someone who's seen you talking about the murder, or it might be the person who broke into your condo tonight. So, take care."

"Wait, what? Did I just hear you say that Matt isn't necessarily the right suspect? Weren't you the one who said you thought he did it?"

"I'm just saying our investigation is ongoing. We can't totally ignore circumstantial evidence. I don't know if it's only one suspect or whether more than one person is responsible. At this point we don't have the whole picture. That's why it's called an investigation."

Ashley turned to me and whispered under her breath, "There it is. Knew the mansplaining would show up sooner or later."

I think Ernie heard her, but maybe not because, oddly, he didn't respond with a snarky comment, as usual.

"Okay, then. Thanks for the warning, Ernie. When's Adrian back in town? Do you know?"

"Don't know. Have a nice rest of the night, ladies."

Back in the car we marveled at the new Ernie.

Ashley was wide-eyed. "Gosh. What happened to him? Did he fall and hit his head or something?"

"Now, now. There's good in everyone. Maybe he's evolving."

"Yeah, right. Evolving into what? A gecko? What's the next stage, a Gila monster? I don't trust him. I think he's trying to psych us out, fake us out, in the hopes of us trusting him, and then wham, the net drops and he's got us."

"Now who has the overactive imagination?"

"Mark my words. Something's up with that dude. Either he's up to something or he's sick or something big happened to put the fear of god in him, because old Ernie wouldn't be caught dead acting the way he just acted."

"Agree. He's usually not as civil as he's been lately." I considered her words as I turned onto the Avenue in the direction of Tender Greens. "The more I think about it, the stranger it seems. Something's up with Ernie. Anyway, let's enjoy the snark-free zone while it lasts."

I parked in a white zone out front while Ashley dashed in for the food. Once she was back, I drove to Benning Brothers, where she'd left her car. I swung into our parking lot and pulled up next to her car, my headlights spotlighting it. We both let out a gasp at the same time. Her tires were slashed.

Chapter 12

I took a swig of white wine. "We clearly were meant to have cold food tonight. Good thing most of our order was salads." I got up off the living room couch and collected our plastic food containers and threw them in the stainless-steel trash container in the kitchen. My type of dinner party—easy serve, easy cleanup.

Ashley tapped her wineglass. "Still good though. Actually, it's never tasted so good."

"What did Adrian say about your tires and the break-in?"

"I haven't told him yet.

"What! Why not?"

"Because I'm too tired to be scolded and warned about being careful tonight."

"You know he does that because he cares deeply for you and—"

"He's a cop. I got it." She flashed me a forced smile, letting me know not to push right now.

It was past nine, and Iris was stretched out on her side on the light oak floor fast asleep. Otis was curled up on a velvet throw pillow on a leather armchair, his black fur blending in with the pillow.

I took another gulp of wine. "At least we got your car to the tire place and it's first up tomorrow morning."

"True." Ashley stretched out at one end of my beige leather couch.

I punched some throw pillows into place and curled up at my end of the couch. "You're spending the night here, right? This way I can drive you to the tire place early tomorrow morning or drop you off at your office if they don't have the tires. How does that sound?"

Ashley set her glass on the glass coffee table. "Sounds like a plan, thanks, Tory. I'm easy. I'm worn out anyway. And we haven't had a slumber party in a long time."

I poured us both some more wine and Otis moved from the chair and regrouped on Ashley's lap. "Let's do some research on Connor,

Rachel, Emma and all the involved parties." I stood and retrieved my laptop from my shoulder bag.

"Oh, fun."

"Come. Let's move to the kitchen."

Ashley obliged and in a few minutes we were sitting next to each other at my kitchen counter with my computer open and ready to search.

My fingers were poised over the keyboard. "Who should we start with?"

Ashley bit her bottom lip as she concentrated. "Um . . . how about Connor?"

"Good choice, I got interrupted on my search for him last time I tried. Let's see what Google says."

I typed in Connor Kringle. "His LinkedIn profile says he graduated college twenty years ago and he's a stockbroker in New York. Clearly, a different Connor Kringle."

"Are there other Connor Kringles?"

"Yep. But none in California or in his age range. Hmm."

"Okay, then. Let's Google Rachel next. More wine?"

"Thanks. Just a tiny bit. By the way, have you heard from Professor Hayes yet?"

"Nope." She checked her phone. "Oh, but here's a text from Adrian."

"What does he want?"

Her face looked scared. "They went over to Barry's house. He's not there. His car is missing too."

"Well, that's a good sign, isn't it? Like he went somewhere of his own volition. My phone buzzed. "It's the SSPD."

Ashley raised her eyebrows. "Answer it."

I took a deep breath. "Hello."

"Hi, Tory."

I mouthed to Ashley, "It's Ernie."

She whispered back, "Put it on speakerphone."

I hit the speaker button and held the phone between us.

Ernie spoke quickly. "I just wanted to give you a heads-up about Emma's murder."

I clutched Ashley's arm. "Yes?"

"We're looking at a lot of people in the process of tracking down the murderer."

"Oh. Does that mean Matt Ortega is no longer your prime suspect?"

"I'm not talking about Matt. Assuming he's home. Or he better be."

"Yes, I'm assuming that too. I mean, I'm sure he is. Who in particular are you looking at?"

Ashley mouthed, "Connor?"

I shrugged in response.

"Like I said, a lot of people. I was hoping you could help me."

I shook my head in bewilderment at Ashley.

Ernie continued. "Do you have Jake Logan's address in Santa Barbara?"

Ashley's eyebrows shot up and she gave my arm a soft punch.

"Why do you need Jake's address?" I gasped softly. "Don't tell me he's a person of interest."

"I'll repeat it again, Tory. We're looking at a lot of people, but we looked at security video outside of Emma's bakery regarding another person of interest and saw Jake lurking around there too."

"What? That's absurd. He lives in Santa Barbara. He's rarely up here. And you do know Adrian is staying at Jake's place right now, right?"

From the long pause at the other end, he clearly did not.

"So why don't you call Adrian and I'm sure he'll set you straight."

I hung up. I was too tired to deal with Ernie and his crazy theories tonight.

Ashley was staring at her phone. Her eyebrows had shot up again. "Oh my god, that Calvin Klein model guy just texted me again."

"You mean 'David'?" I made air quotes.

Ashley laughed. "And here I thought you weren't paying attention."

"Kind of late, isn't it? So, he does have your cell phone number?"

"No, sorry, not text. I meant messaged me on the app." She giggled. "Are you going to text Jake?"

"And ask him what? Why were you stalking Emma? He's a PI, for god's sake. I'm sure there's a good reason."

"True. I'm going to ask Adrian."

She texted Adrian. A few seconds later he texted back.

"Oh, no! They have a BOLO now on Barry."

"Well, that's good. More likely to find him now."

"And they went to Rudders's house, and Rudders still wasn't there. Looks like he's skipped town."

"Sorry, Ashley. After all your hard work to bring the real killer to justice. That's so disheartening. Any idea where he's headed?"

She was busy texting and didn't respond for a minute.

"Gosh. They can't reach one of the other lawyers on Lyle Bubb's team either."

"Is that so unusual? Maybe they're trying to negotiate a bail with a judge or wait for a hearing or something?"

"Hold up. Adrian again."

"What did Adrian text you about now? I didn't think he was involved in that case anyway."

"He wasn't. He just wanted to alert me."

"About what?"

Ashley's eyes looked ready to pop out of her head. "Barry's car was just found."

I squeezed Ashley's hand. "Oh my god. Is he all right? What happened?"

"They don't know. He's officially gone missing now too."

"So, let me get this straight. Rudders and the lead attorney on the team are both missing? That sounds shady. What about Lyle Bubb? The guy who got exonerated? Hope he's keeping safe."

Ashley sighed heavily. "As far as I know he is. He was released and planned to keep a low profile for a few days while he got acclimated. A whole bunch of newspapers and TV stations are after him for interviews, and we got inquiries from several publishers and literary agents who want to represent him and have his story published. So at least there's that and the state will award him compensatory damages for false conviction and incarceration. As they should."

"Okay, well, my head has too much going on right now. I say we call it a night. Come on, Iris. Let's go to bed. Otis, behave yourself."

"Oh, Otis and I are best buds. I'm sure he'll cuddle up later on his own terms. Typical male." She laughed.

I went to my bedroom after I made sure Ashley had towels because she wanted to shower. I brought my computer to bed. I still had some Googling I wanted to do on Rachel and Emma. I got as far as typing in Rachel Downey and my phone pinged.

It was Jake. "You're awake. Hope I didn't wake you up."

"No. I was just looking at my computer in bed. What's up?"

"I heard through the grapevine Ernie told you I'm a person of interest now."

"Don't worry. I set him straight. I figured you were working on a case."

"Thanks. You figured right. I have been working on a case in Santa Sofia. I've been popping up to Santa Sofia about once a week lately." He paused. "Sorry, I haven't been contacting you each time I've been there though."

"No problem. You can do what you like. We're just friends, Jake."

He paused. "I know. But I want to make sure you know I'm honest and I want to be totally transparent."

"Good to know." I was purposely being flippant because I did feel hurt on one level that he'd been in town and not contacted me. I knew I wasn't ready for a relationship. I knew it would be difficult if not impossible to replicate what I'd had with Milo. But still, from the moment I'd laid eyes on Jake I'd felt drawn to him. If being flippant bought me some time to contemplate some of the conflicting emotions I was feeling right now, so be it.

He sighed heavily. "This whole thing with Emma. Life is short. I don't want to be one of those people with regrets for not speaking up just because it's awkward."

"What do you mean?" I had no idea where he was going with this, especially the Emma part.

"Like I said. I want to be totally transparent. And after Ernie called Adrian to let him know he didn't appreciate being out of the loop because Adrian was staying with me, I decided I should come clean with you before you heard it from anyone else."

"I honestly don't know what you're talking about, Jake. But it sounds intense and—"

"It's related to what I told you the other night. About me being divorced. I've been divorced for nearly three years."

"Uh-huh."

"I just wanted to fill you in on the details myself before someone like Ernie did. We both know how obnoxious he can be. I just wanted to let you know it wasn't how it looked with Emma."

"Oh, my goodness. How it looked?"

"I never thought for a moment it might be misconstrued and—"

"That I'd find out? First, I'm offended by how you are under-estimating my Googling skills and, second—"

"No. That it might be relevant to a murder investigation. It was a short work gig. Purely work. At the time I was super busy with other cases. I did my thing, hung out at her residence and place of business to observe who visited her. All pretty routine. I thought about contacting you every time I was here . . . but I didn't want to make it seem like I was pressuring you or making our friendship into a bigger deal than it was."

"Jake, I'm exhausted. Ashley and I had a scare at Milo's condo tonight—"

"You did? What happened? Are you okay?"

"We're fine, thanks. Just a bit shaken up. Someone broke the glass near the front door trying to get in. The security guards scared him off, but the guy got away."

"Is Ashley spending the night, I hope?"

"Yeah. She already went to bed. Speaking of which, I should too. Talk to you soon, bye-bye."

I immediately wanted to tell Ashley. When I peeked outside the room, the light was out in her bedroom. I padded back into my room and wrote her an email with my thoughts since I knew I'd never be able to sleep with them swirling around in my head. I titled it "For a longer conversation" and hit Send.

Iris was asleep next to me feet-up, like a dead cockroach, only a cute furry one. I was about to nod off to sleep when I heard a noise. I laid still, listening for about a minute. Then I heard it again. So did Iris. She sprang to attention and catapulted herself off the bed, landing with a burst of barking, and dashed out the bedroom door.

Ashley stuck her head out the door. "What's going on? Why's Iris barking like a maniac?"

I put my finger up to my mouth. "Shh. I heard something. Iris did too."

Ashley crept into the hallway. She was wearing only the oversized T-shirt top of the pajama set I'd lent her for the night, making her long legs seem even longer than usual. "What did you hear?"

"A noise."

"Work with me here, it's not twenty questions. What kind of a noise? Like someone breaking in?"

"Maybe. I don't know." I ran back to my room and grabbed my phone.

"Are you going to call the police?"

"Not yet." I grabbed Iris. "Where's Otis? I thought he was in your room."

"He was. But he started kneading the bed right next to me like he was playing a pipe organ. Cute, but not when I have to get up early. I need sleep."

"Way to guilt me. Now if it's anything short of a serial killer breaking in, I'm the bad guy preventing you from getting a good night's rest."

"Is this going to be about you too?"

"Too?"

"Okay, okay. We're both scared. What should we do?"

I held up my phone. "Where's your phone?"

"In my purse. Let me grab it."

I tilted my head, straining to listen for any more sounds. Iris was flailing so much I set her down for a moment and she stayed by my side.

Ashley was back in a flash. "I pulled up the keyboard. I'm ready to punch in nine-one-one."

"Good." Our small pajama parade crept down the hallway toward the kitchen led by Iris, whose ears were pricked.

A noise sounded like glasses knocked over.

Ashley gripped my arm. "If Otis broke those wineglasses I got you, his furry little behind is going to be in so much trouble."

All of a sudden Otis whooshed by us from the direction of the kitchen toward my bedroom. Ashley and I both exhaled a big sigh of relief.

Ashley let out a curse. "That little devil."

"Otis! What did you do?" I tried to remember where we'd placed our wineglasses before we went to bed and flipped on the hall light.

There was another noise from the kitchen that sounded like a thud. Ashley and I exchanged wide-eyed glances.

"What the . . ." Ashley swore again, as she tended to do when frightened.

Knowing she was scared made me start to tremble.

She started punching numbers on her phone. "I'm calling nine-one-one."

"Don't let them hear you, for god's sake," I whispered frantically.

She waved her hand and put her finger to her lips and gestured that she was going back to her room to make the call.

I crept toward the dark kitchen. When I got to the kitchen, the light from the hallway was good enough so that I could see the kitchen was empty. If someone had broken in, it appeared they weren't here now. I stuck my head around the corner and the living room looked free of intruders also. I tiptoed over to a kitchen window that overlooked my backyard. I caught a glimpse of what seemed like a reflection of a red light shining in between the slats of the blinds. I couldn't figure out for the life of me what would be reflecting a red light from inside the house. I didn't have a tree or Christmas lights anywhere, nor a power strip light in the vicinity. When I peeked through the blinds to look outside, I saw two red lights on the ground. It was pitch dark outside and the glowing red lights were stationary. They looked to be about a foot apart and just sitting on my lawn. I had my phone in my hand and took a few shots as proof I wasn't going crazy and imagining them. The light was bright and steady and not moving. I doubted it was a man holding two lights to the ground, my initial thought. No, it looked like a UFO. Had an alien landed? My stomach gently flipped. I felt like I was in the movie ET. And then I noticed a little green light in between the two red lights. Could it be a drone? It must be a drone. What else could it be? I didn't think it was an alien mother ship. No, it must be a drone. Was it spying on me? And why had it landed? I took another pic and ran back to Ashley.

"I think there's a drone in the backyard."

"What? Really? How do you know?"

"There are two bright red lights." I showed her the photo on my phone.

"What's it doing?"

"It's just sitting there, not moving at all, and freaking me out. It looks like it's spying on me. Come and look."

We both shuffled down the hall. Iris was oddly quiet. When we got to the window and looked out, it was gone.

"That's weird. It's not there. So glad I took pics." I shuddered. "Ugh. It totally creeped me out. Just like in the movies."

"Okay, crisis averted. I'm exhausted."

"Yeah, me too."

I flipped on the kitchen light. Our wineglasses from last night were intact in the sink where I'd left them, but upon closer inspection they were leaning against each other.

"Otis must have knocked the glasses into each other but somehow they didn't break, thank goodness. All looks well. I'm just so jumpy from the condo break-in and now a drone spying on me."

Ashley yawned. "Get some sleep. We'll discuss it in the morning."

"Call back nine-one-one and tell them it was a false alarm."

Just as I spoke, there was a rap on the front door. Ashley and I both froze. Iris started barking uncontrollably.

"Who can it be this late?" Ashley whispered.

"I don't know. What should I do? Just ignore it?"

We both stood silently for a minute. Again, there was a rap on the door.

A familiar voice followed. "Tory, it's Ernie."

Ashley and I exchanged surprised looks.

I unlocked the chain. "Just a minute." I opened the door slightly. "Hi, Ernie. What are you doing here?"

He gave me and Ashley a once-over with nary a word or an ogle at Ashley's scanty outfit or my off-the-shoulder T-shirt. "When I saw a nine-one-one call was from your house, I wanted to make sure all was well. The dispatcher said there was a loud thud outside in your yard?"

"Yeah. It turned out to be a drone. But it's gone now. We were just going to cancel the nine-one-one call." I got the photo of the drone and held it up for Ernie. "Here it is. I took a photo. It was so weird. I heard a noise. At first, I thought it was the cat. But nope. A drone."

He took a long look at the photo. "Well, glad you're okay. If it happens again, call me directly. It's illegal to fly drones at night. Take care now." He handed me his card.

After he'd left Ashley snickered. "That clinches it. Something's up with Ernie. His gaze was on our eyes, not our bodies, for a change. And he's actually being helpful. What has gotten into him?"

I chuckled. "Maybe that wasn't Ernie. Maybe he's been replaced by a pod, like in *Invasion of the Body Snatchers*. Maybe that wasn't a drone in the backyard. Maybe it was Ernie's mother ship."

Ashley laughed, then said, "I'm out. Pleasant dreams."

"Pleasant dreams to you too. Come on, Iris. Let's try to get a few hours of sleep before we need to get up again."

Chapter 13

The next morning the first thing I did was look out the back window before I let Iris outside. The location where I thought I saw the red lights was empty.

"Okay, Iris. Let's go explore."

Iris trotted around and I made a beeline to where I thought the red lights had been. And then I saw it. A drone up against my wall, about two feet from where I saw the lights the night before. I edged closer. It was a charcoal gray color and looked like a giant spider or a scorpion or Darth Vader's helmet. I still wasn't convinced it wasn't a miniature alien starship. I'd never seen a drone up close and personal before.

I took some pictures just in case it magically disappeared. I didn't want Ashley to think I was losing it. I ran back to the house and called inside the door for Ashley to come and look.

We walked back to where the drone was.

With Ashley near, I became braver and took a closer look. "Oh, it looks like it crashed, and it lost one of its little propellers. Maybe it tried to take off and crashed into the wall."

"I thought you had an alarm system. Did you forget to set it?"

"I do. But not for my backyard."

I took more photos. "I'm going to look up the brand. See what I can find out."

Ashley chuckled. "On the case already. Good job. How is it just sitting in your own house you get drama?"

"Stop. You're starting to sound like Ernie. Speaking of which, I'm going to call him and let him know it's in my backyard."

We walked back to the kitchen, leaving the disabled drone where it crashed.

"Joke all you want. But this is the second incident in as many days. First at my condo and now here. Well, three if you count the first call I got at the condo when I was waiting for the prospective tenant. Could be a coincidence but I'm inclined to think otherwise. I mean, my caterer was just murdered in my tree lot. I almost feel like I'm next. Or maybe I was the intended victim, not Emma."

"Okay. Stop the crazy train right there. I agree. The condo break-in and your drone invasion might not be coincidental. But putting those two events aside, when was the last time you dressed up as Mrs. Claus? I think whoever killed Emma definitely knew it was her and intended to kill her. Unless . . ."

"What? Unless what?"

Ashley looked at her feet. When she looked up, she looked serious. "Unless Emma found out someone wanted to murder you and tried to stop them."

"Me? Why would anyone want to murder me?"

Ashley let out an exasperated sigh. "I don't know, Tory. You're the amateur sleuth. You tell me. You're the one who just said you might be the intended victim. I'm just brainstorming with the material you're feeding me. Maybe some guy you rejected?"

"How can you say that when you know I haven't dated for the last fourteen months. I've gone to dinner with Jake a handful of times and we're just friends. No rejection there. Other than that, I've seen no one. Even Ernie doesn't seem to be interested in ogling me anymore, so that's a dead end."

"Okay."

We both stood staring at each other for several seconds.

"Yes, I heard it, dead end."

"Okay. Nope on the theory you were the intended murder victim. What about Emma? We never got around to Googling her last night. We really don't know that much about her."

"Yeah, I'll try to Google more today. Have you heard from the tire place about when your car will be ready?"

"Not yet. I don't think they're open yet."

"Okay. I have my final meeting of the year this afternoon for the Santa Sofia Hotel Condo project up the coast."

"I have a meeting later this morning. I'll give them a call in a minute."

There was a knock on the door. Iris started to bark and pace. Ashley and I exchanged surprised looks."

"Tory! It's me, Ernie." He knocked again.

"Coming, Ernie." I scooped up Iris and opened the door.

"Sorry to bother you. I got your call and was in the neighborhood. I wanted to take a look at the drone."

I led him to the backyard. He bent down and took some photos of it from several angles.

After a few minutes he stood. "Great. Thanks, Tory. That's all I needed. Got the barcode so we can trace the owner hopefully. It's illegal to operate drones at—"

"—night. I know. You told me last night."

We walked back to the front door.

"Take care, Tory. Don't hesitate to call if something comes up. Have a nice day."

I shut the door and rolled my eyes at Ashley. "Okay, I'm going to get ready."

I quickly fed Iris and Otis and then padded back to my bedroom. Before getting ready I pulled up the photo of the drone I took on my phone and looked up the model number. After a few minutes of looking at the online images I found one that matched. I went to the manufacturer's website. Bingo. The red lights looked the same distance from each other, one on each leg, and a smaller green light in the middle. It matched the photos of the Mavic 2 I found online. Holy cow! It was around fifteen hundred dollars. Equipped with a GPS. And all the other state-of-the-art bells and whistles, apparently. I also looked up laws about drones and verified Ernie's take that it was illegal to fly at night but also illegal to confiscate them. Interesting.

I took a quick shower and threw on some black pants and a black cashmere pullover and returned to the kitchen, where Ashley was eating a piece of toast.

"What did the tire place say?"

Ashley grinned. "It'll be ready in a half hour."

"Great."

"I know. I have to track down Justice Program peeps to see where we stand with things since everyone seems to have dropped off the face of the planet."

"Maybe they all took off early for Christmas break. Are classes over at UC Santa Barbara?"

"Not yet. They're on the quarter system and finals start this week, I think. The quarter doesn't end until this Friday."

Ashley continued looking at her phone. "Hey, what's this email you sent me. Looks like a cross between Dear Abby and True Confessions."

"Thanks. So glad to know showing my vulnerability amuses you."

"You know I like to tease you. Especially when I'm nervous."

"Yes, I know." I chuckled. "Mainly because I'm exactly the same way."

I linked my arm with Ashley's. "Twins."

"Okay, so let me get this straight. You never miss an opportunity to tell me you're not ready for a relationship, yet you stay up late, after a harrowing day, to write me a tome about how you feel disrespected by someone you swear you're not interested in. Can I offer you some words of wisdom?"

"From the girl who has near-perfect Adrian as an almost boyfriend, but swears he's not into you? Sure, fire away. Whatcha got?"

Ashley smiled. "Adrian is nearly perfect, isn't he? But back to you. You, my dear, have a basic case of anxiety."

"What?"

"Yeah. You're overly concerned about all the what-ifs. What if Jake was involved with Emma? What if Jake isn't who I thought he was? What if this means we really are just friends?"

My face heated up and my heartbeat pounded in my ears. I'd heard this exact explanation before from my therapist, Ellen. Stop worrying about the future and ruing the past. Try to focus on the now. Clichéd concepts but they were right on. It all had to do with control. I knew I had no control over my past or my future, yet still I fretted.

"Yeah, you're right. Ellen tells me that all the time."

"Look, I know you're still processing stuff related to your dad and Milo. It takes time. Just do the best you can. Don't worry about other people you can't control. All you can control is your choice of how to react to their behaviors. Like in Jake's instance, I think you owe him a thank-you. At least he wants to be totally honest now, and not try to hide his relationship with Emma if he had one. I mean, Rachel told us Emma might have been seeing someone. We don't know. Maybe it was Jake. I know you are attracted to him and he helped so much last year. But you can't have it both ways, not care and care."

"Hold it right there. Where are you getting this stuff from? All Jake said was that he had a gig with Emma. Like a job. Not a relationship. I thought I made that clear. That was the exact word he used, gig."

"Oh." She flashed me a slight smile. "Never mind, then. I obviously didn't read your email carefully enough. Sorry. In that case, ignore what I said about Jake and Emma. But the other parts still stand. Stop worrying about everything so much. I know it's easier said than done. But try to not overthink things with him. He's attempting to be totally transparent with you. Appreciate that."

"I will try to, thanks. You should take your own advice. It applies to you and Adrian too, doesn't it? We're in somewhat parallel situations. Situations that are preventing both you and me from moving forward. You, because you feel you need more attention from Adrian yet you're afraid to tell him, so he thinks you want it that way. And I have feelings for Jake, but forming a close bond again scares me. I'm afraid of losing it again. Plus, I needed to process my feelings before jumping right into another relationship. So simple yet so complicated."

We hugged. I got up and I peeked out the window to see if the drone was still there. "I keep feeling it's going to disappear, like I thought it did last night." I sipped my coffee while Ashley went to get dressed. Iris wanted to go outside again. We did a couple of laps around the backyard and it felt good to burn off some of the tension my muscles had been holding on to.

When I came back inside, Ashley was pouring herself a cup of coffee.

"I guess I'll have one more cup too." I poured half a cup and filled up the cup with nonfat milk.

"That guy messaged me again."

Again? Just delete the app."

"I did. Somehow, he got my cell phone number."

"Hope the app didn't have some type of malware. Thanks for making me download it."

"It's a popular app. I think it's fine. I think he got it somewhere else."

"Maybe he read about the Justice Program case and recognized you and somehow got you cell phone number that way."

She was staring into space. "Yeah, maybe."

I looked at the news notifications on my phone. "Oh, no. They found that missing student from Santa Sofia. Dead." I read aloud from my phone notification: "'Santa Barbara police are investigating the murder of a UC Santa Barbara grad student who's from Santa Sofia.' Do you think that's the case that Adrian is there for? Because the grad student is from here?"

"I don't know. When I asked, he said it was all hush-hush for now."

"Hmm. I bet this is it. It says the grad student was in law school."

Ashley perked up. "What? UC Santa Barbara doesn't have a law school. Let me see."

I handed her my phone.

"Oh, no. I hope it's not Latrice."

"Who's that?"

"Our Justice Program intern. She was in UCSB's undergraduate law program. She's applying to law schools. I hope it's not her."

"I didn't see a name mentioned."

"I can't find a name either. But if it's her, I'm sure Barry would have . . . oh my goodness. Maybe that's why Adrian wanted his number. To get her emergency contacts."

"Your professor can't be a suspect, can he?"

"Barry? Never. He's the straightest arrow I know. I'd trust him with my life."

"Good. Because it's starting to sound like the TV show *How to Get Away with Murder*. Good thing your professor isn't Annalise Keating."

"Love that show. But no, he's an open book. Still, I don't like it one bit he's MIA and now this news about a murdered law student. A little too close for comfort."

I checked the time. "We better get going. You ready?"

"Yes, let's go."

I'd just gathered up my computer and purse when there was a knock on the door. Iris commenced to bark her fool head off again. I peeked through the peephole and there was a guy who looked like he was about in his late thirties or early forties at my door.

Ashley tugged on my sweater. "Who is it?"

"I don't know. Some guy."

He knocked again.

I spoke through the door. "Yes? How can I help you?"

He said something in reply, but Iris was barking so loudly I couldn't hear a word he said. I hissed at Iris to be quiet, which got her even more frenzied. I tried again. "Sorry, what did you say? I couldn't hear because of my dog barking."

He said something, most of which I didn't hear again. What I did hear was "drone."

I whispered to Ashley. "I think he's come about the drone."

I cracked the door open. He was an average-looking guy. Wearing jeans and a shirt. Nothing really distinctive about him. Familiar-looking, even.

"I'm sorry but I think my drone is in your backyard. I don't know what happened. It's never happened before. All of a sudden, I lost it. And the GPS says it's in your backyard." He was affable and polite.

I had mixed emotions. This guy had been flying at night illegally and nearly gave me a heart attack. But I'd figured with it being that expensive, no one would have abandoned it, even with a broken propeller. "You scared the daylights out of me last night. I had no idea what it was at first."

"I'm so sorry. It's never happened before."

"What were you doing? Why were you flying it over my backyard?"

"So sorry. I was working on a project."

"Okay. Wait here." I closed the door. "He wants his drone back."

Ashley was holding Otis. "Are you going to give it to him?"

"I guess. With my luck, if I don't, he'll probably sue me."

"You're right there."

Iris and I went to the backyard and retrieved the drone. It was lighter than I expected. And I still didn't trust it. I felt like it might activate again.

I set the drone down on the floor and grabbed Iris. Then I opened the door halfway and picked up the drone and handed it to the guy.

"Thank you so much." He looked elated to see it and then got serious when he saw the broken propeller. "I'll be able to replace the propeller. Thanks again."

As soon as I closed the door I thought, I've seen that guy before. But where? And what type of project was he working on? I kicked myself that I hadn't asked him, but the truth was he made me nervous and I just wanted him to go away.

When I looked at Ashley her eyes looked ready to pop out.

"What's the matter?"

"I know that guy?"

"What? From where?"

"I don't know. I can't remember. But I'm getting a bad vibe."

"Huh. Yeah, I feel like I've seen him before too."

But we both wracked our brains the whole way to the tire place, and neither of us could put our finger on where'd we'd seen him before.

Chapter 14

I dropped off Ashley at the tire place to pick up her car and I headed to my office. The first thing I did when I got to my desk was to Google the Kringles. I was curious about Connor and his grandpa Chris for several reasons. Where had Chris gotten the bail money for Matt Ortega and how had he even known so quickly that Matt had been detained? I Googled Connor first. I still couldn't find anything on him. I found an Instagram account, but it was for a different Connor Kringle.

The prospective tenants who were lawyers to whom I'd shown the condo had sent me their rental application. I ran background and credit checks through an online service. Their credit scores were exceptional and there were no red flags in their background checks. We had a winner. I sighed with relief. One less thing on my to-do list.

All the background checking got me thinking about Emma. I didn't know anything about her background. I Googled Emma Evans. If we wanted to find out who had murdered her, we needed to find out more about her. All I knew from my brief interactions I'd had with her over the last year was that she was ambitious, funny, organized, and a fabulous cook and baker. Beyond that, we'd never really talked about anything personal like family or relationships.

Hmm. As I scrolled through the sites the Google search had yielded, I wondered why we had never discussed family or relationships. Oftentimes, women bonded over personal small talk. With Emma we had almost exclusively stuck to the business at hand. In other words, professional. A good thing, right? Or was she hiding something?

On the sites that collected public information, listed were estimates of an individual's personal worth, their marital status, political affiliation, and religion. Emma was currently listed as single. I wondered if Evans was her maiden name or possibly her married name if she had been married or was separated. Listed under Emma's name were her aliases, which the site called "also known to go by" and people associated with her, among whom were a couple of males, including one with a different surname. It looked like Emma Evans was her maiden name. I assumed the different surname was possibly an ex-husband's. As I pieced the information together, I thought it was safe to surmise Emma had had an ex. I wondered if he wanted her dead. If they were divorced, he probably didn't want her dead. The cases that made the headlines were the ones where the husbands chose murder over divorce, usually because of money. I'd have to see if Emma was divorced from her ex or not. If not, then we might have our suspect.

I tried Googling all the other people's names she'd been associated with and her other names listed, but nothing revealing came up. One of the names associated with Emma's was a Nic Evans. Maybe he was her ex-husband. Or he could have been her father or brother too. But then I noticed there was a Nicole Evans listed too. So possibly a sister or mother. Or maybe even her daughter. But she'd never mentioned she had children.

I knew Ashley and her network of legal contacts could help me out. I made a mental note to ask her the next time we spoke to see if she could find marriage and divorce records for Emma. I'd always been amazed at how much personal information you could find online if you knew the right sites, but I'd found the sites not to be foolproof. Often the compilation of data had errors and confused identities.

I wanted to explore more and also look up Rachel Downey, but I had my Hotel Santa Sofia Condo presentation in the afternoon. I would resume my Google search after I prepped more for my client meeting.

I worked steadily for about an hour going over the planting palette plans and specifications for outdoor hardscape. I'd already sent the updated plans to the sub-consultants, the engineers and architects, for their review. This meeting was a presentation to the executives of Hotel Santa Sofia Condominiums to update them on the project's progress for the landscape design and plant installation. When I'd finished prepping, I strolled over to Uncle Bob's office down the hall. He and Aunt Veronica only came in a couple of days a week now, so I had to plan our joint work accordingly.

His door was wide open. I knocked lightly. "Hi, Uncle Bob!"

"Tory! How are you?" He raised his portly frame out of his desk chair as I walked toward him to give him a big hug.

Aunt Veronica was in the adjoining office. "Is that my Tory I hear?" She came rushing through the alcove between their offices, her blond highlighted chin-length bob perfectly coiffed as always, and also gave me a big hug. "So sorry about you having to find Emma's body, sweetheart. Adrian told us all about it. Did you know her well?"

"Professionally. I knew her fairly well professionally. But the more I think about it I realize how little I really knew about her personal life. I've been doing some digging online and it appears she was divorced, which she'd never mentioned to me."

As I listened to my own words, I realized due to Milo's murder my life was pretty much known to anyone who could read. The last year had seen my name plastered on websites all over, even the *Daily Mail*. It occurred to me that Emma and everyone else already knew all about me. They felt like they knew me because in a way they did. I, on the other hand, had to actively ask them or search online. And just like that, I had an insight.

Maybe I had to take a more proactive role in getting to know others and making new friends. Here I'd been trying to gauge other people's interest in me by the questions they asked of me, never realizing they'd probably read about my whole life story in the news. Applying this insight to Emma, maybe we were more acquainted than I'd thought. And applying this insight to Jake, maybe he wasn't distancing himself from me, maybe it was me doing the distancing. With this little nugget of self-discovery now expanding my self-awareness, I suddenly felt better equipped to communicate with Jake. I vowed to initiate questions about his divorce next time I saw him.

Aunt Veronica put her arm around my waist. "Everything okay, Tory? You seem particularly pensive today. How upsetting it must have been for you to find your friend's body. So glad you had Ashley with you and Adrian. We'd love to see you out of the office for a change. How about coming over for dinner on Thursday? You haven't even seen our tree yet, so we'd love for you to come over for dinner."

Uncle Bob smiled. "Why not make it a party? We'll see if your aunt Marian is free. Please ask Ashley if she's free too."

"And Adrian. Although with Emma's case, might that be a conflict of interest, what with Matt being a suspect?"

"Adrian has been working on a case in Santa Barbara and staying there."

"Oh. Is it about that murdered college student? She's from Santa Sofia, and there's a missing professor I think too. Hope it's not a serial killer."

"Now, Veronica, we don't even know if the two are related. We don't know whether or not the professor has been murdered." His face turned beet red as soon as the words left his lips. "Sorry, Tory. I wasn't thinking." He rubbed my shoulder.

"That's okay. It sucks that every murder brings everything back but it's certainly not your fault, Uncle Bob. I don't want you to feel like you always have to walk on eggshells around me."

"Anyway, invite Ashley and Adrian and let me know if they can come."

Back at my desk, I texted Ashley about my aunt's dinner invitation and told her Adrian was also invited.

Cool.

It was so uncharacteristic of Ashley to give a one-word response. She loved my aunt and uncle and loved their ranch-like property. *Is everything okay? You're awfully muted.*

Actually, no. Not okay at all. Still can't seem to locate Barry and just found out the murdered student was Latrice, our intern. This is giving me a nervous breakdown. Since when are Santa Barbara and Santa Sofia crime capitals?

I'm so sorry, Ash. How awful. Do you think Barry's disappearances is related to Latrice's murder?

I don't know. But I can't get anything out of Adrian, which makes me think this is why he's down in Santa Barbara.

147

Well, she was from Santa Sofia, wasn't she? So, it could just be related to that. Not necessarily all related, right? But as I texted her, I thought they must so be related. *Did that guy Rudders ever turn himself in?*

No.

I felt my stomach flip.

What about the guy who was released?

You mean our third missing person, Lyle Bubb? Adrian said he fell off the radar right after he was released.

Hmm. So strange. Try to stay calm and keep me posted. I have my meeting soon. I'll call you when it's done.

Chapter 15

After my meeting I got a call from the current condo tenant. I'd called them about the attempted break-in and assured them none of their belongings had been touched. I apologized, suggesting I might have a stalker because it was the second time there'd been an incident in two days, one at the condo and then the drone incident at my place. I told them it all started when the phone rang in the condo when I was there on Sunday night, waiting for a prospective tenant who ended up being a no-show.

The current tenant then proceeded to tell me a story that stunned me. They said the prospective tenant I was supposed to meet, a friend of theirs, had called the condo hoping to leave a message for them. The prospective tenant had lost or deleted my phone number somehow and called the condo's landline hoping to leave a message for the current tenant to pass along to me that they wouldn't be coming to view the condo because they found another place. Apparently, the mailbox was full. The prospective tenant got a hold of the current tenant by cell phone finally and let them know their voice-mail box was full and the current tenants cleared the mailbox remotely.

"Thanks for letting me know." As soon as I got off, I reflected. Okay, so when the phone rang at the condo when I was there alone, apparently it was my no-show prospective tenant trying to reach me in a roundabout way through our current tenant, not a stalker. So that meant the stalker only called on the night of the break-in. Hmm. Was the stalker the hooded figure Ashley and I saw running away from the condo? And was the stalker the same guy who came to pick up the drone? He looked familiar. But I still couldn't place him.

I called Ashley to tell her about what my tenants had told me.

"Hmm. So at least one less possible stalker incident. Cool. Meanwhile, in other news, Rudders still hasn't turned himself in and we still haven't heard back from Lyle Bubb. We're all starting to get worried. The judge vacated Bubb's conviction, so Bubb is officially a free man and totally exonerated now."

"Well, he must have showed up for that, right?"

"Yes, he did. But nobody's seen him since."

"Well, then, that's not that bad. Sounds like he's just lying low, not missing. Let's not spiral and blow this out of proportion."

"Tory, Barry is missing for sure. Our intern was murdered. Rudders is MIA. I'm hardly blowing it out of proportion."

"Sorry, sorry. Wrong word choice. I know it's a really bad situation, I just meant don't make it worse than it is. Because Bubb was just in court and obviously fine."

"Yeah."

"You know, I've only read the headlines about your case. And I know you've told me before, but who was Bubb accused of killing again? His ex-wife?"

"No, his current wife at the time, Nicky Bubb."

"Wait a minute. I've heard that name before."

"Duh. I told you before and it's been all over the news for the past several days."

"And why did they think Lyle killed Nicky?"

"Because the husband is the one they always suspect. He never signed a confession, but he claimed the cops twisted the words in his statement to implicate him, causing the jury to think his backpedaling from the statement was evidence he was lying, and that he killed her. He spent fifteen years in prison for a crime he didn't commit. The judge apologized to him and to Nicky's family for allowing the real killer to be free all these years. The judge feared the real culprit might have committed other crimes during that time."

"Wow. That's truly awful. How can that even happen?"

"It happens more than you think. Unreliable scientific and medical evidence, prosecutorial misconduct, police misconduct, and false testimony, aka a setup. Not to mention lack of financial resources for good legal representation."

"But why?"

"Dirty cops, corrupt lawyers. Dwayne Rudders, Nicky's actual murderer, was her ex-boyfriend who she'd dumped before she even met Lyle Bubb. But that didn't come out at the trial. The cops rushed to judgment early about her husband, Lyle, because he had a jealous streak and a criminal record, so he was convicted."

"That's so unfair."

"Tell me about it."

"So how did Barry choose this case to champion?"

"One of the cops who'd worked the case came to see Barry. The cop said he was a different person now and realized how his inaction back then had contributed to Bubb's conviction. The cop said he didn't know for sure whether Bubb was innocent or not, but now that he was older and wiser, he felt compelled to come forward and confess that some evidence was never used at trial that would have helped Bubb's case."

"So now what? How are you going to get Rudders to turn himself in?"

"His lawyer had supposedly been working on conditions for his surrender. But his lawyer hasn't been heard from now either."

"Great. What about Bubb and his family? They must be nervous with that guy on the prowl."

"They have mixed emotions. Yes, there's definitely some anxiety, but I'd say the overwhelming emotion expressed has been anger. There's more, but I'm not at liberty to share."

"I hate when you tease me like that."

She laughed. "I know. But seriously, we want to stick to the rules to make sure we've got all our ducks in a row if and when he's found. We are afraid of leaks to the press that will show our hand. Adrian gave me strict instructions about confidentiality."

"Fascinating case."

"I'll send you the article from the *Los Angeles Times*. It's got all the details."

"Great. Thanks."

"Hold on. Let me find it and I'll email it to you."

I stayed on the line and checked my computer for messages while I awaited her email.

Ashley came back on the phone. "Okay. I just sent you the Rudders article."

I opened the email and there was an old mug shot of Rudders at the beginning of the article. "Wow. He seems so familiar." And then it clicked. I studied the picture more closely, trying to imagine him with sharper features and hair in a more current style to reflect aging by fifteen years. Yep. I was sure of it.

"Ashley, I have seen him. And you have too. It's the drone guy. The guy who showed up at my door wanting his drone back."

"Get out. Are you sure?"

"I'm positive. His hair has thinned. It's cut short now, not long like in the mug shot."

"Hold on. Let me take another look."

I waited while she studied the photo.

"Holy crap. I think you're right. I remember you saying he looked familiar. But, to be honest, I only got a brief peek at him because you had the door half opened."

She was quiet for about a minute.

"Are you still there?"

"Yeah. I'm still looking at the mug shot. Not gonna lie. It freaks me out if he came to your door. If that was him. But the more I look at this old mug shot, I'm not so sure it was him. And why would he be stalking you?"

"Well, I think it might be him." My certainty was starting to waver.

I checked Twitter to see if there was anything about Dwayne Rudders in the news with a current photo while Ashley kept looking at the photograph.

"Oh my god!"

"What?"

"I think he was on the dating app. But I didn't swipe right so he's not in my rotation anymore and I can't compare his photo to the mug shot."

"You're kidding. That's so creepy. But then Santa Sofia's dating pool is pretty small. So that's not that surprising that a single person might be on a dating app."

"Still not sure, but it seems that it was somewhere else I'd seen him, and it was fairly recently."

I stared into space as my mind traveled back in time trying to retrieve where I'd seen him before. And then a vision came into focus. "I remember now. He was hanging around the tree lot last Friday afternoon. I remember because he seemed to be looking for a tree but then I saw him leave without one. That doesn't happen that frequently. Usually people come, they look, they buy a tree."

"Last Friday? That's the day before he was supposed to turn himself in."

There was a silence on both ends of the phone as I connected the dots and assumed Ashley was doing the same. Friday was also the day before Emma was murdered.

Chapter 16

With the possibility that a suspected murderer was hanging around our tree lot a day before Emma was murdered, I had a lot to process. After the last few days of harrowing ups and downs, I was really looking forward to spending some time with my family later in the week.

Meanwhile, I sent the new tenants a copy of the lease. All they had to do was sign and return it with a check for the first and last month's rent and security deposit. If all went well, move-in would be the first week of January. I pulled up the lease I'd used last year, made the appropriate name and date changes, made copies for me and the tenants, signed all the copies, and stuck them in a large envelope with a note requesting they sign them all and return one signed copy to me. I put it with the company's other outgoing mail in a tray on our receptionist Claudette's desk and poured myself a cup of coffee, pleased to have that off my to-do list.

I ambled back to my office and sat down at my desk with a satisfied sigh. The condo was rented for another year. One down and one to go. I idly checked my emails to find one from the general contractor doing the work on my father's house to let me know all the work was completed—the house was ready to show. I sat up straighter and felt energized. Now I had to find a tenant. My father's house was located in the exclusive Santa Sofia hillside neighborhood of Sycamore Canyon. I'd spent last year overseeing updates to the kitchen and bathrooms and the renovations were scheduled to be completed by the end of the month. How often did a contractor finish ahead of schedule? Never, right? Same in this case. Renovations were first estimated to be completed in early summer, then late summer, and finally, at long last, December. But I couldn't complain. The contractor was a dear friend of my late father and was cutting me a phenomenal deal, so I figured it taking a little longer was a reasonable trade-off. I couldn't wait to go up to his house to see the final results. I emailed the contractor back and he responded right away. We set up a time for the final walk-through. I would meet him in an hour.

To bide my time, I resumed my Google search of Connor Kringle. Ten minutes later, my search yielded nothing new. I switched to Emma Evans again. I tried something new with her Google search and clicked images. I scrolled through photos of her, most from the Facebook page where she promoted her food truck. Then I stopped dead. My mouth fell open. It looked like she was at a party and a guy had his arm around her. He wasn't tagged but I had no doubt who it was. It was Connor Kringle. So, he'd lied about not dating Emma. I couldn't wait to tell Ashley. I took a photo with my phone of the Facebook post and texted it to her.

• • •

The drive up to my father's house in Sycamore Canyon was one I always looked forward to. I'd grown up in a smaller house in the flats of Santa Sofia not far from Sycamore Canyon, but after I went away to college my father had bought a house nestled in the foothills of the Santa Ynez mountains with sweeping views of the ocean. He'd planned to renovate it and had even commissioned an architect friend of his to draw up the plans but, alas, it never happened.

As soon as I turned onto Sycamore Drive I entered a long tunnel of overarching tree branches now nearly bare. The burnished leaves they'd shed now formed a golden carpet along the roadside that made me feel as if I was entering a magical forest. At the fork in the road I branched off to a higher and narrower road and continued climbing up into the denser foliage of the hills until I came to my father's house.

The gate was open. I drove up the steep and winding driveway to the small motor court area at the side of the house near the garage. Victor, the general contractor, said he'd meet me at two. I checked my phone and it was ten minutes to. As I unlocked the front door, I imagined how beautiful one of our big blue spruce wreaths with cedar and eucalyptus accents would look on it. The two-story red tile foyer with its star-shaped, leaded-glass light fixture opened up to a circular staircase flanked by the living room and dining room on the right and the family room on the left. Recessed lighting lit the open floorplan. What I loved about his house was its simple Mediterranean style blended with modern amenities. The streamlined kitchen stretched from the dining room to the family room.

I strolled into the large living room. An arched picture window was in the center of the wall facing the front yard. One of our big noble firs would look gorgeous there. My father had a standing order for a nine-footer each year. I made a note to follow up on its delivery and added white twinkle lights to my list of things to do before showing the house. Like any good realtor knew, making a home inviting helped people envision living there.

I walked to the back of the living room and continued through the wide arched doorway that opened into the dining room and then to the kitchen beyond. Victor had come through. From the light oak hardwood floors, white granite countertops, white cabinets with blond wood, and stainless-steel Viking and Miele appliances, it was perfection. What a transformation from the older yellow-and-green-tiled kitchen with leaky fixtures and dated appliances it had before. The kitchen addition alone would increase the rental value by about a thousand dollars according to one of Ashley's realtor friends. Before it got rented, we'd have to christen the new kitchen with a small get-together, but with take-out food so we wouldn't get the perfect kitchen dirty. We could sit at the island, eat Tender Greens salmon and salad, and toast the new year. Maybe we could even have a small intimate New Year's Eve party here, although as soon as I thought that I realized I didn't have a date, not a biggie, but that Ashley probably would. Probably Adrian, but who knew, given her recent dating app game. I didn't want to be a third wheel. I'd think about it.

Lost in my reverie, I climbed the circular staircase to check out the upstairs when my phone pinged. It was a text from Victor apologizing for running late. He was on his way. ETA was in ten minutes. I heard a car outside. If it wasn't Victor, who the heck was outside? I skipped up the rest of the stairs so I could peek out an upstairs window undetected. From the master bedroom I saw a white pickup truck parked in back of my car. Pretty much blocking my exit. But that wasn't the worst of it. The truck's flatbed was covered in a tarp. It looked like it was covering a body. Resting on the truck's front passenger seat was a drone. My heart palpitated. I texted Ashley. *I'm at my father's to meet my contractor and someone else is here. With a drone!*

The doorbell rang. I froze in place even as my body overheated from fear, sweat moistening my forehead and underarms. I sure as heck wasn't going to answer it. Who would block my car like that? That was no accident.

There was a loud knock at the door. It was a confident knock. Like someone obviously knew I was there because of my car and wasn't going away until I answered. Already I hated whoever it was for their bullying behavior. It was my house, and if I didn't feel like answering the damn door I wouldn't.

Ashley wasn't texting back. That usually meant she was in an important meeting. What was the point of having a phone if she didn't check her texts? Now I was also annoyed at Ashley in addition to the stranger at my door.

Another knock on the door and then some action with the doorknocker. Then whoever it was rang the doorbell five times in the row. Hitting it over and over. Like that wasn't rude. By now I was trembling, half frozen with fear, half mad that someone was making me scared in my own home. At least Victor would be here soon. Hopefully he would scare whoever it was away.

It'd been a full minute without any knocks or ringing. I peeked out and saw a man walking around the motor court. Was he looking at my car? I couldn't tell. When he turned around, I saw his face. I gasped. It was Connor Kringle. What was he doing here? He looked up at the second-floor windows and I dipped backward. Had he seen me? Probably.

The doorbell and door knocking resumed. Yep. He'd seen me all right. I texted Ashley. *Connor Kringle is here for some reason. Please text me back ASAP.* How long can a meeting last?

All my Googling flashed in my head. Had he somehow figured out I was on to him? That photo I found of him and Emma showing so clearly that they'd been a couple at some point. Why had he lied about that? And why was he at my father's house now? He must have followed me here, otherwise why would he randomly just be dropping by? It must be to intimidate me. To find out how much I knew. Or worse. I needed to sit tight until Victor got here.

My phone pinged again. It was Victor. He'd stopped by another job because of a minor emergency. He'd be here as soon as he could. Oh. Come. On. Victor.

I heard footsteps inside. Connor's voice echoed through the house. "Ms. Benning? It's Connor. I need to talk to you."

Footsteps started up the steps. Last thing I needed was to get cornered upstairs. I stood at the top of the stairs. "Connor, how'd you know I was here?"

"Matt Ortega told me you were here."

"Matt Ortega?" My head was spinning. Why on earth would Matt Ortega know where I was? And why would he tell Connor? Had I been wrong about Matt? Were he and Connor in cahoots? Had they conspired to kill Emma? Was Connor Matt's hit man? Oh my god, was Connor here to kill me? He backed down the stairs. I had to admit, though I was terrified, I'd somehow been able to muster a commanding tone to my voice.

"What are you doing here?"

He reached in his pocket.

I held out my hand. "Hold it right there. My contractor will be here in a few minutes."

He nodded slowly. "Okay."

"He's a big guy. About six two or three. Strong. Protective. And prone to violent outbursts."

Connor's eyes widened like a cartoon character's eyes ready to pop out of their sockets. "Um, good to know."

Okay. He was going to play it coy. I could do that.

He turned toward the front door. "I think I'm going to call Matt."

"Why?"

"To ask him what I should do."

"Don't do that."

Connor winced. "No?"

"No."

"Okay. Um, I'm going to get some water in my truck then. I'm thirsty." He started to sidestep out the door while keeping his eyes on me.

A likely story. He was going to call his apparent accomplice, Matt Ortega. But this was my perfect opportunity. My car might be trapped. But I could run. I inched down the stairs as he walked toward his truck. Or did he have a rifle there? I needed to make my break.

Connor's phone rang and he answered it. "It's Matt. Uh-huh. Uh-huh."

I pushed past him and ran out to the motor court.

"Ms. Benning, wait!"

Said the spider to the fly. That was all I needed to give my escape a power surge. I ran down the windy drive so fast I was in danger of going head over heels. By the time I reached the street I didn't hear Connor any longer. The sound of a vehicle approaching on the street paralyzed me for a second. Was it Matt on his way to corner me along with Connor? A truck appeared. In the driver's seat was my general contractor, Victor. I'd never been so happy to see him.

I flagged him down. "Victor. Thank goodness you're here finally."

"Yeah, sorry. Matt Ortega wanted me to take a look at something for him." He smiled knowingly.

What! Were there three of them in on it now? Matt, Connor, and Victor too? Like an old *Twilight Zone* episode where no one is who they claimed to be.

Connor's footsteps rustled on fallen leaves on the gravel drive behind me. "I just got off the phone with Matt." He flashed a wary smile in my direction. "But he said you'd already given him the intel."

Intel? Was it a spy ring? A drug cartel? What were these three up to? And how did it involve Emma's murder?

My phone vibrated. It was a text from Jake. *I think we should talk.*

I bet he did. Not the time for chitchat.

Victor gave me a smile. "Yes, I already knew."

"Knew what?"

Victor laughed. "I told him nine feet, tops."

Was he referring to my grave? Nine feet under? To ensure no discovery?

Victor smiled again. "Let's go up to the house now. I have another client to see in a half hour."

And by "client" he meant hit? After a quick assessment, two guys against me, I thought I should at least pretend I was going along with them. That way I'd be better able to get them off their guard and then make a break for it again. If I ran now, Victor's truck was right here, and Connor looked like he was a fast runner. With my luck, he'd probably been a damn high school track star.

I also wanted to find out why Emma was killed. "So, Connor, I was doing some online snooping, as I do, and found pictures of you and Emma together. I thought you said you were never a couple."

Both men snapped their heads toward me.

Connor was taken aback. A flash in his eyes belied his calm demeanor. "Excuse me?"

"I found a Facebook post that tagged Emma. I saw pictures of you both. Together. It looked like a barbeque or party of some sort. I thought you told me you never actually dated."

"Well, I think I said we didn't date long."

I nodded. "Mmm. Right."

"And we didn't date long. A couple of weeks max. I thought I'd made that clear when I said she found me too young. She had family stuff going on too. That's actually why she said she didn't want to see me anymore. She said maybe in the new year, but it wasn't a good time."

"But you thought she just said that to spare your feelings, about the age gap."

"Totally."

"I see. Did she happen to mention what the family stuff was?"

"Nope. She got very closemouthed when I asked her. That's why I thought it was just an excuse because of my age. She got a weird look on her face. Almost like she was afraid."

"And you took that fear as fear of what?"

"Of hurting my feelings. Because of the age thing."

I let all of that marinate for a few seconds.

Victor said to me, "Ready for the walk-through?"

I wasn't sure how I was going to avoid going back to the house. And now there were two of them. Should I ask Connor to move his truck? Or should I make a run for it right now?

Victor put his hand on Connor's shoulder. "Let's show Tory what you got. I think it will take her breath away from what Matt said."

I sucked in air. What were they talking about?

Connor broke into a wide smile. "It was the last one. That's why I decided to drive up here. Didn't want someone else to get it. That doesn't happen too often, but it does occasionally if no one sees the tag. It's all set on its stand and ready to go."

He turned to me. "It's a real beauty."

"Wait a minute. What are you talking about?"

"The nine-foot tree I brought. Matt wasn't sure how high the ceilings were, so he called Victor. I'd already loaded and left but it wasn't until Victor called us that we knew for sure."

"Ahh."

Victor winked. "Let's do the walk-through."

I breathed a sigh of relief and walked myself back from the emotional ledge I'd spiraled onto. Man, my nerves were on edge. Pretty much the understatement of the year. My imagination was on overdrive, telling me in no uncertain terms I wasn't at all in control of the current situation, to the point I was concocting conspiracy theories where there were none. Connor didn't lie. He and Matt weren't planning my hit. And Victor was not their wingman. He was just a contractor who wanted to do the walk-through and get paid.

Connor hauled in the nine-foot noble fir. He'd even brought new twinkle lights and put them on the tree to save me the time and effort. After the walk-through there were just a few tweaks that needed to be addressed. Nothing major. Minor things like a paint drop they missed on the kitchen window and some missed spots on the bathroom baseboard.

After Connor and Victor both left, I was able to access my car. While driving down the winding driveway and then down the canyon road on my way home, I reviewed all the misunderstandings of the afternoon. And then one piece of information Connor had revealed popped into my mind. Before I could think about it anymore, Jake called.

"Hi. I've been texting you."

"Yeah. Sorry. I was tied up. Luckily, only figuratively."

He chuckled. "Okay. That sounds like a longer conversation. For now, I just wanted to let you know I'm probably going to be up in Santa Sofia in a day or two. Could we grab dinner? There are some things I'd like to discuss regarding Emma."

"Can't we do it over the phone? Why the intrigue?"

"Because I'm not sure how secure our phones are. I'd just prefer to talk to you in person."

"Well, now you have my attention. Sure, let me know when things firm up and hopefully we can rendezvous." Rendezvous? I shook my head. Who was I? Veronica Mars? I needed a good night's rest.

Chapter 17

I returned to my office feeling better after a session with my therapist, Ellen. I'd gained some insights about my feelings toward Milo's death and my need to take an active role to find out what had happened to him. Our session had helped clarify how all of that related to my current state of mind and my need to find Emma's killer. I knew now that wherever my search for Emma's killer led, I was doing it not just for the sake of justice but for my own mental health, to help me deal with her murder like I'd done in Milo's case. Talking to Ellen had also helped me sort out my mixed emotions about Jake and his text about wanting to talk.

Just when I was feeling more clearheaded and hopeful than I had in a while, I got a call from Ernie.

"Tory. Glad I caught you. I just wanted to update you on our investigation into Emma Evans's murder."

I had no words for this new Ernie. His changed attitude, seemingly helpful instead of adversarial, had taken me aback.

"Tory? Are you there?"

"Yes. I'm here."

"You'll be happy to hear we won't be charging Matt Ortega with murder."

I took a deep breath and exhaled. "That's great. So good to hear."

"Also, we've been able to obtain some additional security footage from stores around Emma's bakery. I've gone over about the last three weeks or so of tape. But I wanted to share with you what we've found so far."

"Okay."

"Remember when I'd mentioned that your PI friend Jake Logan had been seen in the first video we looked at initially?"

"Yeah."

"Well, turns out that wasn't a one-off incident. Our weeks of footage show he'd been hanging out around her bakery for at least three weeks. At all hours of the day and night."

I fell back in my chair hard. My head was reeling. Had Jake been lying when he told me he'd only been in Santa Sofia a few times? Define a few. Fourteen to twenty-one days. Hardly a few.

"So why are you telling me? What does it mean?"

"Well, your own safety primarily. We haven't figured out his role in this yet, whether he was on the job or whether it was something more personal . . ."

"We?"

He paused. "Well, it's been me mainly up to this point. Adrian's in Santa Barbara and we don't have that many other officers on this case at the moment given we're narrowing it down."

"Narrowing it down?" Since Matt Ortega was no longer a suspect, the other possible person of interest must be Connor, because who else would it be? Very interesting. I clucked silently to myself, proud that my amateur sleuthing deductions were jibing with those of professionals.

"Yep. And my bet is one of them will end up being our prime suspect. We just have to methodically build our case now. Collect our evidence. Interview witnesses. Do everything by the book to help ensure the prosecutor can move forward."

"Okay, you might just try asking Jake why he was hanging out around her house. Or ask Adrian to ask him. You know Adrian's staying with Jake while he's in Santa Barbara."

"Not anymore he isn't."

"He isn't? Since when?"

"Since we saw Jake on all these tapes. Adrian respectfully declined Jake's invitation to stay more nights. He's on his way back to Santa Sofia anyway."

I wondered if Ashley knew Adrian was coming back to Santa Sofia. Or that Connor was now a person of interest. "Wait a minute. You said 'one of them.' You think it's one person acting alone?"

"Oh, yeah."

"Do you think the person who killed Emma was the person who also hacked into our computer system?"

"Definitely. That's my theory."

If Connor was the murderer, as Ernie thought, how did he manage to hack our system? Maybe Emma had found out Matt Ortega's password when she dated him and then somehow Connor found it when he dated Emma. No, that seemed like too much of a stretch. Just thinking about that scenario made it seem highly unlikely.

"The main reason for my call was to update you."

"Thanks."

"But, also, to warn you."

"Warn me? About what?" A little late. I'd already been alone at my father's house with Connor, and I think my aggressive stance had given him a healthy respect for me. He'd backed off. *I could handle him, Ernie. Don't you worry about me.*

"I know you consider yourself a pretty good sleuth after solving Milo's disappearance."

"Um, thank you, Ernie, for saying that. I appreciate it. It was a team effort." No thanks to Ernie, though. But I was feeling magnanimous.

He whistled. "I have to tell you, Tory, you're a cool cucumber. You don't seem very upset."

"Why should I be? I've already been alone with Connor and lived to tell the story. That built my confidence. I think my attitude kind of scared him, actually."

"Who's Connor?"

"Connor Kringle. Your other person of interest." Sometimes Ernie could be so annoyingly coy.

"Connor Kringle?"

"Yeah. Connor Kringle. One of your persons of interest along with Matt Ortega."

There was a long pause from Ernie. Was he a slow processor—a definite possibility—or was he recording our call and choosing his words so as not to incriminate anyone?

"Where did you get that idea?"

"You just told me."

"Told you what exactly?"

Okay. This was getting too much like a "Who's on first" routine. I sighed in exasperation. "Look, Ernie, you just said you had narrowed it down to a few persons of interest, Matt Ortega and Connor Kringle."

"I did say we were narrowing it down. I'll give you that. But I told you we will not be charging Matt. I assumed you knew who I was talking about, but I guess I assumed wrong."

I could hear his signature mouth breathing over the line.

"Okay. I give up. I don't have time to play *Jeopardy!* Who's the other one, if not Connor? Surely not Fuji? As far as I know he doesn't even know Emma except to say hi."

"You're kidding, right?"

"Ernie! Who is it?" I had one nerve left.

"Okay, sorry. No need to shout. I thought you knew and were kidding around. It's Logan. Jake Logan."

Chapter 18

"Ernie, I thought Adrian set you straight about Jake already. What was his motive?" As the words left my lips, one possibility popped into my mind. Had Jake's involvement with Emma been more than professional? Otherwise why would Ernie consider him a suspect?

"Tory, you know I can't go into details. It might affect the case. But I wanted to warn you because I know Jake Logan is your friend. I wouldn't want you to get hurt in any way by him."

"He wouldn't hurt me."

"People can behave in surprising ways if they feel cornered."

"Does he know you still consider him a person of interest?"

"Not yet."

"Then why tell me? I thought you didn't want your case affected."

Ernie emitted a soft grunt, as if frustrated with my fondness for logic. "Because even though we're not certain, I don't want you to get caught in the cross fire, so to speak."

"No one's having a shootout, Ernie. Anyway, thanks for the heads-up. For the record, you're barking up the wrong tree thinking Jake is a murderer."

"For your sake, I hope so."

What was this transformation? "Ernie, I have to say you surprise me sometimes. After our history . . ."

"People can change, Tory." He paused. "I have a few regrets regarding my past behavior, but I will say going forward I will let no stone go unturned. Because lives are at stake."

"Sounds like you've been talking to Ashley. That is the whole push behind the Justice Program she volunteers for."

"You've been talking to Ashley?"

"What? Of course I've been talking to Ashley. She's my best friend."

"What have you been talking about with her?"

"What?" I pulled my chair up closer to my desk.

Ernie cleared his throat. "I mean in terms of her work on the Justice Program."

"Oh. Just how the guy who was supposed to turn himself in never did." I checked my Twitter feed.

"You mean Dwayne Rudders."

I scrolled through Instagram to see what was new. I mainly followed landscape and animal rescue accounts. "Yes."

"I heard his lawyer doesn't know where he is either."

"Yeah. He's not the only one. Ashley's former professor who heads the Justice Program can't be reached either."

"I thought they'd tracked down his number and reached him?"

I sat up straighter. "Really? I don't think so. Adrian will probably have the latest on everything, don't you think?"

"Yeah. Let me know if Ashley hears from Professor Hayes. And I'll keep you posted on Emma's murder investigation. I don't know Connor, what was his name again?"

"Kringle."

"I don't know him. But I'll look into it. Thanks for the tip."

"Sure."

When I hung up, I reflected on my conversation. I sat deep in thought, staring at a cute Pomeranian just saved by a rescue. A soft knock on my open door startled me.

Matt Ortega stood in my doorway. "Hi, Tory. Didn't mean to startle you. Just wanted to give you an update. The lot is low on inventory. I'm hoping business picks up, and if it does, we'll need more inventory. I sent two of our guys out to the tree farm to pick up some fresh trees."

Many of our trees got shipped in from tree farms in Oregon, but some varieties, like our Monterey pines, we bought locally from regional tree farmers in Santa Barbara and San Luis Obispo counties.

"Okay, that doesn't sound too bad."

"With two guys out, I have the other two guys running the lot and one the nursery. And I just got a call from a customer reporting an incomplete delivery. Fuji dropped off her tree but somehow the custom wreath she ordered didn't make it to their truck. They searched their truck and no wreath. I thought maybe they had dropped off the wreath at the wrong address. But when I poked around, I found the wreath near the loading area. It never got loaded onto the truck. Anyway, bottom line, she needs her custom wreath, stat. She's hosting an open house tonight. She'd wanted it delivered the day of her open house so it would be fresh."

"Fair enough. But you don't have anyone free to run it up to her?"

"Correct."

"I'd be happy to do that. What's her address?"

"Thanks, Tory. I'd run it up myself, but Adrian wants me to come in for a few more questions if that's okay with you. The guys have the lot and nursery covered."

"Of course. Questions about what? Did he say exactly."

"No. He just said to come in and get someone to cover for me because it was important."

Matt said he'd meet me at the nursery, so I got in my Lexus and drove over there. I jumped out to meet Matt and help him arrange the huge wreath in the hatchback, laying it carefully out so it wouldn't get damaged. He closed the hatchback and I climbed into the driver's seat. The smell of Christmas filled my car.

"Let me know how it goes with Adrian. Good luck."

As I pulled away slowly, I reminded myself to be mindful and drive carefully because the wreath was a tad fragile with its berries and pine cones. I didn't want to deliver a wreath with broken branches and missing parts. The customer who the wreath was going to was up in the hills of Sycamore Canyon not far from my father's house. But this address was farther up the ridge road, almost at the top of the mountain. The roads were windy with straight stretches in between as I climbed higher and higher into the hills.

I'd never had much involvement in the nursery side of Benning Brothers before my father died. I was strictly on the landscape design end. That was still my primary focus, but now as joint owners with Uncle Bob and Aunt Veronica, it was good for me to find out more about our nursery business too.

There were a few more curves and I came to a walled and gated property at the top of the mountain. I pressed the intercom at the gate and was buzzed in. I drove up a driveway that was at least twice the length of my father's driveway.

I parked in the large motor court, got out of the car and opened the hatchback. The wreath still looked gorgeous. My careful driving had preserved its perfection. I tried to sling my shoulder bag around my neck messenger-style and nearly strangled myself in the process, knocking my sunglasses to the ground. My shoulder strap wasn't long enough for that to work and it looked like I was wearing a feedbag. I stuck my sunglasses on my head like a headband. After a few seconds I decided to just dangle my purse from my wrist. It was awkward but at least it freed my hands and it wouldn't bang into the wreath and knock off needles and berries like it would if it was over my shoulder.

I carefully worked my hands through the center of the wreath to gently lift it from underneath. Then I grabbed the wreath's wire frame and hooked my fingers under it, supporting the whole wreath with my other hand. I set off toward the mansion's front door, eager to present this beauty. At the front of the house was a gated courtyard. I stood at the gate, gripping the wreath frame tightly and using my support hand to lift the gate lever without hurting the wreath. This took a full minute. I had to shift the wreath to lean on my leg while I kicked open the gate.

Dogs started to bark from somewhere on the property. And they had the loud, husky barks of big dogs. I was hoping friendly big dogs. I moved slowly toward the front door. Just as I stepped onto the doorstep, the front door opened. Connor Kringle stood before me.

"Oh, my goodness, Connor. What are you doing here?" Again, like at my father's house, I tried to reconcile the odd man out in this situation. Was he indeed stalking me? What was he doing here? Had he hurt or taken the occupants hostage just so he could trap me? I started to tremble ever so slightly and hoped he didn't notice. But the two large pit bulls behind him were harder to fool. I was sure they smelled my fear. One growled.

"Your dogs seem nice." The high-pitched voice was mine.

He laughed. "Don't be fooled by that growl. That's Grandma. It sounds like a growl but she's really just saying howdy."

I bowed to Grandma and put my best foot forward. "How you doing, Grandma?"

Grandma howled. It sounded like a drawn-out growl and ended with a grunt. But her eyes twinkled, and it actually seemed like she was smiling at me.

"Pleased to meet you too."

Connor laughed. "Now Killer here isn't as outgoing as Grandma."

A dog named Killer owned by a suspected killer, duly noted. I didn't know what to make of the choice of Grandma. Granny issues. Like Mommy issues. Like *Psycho*. I was spiraling inside but had a frozen smile plastered on my face the whole time.

"Well, I'm here to drop off this wreath but not sure I'm at the right place. I'll just sidle back to my car and check the address. Sorry to bother you." I turned to go.

"Stop."

I looked back, expecting him to have pulled a gun on me.

"You're at the right place. Sorry to have inconvenienced you. I would have brought it here myself, but I worked at the Santa's Helpers lot today and was a minute away when my mom called."

His "mom." Okay. This was getting awkward. I suspected Connor was really his middle name and his first name was Norman. "I don't quite understand." I didn't have a clue what he was rambling about, but I thought this was not the time for being blunt.

He laughed. I guess it was a normal laugh. But he threw his head back slightly. Bordering on diabolical laugh for sure.

"Anyway, so sorry we didn't deliver this with your tree. Matt told me your mother was anxious to have this wreath. Is she here?"

"No. She got called away."

And then I got a weird vibe. Like I did at my father's house. Was I being paranoid? Or was Connor really the son of the owners of this house? Or did he just give me a cock-and-bull story.

"So, you're having a big party tonight?"

"What?"

"Your mother's Christmas open house."

"Yeah. Right." He bit his lip.

This response did nothing to assuage my paranoia. He seemed like he'd not heard of a party.

An awkward silence followed.

Connor scratched his head. "I can take the wreath any time now."

"What? Oh, yes. It's why I'm here. Sorry."

We made the transfer, both of us careful not to crush or break anything.

"One thing, before I head out." I decided to go for it. "Who do you think murdered Emma? I'm assuming you talked to each other still even though you no longer dated?"

His eyes popped again like they had at my father's house. Startled by my directness, no doubt. He made a sly recovery though, barely missing a beat. "Totally amicable. We still talked when the food truck was at the lot."

"You of all people must know what was going on in her day-to-day life. Was anyone bothering her?"

"She was using a dating app. But more as a device to amuse herself than looking for anyone to date. The other day she told me one guy was coming on way too strong."

"Really. Did she have a name for this guy?"

"Nah. She never told me his name. All she did was flash me a quick look at him on her phone."

"Oh. So, you actually saw him? Did you recognize him as someone you'd seen before?"

"Now that you mention it, he did look like I'd seen him before. But where, I couldn't tell you."

"What did he look like?"

"Couldn't really tell. All I remember was he was wearing a Santa hat."

I froze. Santa hat. Like the guy that was bugging Ashley. "Did she show you any other guys on the app?"

"Yeah. All a bunch a posers if you ask me. All looked like trainers or models."

"Uh-huh." I nodded and thought for a second. "Any others wearing a Santa hat?"

"No. Just the one who kept bugging her."

"What do you think about Matt as a suspect?"

"Definitely couldn't be Matt. He's one of the nicest guys I've ever known. I've never seen him get really angry either. He's a pretty level-headed and chill guy."

"I know. I feel exactly the same way. I could never imagine him resorting to violence."

"I couldn't either. The cops are on the wrong trail there."

"Who do you suspect then?"

"I really don't know. We had only started to get to know each other, we weren't exclusive, and she didn't really tell me much about her past relationships or her past in general, for that matter."

"Hmm. Interesting." I thought about Jake. Was he part of that past she didn't talk about?

"All right. Hope your mother likes the wreath."

Again, he gave me an odd look I couldn't figure out.

I got in my car and drove down the driveway with thoughts of potential suspects whirling in my head. Why was Emma secretive about her past? Was Connor telling me everything he knew?

Just as I pulled out of the driveway, a silver Mercedes coming from the opposite direction slowed. The driver was an older woman, around fiftyish I'd guess, with a square determined jaw. Like Connor's. I slowed and, sure enough, she turned and disappeared as she headed up their driveway. I wondered what she knew about Emma or if she'd even met Emma since Connor said they weren't exclusive. I reached for my sunglasses, then realized they were no longer on my head. Shoot. Did I drop them? Then I remembered I'd pushed them up on my head when I struggled with my purse. They must have slipped off in the commotion.

At the next flat stretch in the road I made a U-turn back to the house. I pulled up in front of the property and got out of my car to take a look on their driveway. The gate was bordered by two stucco posts. The wall of hedges allowed a tiny space between the gate and where the wall began. I slipped through and started up the driveway. There they were. Right in the middle of the driveway. Thank goodness the woman's vehicle hadn't touched them. I tiptoed up the drive, hoping Grandma and Killer would remember me if they were loose. As I got closer, I heard Connor greeting his mother.

The woman hugged Connor. "Isn't that the second time that Benning woman has supposedly run into you in as many days?"

My face heated up and prickled. You got it wrong, Mom. Your baby boy has been turning up wherever I have been.

His mother continued. "Someone's got a fan. Just be careful. These older women want more than a boy toy. They want a meal ticket too."

My face prickled with rage. I didn't know which comment aggravated me more, the insinuation that I was a gold digger or the crack about being an older woman. I had tops five years on Connor.

"Relax, Mother. You're paranoid. Always thinking everybody is after me because we're rich. Listen, she acts weird and nervous. I'm not sure she even knows who I am."

"Well, just don't be gullible. That food truck woman certainly had her sights set on you. I could practically see the dollar signs reflected in her eyes."

"Oh, Mother. You're such a drama queen."

They both laughed and went inside.

I scrambled back to my car with more ideas about why Emma had been murdered than ever before.

Chapter 19

The next day flew by. I finished all the needed correspondence for my various projects for the year. I clicked Send on the last email and sighed with satisfaction. All done until next year.

I drove home and Ashley called as I turned onto my street.

"Hi. Just got home and wanted to know what you're wearing to your aunt and uncle's tonight."

"Something festive. I have two things in mind. But I think I'll end up wearing black velvet pants and a cranberry cashmere pullover. What about you?"

Ashley laughed. "We might be twins. I have planned black velvet skinny jeans, a burgundy blouse and my black faux leather jacket."

"I'm going to wear my black faux fur jacket, so at least when we arrive, we won't look like identical twins."

"Totally fraternal twins though." She laughed. "See you there."

Iris started barking as I walked up my front path.

"Iris, settle down!"

As was often the case, my command had the opposite effect on my headstrong Pom and she doubled down on her manic howls. As soon as I opened the front door, she jumped up around me, pawing my legs for pets. A dog whisperer I was not.

I crouched down to pet her and let her lick my hands. "Hi, pommie! All is well. I didn't abandon you. I've returned, just as I told you I would when I left."

Otis didn't surface for about five minutes. He looked very sleepy when he ambled out of the bedroom. "Hi, Otis. I'll get your dinner in a minute. Iris, let's go outside and take a walk."

I opened the door to the backyard to let Iris out and she galloped back in for dinner a few minutes later. I scooped some kibble for Iris and Otis and gave them fresh water. Then I hurried into the bedroom to change. Decked out in my holiday apparel, I emerged from my room to Iris's anxious stare and Otis's disdainful disregard. I rummaged through my collection of gift bags in my office, found a Christmassy red foil one, and stuck a bottle of wine in it for my aunt and uncle.

"Okay, kids, Mom has a Christmas party to go to. Well, it's not really a Christmas party, more a small get-together to see Uncle Bob's and Aunt Veronica's tree and partake of their delicious holiday fare. Before you know it, I'll be back, and then we can snuggle. Now you both can have a nice nap."

Iris listened to me intently, turned, and walked to her bed, resigned to the idea I was leaving again.

"I won't be gone long. Promise."

The night was crisp and the frosty sea mist stung my cheeks and frizzed my hair, as it was wont to do. The drive to Ryder Ranch, the rustic neighborhood where my aunt and uncle lived, took me past houses decked out in Christmas lights and decorations appropriate for Santa's Village, replete with lighted reindeer and sleighs. Their house was aglow with white twinkle lights, and their tree with multicolor lights was showcased in the big bay window in their living room.

Ashley was getting out of her car as I pulled up and walked over to my car while I parked. She waited at my door and we exchanged hugs when I stepped out. "Perfect timing."

The wreath-adorned upper half of their Dutch door was open, with my smiling Aunt Veronica standing watch near the doorway. She threw the bottom half of the door open and hugged us both. "Welcome, girls! So good to see you both." She gestured us inside and we followed. When she turned around, her straight blond highlighted hair, which I envied greatly, swung like a model's in a shampoo ad and the ivory silk blouse and forest green velvet pants she wore completed her cover girl look. Goals for me when I reached retirement age one day.

Uncle Bob strolled into the foyer. He wore a sweater with a reindeer on it that did a good job of disguising his substantial paunch. "Tory! Ashley! Merry Christmas! What can I get you to drink? We have your aunt's famous mulled wine. We also have regular wine and beer. Also, eggnog."

"I'd love some eggnog with a bit of sherry, please."

"You got it. Ashley, what about you?"

"I'll have what Tory's having. Sounds so good."

We were the first to arrive. Aunt Veronica ushered us into the living room.

Their tree was laden with ornaments. "Oh, my goodness. What a beautiful tree!"

Aunt Veronica beamed as she pointed out a few of her favorite ornaments she'd collected over the years. "We got this one in Santa Barbara." She pointed to a quilted white starfish with Santa Barbara stitched on it in red yarn.

The doorbell interrupted her commentary on Christmases past and Aunt Veronica went to the door.

Uncle Bob glided in with a glass of eggnog in each hand. "Here you go."

"Merry Christmas." Ashley and I toasted each other.

The doorbell rang again, and Aunt Veronica greeted someone loudly. "Glad you could make it." Seconds later she was back in the living room. Trailing behind her was Jake Logan.

"Jake! What are you doing here?"

"Good to see you too." He flashed a dimpled smile at me. Your aunt and uncle graciously invited me over to see their tree.

"I see."

Ashley smirked and elbowed me before tipping her glass to finish off her eggnog. "That was so good, Bob. Perfect ratio of nog to sherry."

I took another sip myself since Jake's presence threw me. I had to agree with Ashley. "This eggnog is superb. Well done, Uncle Bob."

"Thank you, thank you. Who's ready for a second? Jake, what can I get you?"

"Who could resist those testimonials?"

"So, three eggnogs?"

We all nodded.

"Great. Three eggnogs coming up."

"Thanks." Jake walked over to the tree. "One of the most beautiful Christmas trees I've ever seen."

Aunt Veronica gushed a thank-you. "I was just telling the girls about the history of a few of my favorite ornaments. We got this one from Carmel when our son Sam was four years old." She pointed to a wooden ornament in the shape of the number four with a reindeer on it. "Sam was supposed to be here tonight but got invited to another open house being thrown by the parents of the girl he's been dating up in Carmel. He's been staying with my sister in Carmel and will be home for Christmas. Happy to report he's been thriving in Northern California this past year. Nothing like a change of scenery to help heal your wounds, especially when you're young."

Jake patted my aunt on her shoulder. "Good to hear he's doing well."

I sighed in relief upon hearing Sam's name. We'd all had such a difficult time last year with the deaths of my father and Milo, but perhaps it affected Sam most, on a variety of levels.

"Such good news, Aunt Veronica. He's always been a good kid. He lucked out with you and Uncle Bob."

She blinked her eyes at me twice in a double wink that I affectionately called a twinkle.

Uncle Bob came back holding one eggnog and a plate of appetizers. He handed the eggnog to Ashley. "Anyone hungry? Want to make sure we balance out our imbibing with some tasty hors d'oeuvres. Tory, your eggnog and Jake's are on the counter in the kitchen."

"Thanks." I headed to the kitchen. Jake followed me.

I picked up a glass of eggnog. "So, this was a surprise."

"For me too. I didn't know you were going to be here."

"Same."

Our gazes locked. We both smiled, realizing at the same time my aunt and uncle were probably guilty of attempted matchmaking.

Jake took a sip of eggnog. "Well, the good thing is, I wanted to see you to talk."

"Yes. Killing two social obligations with one stone, right?"

"Obligations? Hardly. More like a double bonus." He blushed and took another sip of eggnog.

The doorbell rang again. Now who?

By the bubbly voices of my aunt and uncle I guessed who it was. My other aunt, Marian. My late mother's sister. She was head librarian at the Santa Sofia library.

Aunt Marian walked in with a pretty red sweater and the apparently obligatory black pants.

"Hi, everyone."

After Uncle Bob had gotten her drink order and we were all back in the living room seated around the tree, Aunt Marian started pumping me for information regarding Emma's murder.

"Such an awful business. So young too. Any closer in finding out who did it?"

"They had designated our nursery manager, Matt Ortega, as a suspect, then downgraded him to a person of interest. I really don't know of any other developments." That last part had trouble leaving my lips when Jake, a person of interest according to Ernie, was seated right next to me on the sofa. Awkward.

I turned to Jake. "Have you heard anything new from Adrian?" My gaze met Ashley's. "What about you, Ash? You both speak to him more than I do I would think."

Both Ashley and Jake mumbled a "no" while shaking their heads.

Aunt Marian nodded at me. "What about Connor? Wasn't he interested in Emma at one point and then she rebuffed him or something like that?"

"Yes. How did you know that, Aunt Marian?"

She flipped her silver hair at me. "I'm a librarian. I know everything."

I laughed. "I don't doubt that. Anyway, Connor's definitely a suspicious character in my book. Always seems to be turning up anywhere I go." I turned to Uncle Bob. "Wait. You didn't invite him over here tonight, did you?"

Ashley guffawed.

Aunt Veronica came into the room with two trays of cheese and olives. "Who is this you're talking about, dear?"

I sprung up to help her with the trays. "Connor Kringle. Chris Kringle's grandson. Chris Kringle is the owner of the Santa's Helpers tree lot, as you know."

Aunt Marian laughed. "You're slipping on your sleuthing, young lady. You mean Connor Kemp." She winked at Aunt Veronica.

I did a double take as I processed her words. "Say that again. Connor Kemp? Like the Kemps who own St. Nicholas Vineyards and St. Nicholas winery and the St. Nicholas Inn?"

Ashley piped in. "And Frost wines too."

Aunt Marian nodded. "Yes. Connor's mother is a Kringle. Marissa Kringle. Goes by Marissa Kringle Kemp, I believe. Why on earth would he want to murder Emma if she turned him down when he's the most eligible bachelor in Santa Sofia?"

No wonder I couldn't find anything on him when I Googled him. I had the wrong name. Everything I'd known or thought I'd known about Connor suddenly flooded my brain. And now it all made sense. Connor wasn't stalking me. If anything, I was the one stalking him. He probably thought I was purposely waiting for him when he made a delivery at my father's house. And then when I personally delivered the wreath to his mother's house. He must think I was totally after him. No wonder he always looked awkward. If I wasn't so mortified at what must have seemed like my own shameless hussy-like behavior, I'd be rolling on the floor laughing at my comedy of errors.

Aunt Veronica leaned in. "I'm a bit confused, Tory. You were worried about Emma being hounded by the town's winery dynasty scion?"

I nodded. "Pretty much."

"In Tory's defense," Ashley put in, "sometimes those rich kids don't take no for an answer. I've read about spoiled brats who are offended when the poor girl they like doesn't like them back."

Jake gulped hard. "I've heard stories like that for sure."

I spoke slowly. "So then if Connor has no apparent motive—"

Ashley quickly jumped in. "That's why the cops don't view him as a person of interest."

Aunt Veronica jumped up. "Whoops! I'm so engrossed in the conversation I almost forgot about dinner. Don't want to overcook everything. Better get the food out of the oven."

"Need some help?"

"Thanks, Tory. Just to deliver the food to the island and the sideboard would be great."

Jake and Ashley also offered.

"Thanks, but Tory will be fine."

I followed her into the kitchen. She opened the refrigerator and started handing me bowls of salads. One was a mix of grilled winter vegetables, one was a Waldorf salad with walnuts and cranberries, and another was a pasta salad with basil and dried tomatoes.

"I didn't make these. Ordered them all from Clementine's. Put these on the pass-through counter please."

"Yum."

"And then I have a ham and some sides heating in the oven."

She slipped her hands into oven mitts and pointed to another pair for me.

"Could you please deliver these to the sideboard in the dining room and look for serving spoons and forks in the top drawer."

Once we were all set up, Aunt Veronica announced "Dinner is served" to everyone in the living room. "Help yourself, please. We've got plenty. And let Bob know if you need something to drink other than the wine at the table."

We all grabbed plates from the stack on the pass-through counter and served ourselves and then sat down at the dining room table set for six. Aunt Veronica had set the table with cute red place mats with reindeer on them and white napkins with the names of Santa's reindeer embroidered on them rolled into red jingle bell napkin rings.

Dinner was jovial, partly due to the pleasant company and partly due to the wine that flowed and the delicious food for which we'd all expressed gratitude. For dessert Uncle Bob had made his famous trifle, layers of pound cake alternated with sherry-soaked peaches, pears, oranges, bananas, and vanilla pudding. It was topped with whipped cream dotted with kiwi slices and strawberries—a perfect Christmas-themed confection.

Aunt Marian was the first to leave. Then Jake, Ashley, and I all left together after many thank-yous and hugs.

I'd expected Jake to linger behind after Ashley left since he'd mentioned he'd wanted to talk to me, but he said goodbye first and Ashley and I said we'd touch base in the morning. I got in my car and drove down the street about a half block when I heard a clunk in the backseat. The wine. I'd forgotten to give my aunt and uncle the wine I'd brought. At the next fork in the road I made a U-turn and headed back to their house.

As I approached my aunt and uncle's house, Jake and Ashley were still outside talking. What was that about? I was so surprised I kept driving past the house. After a minute I decided to turn around and just park and drop off the wine and stop making drama where there was none. I pulled into a driveway and then headed back toward the house. They'd both left in the few minutes it'd taken me to turn around. I grabbed the gift bag and ran up to the door. Aunt Veronica looked surprised to see me. But not nearly as surprised as I was as I drove home wondering what Ashley and Jake had lingered to talk about.

Chapter 20

When I got home the animals were super excited to see me, as I was them. I took a warm shower to unwind and think about what Jake and Ashley could have been talking about. It had to be about the case. Ashley already had some professional connection to Emma. She'd told me so herself. I bet Jake did too. And I bet neither could divulge anything to me because of client confidentiality. I knew Ashley was totally in love with Adrian. Jake, who knew? I couldn't imagine that they'd have any romantic interest in each other. I'd trust both of them with my life. So, it had to be about Emma's murder. I was sure of it.

I cuddled with Iris and Otis on the bed for a few minutes. Otis soon had enough, and Iris started scratching a spot on my red and green polka-dot flannel duvet to settle down for the night. I looked at the news online—no new developments apparently in the Justice Program suspect search. Rudders still hadn't turned himself in and his lawyer was still saying he would, and that they were in negotiations for the terms of Rudders's surrender. There was a brief mention that Lyle Bubb hadn't been heard from since he'd been released. Well, that was understandable. Unfortunately, I couldn't find any updates on Ashley's missing mentor, Professor Barry Hayes of the Justice Program, the man who was responsible for Lyle Bubb's release.

I kept thinking about Ashley and Jake lingering outside my aunt and uncle's place after we all had said goodbye. The more I thought about it, the more it seemed as if they had purposely waited for me to leave. I couldn't stand it any longer. I had to know what was going on.

I called Ashley.

"Hi. Everything okay? It's late."

It was five minutes past midnight.

"Sorry. I didn't check the time. But I just couldn't wait until tomorrow. I had to know."

"Had to know what?"

"You know."

She spoke slowly. "No, Tory, I don't know."

"OMG, did I wake you up? I'm sorry."

"Yeah, kind of. Definitely. I was just nodding off."

"Sorry. But I have to know what you and Jake were talking about after we left my aunt and uncle's tonight."

Silence.

"Are you there?"

"Yes."

"Well?"

"Tory, I'm half asleep. Cut me some slack. I'm thinking."

"What do you mean?"

"I mean how I'm going to tell you something that I've been sworn to secrecy about, but knowing you as I do, now that you suspect something, not telling you will put you in more danger than telling you."

"Well, you've certainly gotten my attention. Tell me what exactly."

"Promise you won't tell a soul?"

"Promise."

"Okay. It's about Emma's murder. Adrian told me that the cops have two suspects."

"Old news. That's what Ernie said too. Who are they?"

"Adrian wouldn't tell me. But he said only one is a real suspect. The other suspect is a decoy."

"What do you mean, a decoy?"

"Well, according to Adrian, the real suspect is a big flight risk. So, they don't want to show their hand too early, fearing he'll get wind of it and leave town."

I sucked in air. "So, it's a sting. And I'm assuming Matt Ortega is the decoy?"

"That's what I think too."

"And the other suspect, the real one, who is it?"

I held my breath waiting for her response. And exhaled loudly. "Well?"

"I told you, he wouldn't tell me."

"What! You tease me, leading me to believe you know who their suspect is and then you tell me you don't know? Are you being honest? Please tell me if you know."

"Tory, I'm telling the truth. He said no matter how good an actor I think I am, he couldn't risk telling me in case I gave it away. He also said he knows I'd probably tell you. And we're all safer this way."

"Rude."

She chuckled. "I know."

"And he didn't drop any hints? Do you think it's Connor? I mean, we were thinking it was him until we found out more about his background in terms of motive. Just because he's wealthy doesn't rule him out necessarily. Maybe he had another motive other than financial. Clearly, Rachel had an ax to grind by implicating him. Adrian referred to the real suspect as a him though, correct? So, it's not Rachel."

Ashley yawned. "Yes. He definitely referred to the real murderer as a male."

So that ruled out Connor's mother, Marissa Kemp. "Okay, so it could be Connor after all. Maybe I've been right all along."

"Who else could it be? None of the other Benning Brothers peeps knew her that well, did they?"

"Not that I know of."

Ashley yawned again. "Ooh. I know. Didn't she say she used a dating app? Maybe it was some weird guy she met online."

I rearranged my pillow. "Hmm. That's scary. Connor mentioned that Emma was on a dating app too. And he told me the guy she showed him on the app was wearing a Santa hat, like the guy in the Santa hat who's been bothering you."

"OMG, Tory. Who isn't wearing a Santa hat this time of year? Stop being overly dramatic."

"All the guys on the dating app who aren't pestering you, that's who. By the way, he hasn't contacted you recently, has he?"

"We should ask Rachel if Emma ever mentioned specifics about the guys she met on the app."

"Good idea. I'll call her tomorrow. And you never answered my question."

"What question?"

"You know very well what question, Ash. Are you still getting badgered by that guy who left you a ton of texts?"

She paused. "Badgered, no."

"Phew, that's a relief."

"But—"

"Don't tell me you're still communicating with him?"

"Relax. We've had several long phone chats. He's fine. He's normal. He just has had women ghost him and that's his pet peeve, so he wanted to make sure I wasn't ghosting him."

"Are you listening to yourself?"

She hesitated and then responded by stretching out her words. "I am. Oh my god, he's a manipulator, isn't he?"

"Ya think? I don't know how a smart woman like you falls for that. Jake told me about this group of women that monitor online dating sites looking for bad guys. Called the Valentine Vigilantes or something like that. I never looked them up, but you should."

Ashley paused before responding. "Actually, I do pro bono work for them."

"You what?" I couldn't believe my ears.

"Yep. In fact, my dating app interest is partly personal and partly professional. So believe me when I tell you I'm being careful. I'm well aware of the weirdoes out there. But also aware not all the guys on apps are predatory."

"I can't believe you never mentioned you did pro bono work for them."

Ashley chuckled. "Well, I try to provide some modicum of discretion for my clients, believe it or not. When they contacted me a couple of weeks ago for advice I was intrigued. That's when I offered my services pro bono. They're a new nonprofit and they just want to make sure they don't get sued by some guy on an app. And then I thought the best way to find out what my client was about was to sign up myself."

I was speechless. "Aren't you full of surprises?"

"Anyway, don't worry about me."

"But I do. You don't even know for sure if that photo is even of him."

"Well, he's not on the Valentine Vigilante site, so that's a plus."

"Yet."

"Let's not be so negative. The photo is him."

"How do you know?"

"Because he told me. He models part-time."

"Of course he does."

"Okay, okay. I'm hearing it. I got swayed by his good looks. I wanted to get Adrian jealous."

"What did Adrian think of your dating app guy?"

"Haven't actually told him yet. I'm waiting for an opportunity when we were together and I get texts from the dating app guy."

"Solid plan. Not. Honestly, just ease out with that guy. I have a bad gut feeling about him."

"Okay. To be honest, I already have been. After I talked to Adrian the other day and he was so nice, I realized my own insecurity was raising my defenses, rather than something he actually said or did."

"Finally. You're starting to see the light. Yay."

She laughed. "Okay, this princess needs her beauty sleep. Glad we cleared the air. Let me know if Jake tells you anything more about who the real suspect is. And I'll let you know if I hear anything."

"Deal."

After we hung up, I sighed and crawled under the covers. Iris was sound asleep with her head buried in the pillows and Otis had padded back into the bedroom and curled up in Iris's dog bed. I shut off the light and closed my eyes thinking about Connor. I wondered about dating app strangers lurking around online and in real life and wondered whether Emma had offended someone inadvertently or purposefully online. And I thought about Jake. Why on earth had Ernie pegged him as a second suspect? I wondered why Adrian stopped staying at Jake's place in Santa Barbara. Maybe he had a per diem and preferred to stay at one of Santa Barbara's many cute hotels or bed-and-breakfasts. But he and Jake were friends and more or less in the same business with a lot in common. That's why he seemed so stoked to stay with Jake in the first place. Why wouldn't he want to stay with Jake anymore? I tossed and turned trying to get comfortable as all these thoughts popped in and out of my consciousness. I was about ready to nod off to dreamland when a horrifying thought occurred to me. What if Adrian agreed with Ernie? What if Jake was Adrian's prime suspect too?

Chapter 21

The next morning, I was power walking laps in my backyard as Iris romped around running from tree to tree in search of squirrels. Eventually Iris took up her usual perch, at the driveway gate that extended from the house to the wall between my house and that of my neighbor, Katie Omstead. As I circled around for the fifth time, I thought about what Ashley had told me last night. The more I thought about it, Connor didn't add up as Emma's killer. First, he seemed to be well-liked, judging by the way I observed him interacting with other employees and customers on the tree lot. Second, he was always polite to me, even when I was grilling him. And third, he and Emma had never been in an exclusive relationship. Despite what Rachel had said, Emma and Connor by every other account were just good friends, as the saying went.

That left the dating app guy and Jake as the two remaining suspects. The dating app guy was just a hunch but seemed the most promising to me. As far as Jake being a suspect, I honestly didn't know what to think. I trusted him, or had trusted him, until recently. What had made me feel less trusting? Was it really less trusting? Or was I protecting myself and putting my guard up because I really liked him a lot and didn't want to be hurt by him? But why would Ernie suspect him? Granted, Ernie had a history of leaping at potential suspects before looking at them carefully, but he said he wanted to warn me about Jake, as if he really believed Jake was a suspect. And then, of course, he claimed there was a video showing Jake hanging around Emma's place. So maybe Jake had dated Emma? What if he did? Was that really anyone's business? Except now I guess it really was since she'd been murdered. She didn't have any hidden wealth that I'd heard of, so I doubted that money, a common motive, was it. With greed off the table, that left business dealings, relationships, and revenge as possible motives.

Hmm. I'd already talked to Cynthia, her only food truck competition, and they seemed to have had a friendly working relationship by all accounts. I guess it could have been a rival caterer, but I was not aware of any. Her business dealings with me had been impeccable. That was why I'd liked her. Quality and integrity. A winning business combination in my book. So that left relationships and revenge.

Assuming I believed Connor, that left only Jake in the possible relationship realm.

So had Jake dated Emma? As I neared my back door, I made up my mind there was one direct way to find out—I'd simply ask him. Inside I poured myself a cup of coffee, and just as I got ready to grab my phone, it rang. It was Jake.

"Hi. What are you up to this morning?"

"Nothing much. What about you?"

"Same. I wanted to know if you were up for taking a hike and then we could grab breakfast afterward."

"A hike. Hmm. Where were you thinking?" I loved to hike, and my hair had already surrendered to the misty weather, so I had no excuses.

"I've discovered a special spot. I can pick you up and that way we avoid any possibility of you getting lost." He chuckled.

"When have I ever gotten lost? Anyway, sure."

"Great. I'll be over in about ten minutes if that's okay."

"That's fine. See you then."

As soon as I hung up my stomach flipped. Was it nerves because I liked Jake and was nervous to see him? Or was it a gut-level reaction to going on a hike with someone at least one cop I knew considered a murder suspect? I repressed both thoughts while I changed into a pair of camo-patterned leggings, a long-sleeved olive green T-shirt, a charcoal gray puffer vest, and boots, with Iris swirling around me, full of anxiety in anticipation of another possible separation, as usual. I texted Ashley to let her know I was going on a hike with Jake. After Milo's disappearance, she and I, both iPhone owners, had put each other on the Find My Phone app so we were each other's backup person. We'd always know where the other one would be. Both of us admitted we were too lazy to check on a regular basis, but it was times like this that I was happy we both used the same phones to benefit from this technology.

Ashley texted me back with a winking emoji and a heart and said to "have fun." Ever the matchmaker. This was my chance to be straightforward with Jake and ask him about Emma in the context of her murder. That way I could then tell Ernie that his theory was full of holes, and at the same time I'd hopefully be able to get a better understanding of Jake's intentions about our friendship.

He pulled up in his white Tesla and I ran out and jumped in. Jake was wearing a red sweater and jeans.

"Aren't you festive this morning?"

He laughed and surveyed my outfit, his eyes lingering on my camo leggings. "We're just going on a day hike. But I see you're prepared in case we need to emergency bivouac?"

"Very funny. Perhaps if you had more fashion sense, you'd know camo is trending right now."

"I'll take your word for it. You're going to love this place. I accidentally discovered it while working on a case. It's near Eucalyptus Grove. Are you familiar with the area?"

"Kind of. It's up in the hills around Sycamore Canyon where my dad's house is, isn't it?"

"It's in Brook Canyon, the next canyon over. From the ridge road there's a spot where the view is to die for."

Strange wording, given Ernie's suspicions. "Sounds great. Hope the marine layer burns off by the time we get there or there won't be much of a view of anything."

We drove further and further into the foothills while chitchatting about the dinner at my aunt and uncle's the night before. Jake was sweet and entertaining, as usual.

"By the way, I was glad to hear Sam is doing well."

"Yep. He's been staying in Carmel with Aunt Veronica's younger sister, as you know. She has two teenagers herself. The kids all bonded over surfing. His cousins introduced him to all their friends, and he adjusted pretty quickly."

"When did you see him last?"

"At Thanksgiving. My aunt and uncle miss him a lot. They drive up to see him every other month and he flies down on alternate months. It's worked out amazingly well for everyone."

"That's all good to hear. His age is such a fragile stage to have gone through the grief of losing your father and Milo. Speaking of which, how are you doing in that regard?"

I laughed. "Do we have that much time? It would take hours to describe my mood swings and the host of emotions I experience from time to time. At least it's not daily anymore so the swings are diminishing in frequency and, I guess, in intensity too."

When I turned to see his reaction, I caught him gazing at me with those intense blue eyes of his.

"What's the matter? Sorry, did you want the 'I'm fine, thanks' version?" I ended with a nervous chuckle.

"No, no, not at all. I was just contemplating everything you've been through, everything we've all been through. And now we're at the other side."

I nodded to acknowledge his answer, but I didn't know what to say.

"You know, I started a conversation the other day but then we got interrupted."

"Oh? What about? Your divorce?" There. If that wasn't what he was aiming for, too late now.

"Yes, that, and Emma. Mainly Emma though."

What on earth did that mean?

He slowed down the car. "Hey, we're here."

All the time we'd been talking I'd hardly paid attention to where we were going. Thinking about Sam had taken me back fourteen months and thinking of Jake and his divorce had me thinking of the future of our friendship. And how Emma had or will figure in, going forward. Consequently, I had no idea where we were. All I knew was it was isolated.

"So where are we exactly?"

"Brook Canyon is the general locale. But we're on the top of Mount Cedar."

"Of course. I was momentarily disoriented. I've seen Mount Cedar from afar all my life and have even flown over it in a plane. But I've never been all the way up to the summit."

"Well, then. You're in for a real treat."

We parked in a small parking lot and exited the car. Jake led the way to a trail, and we preceded to climb upward.

"It's not too far to the top. That's the best part."

We hiked for another ten minutes, focusing on the trail. I hated snakes so my eyes were glued to the ground. Before I knew it, we came to a clearing and the most breathtaking view ever.

"We're on top of the world."

"I know. Right?"

"It's so amazing. Let me take some pics."

"Don't do that." He grabbed my phone out of my hand.

I was taken aback by the change in his tone. What was going on? "Why not?"

"Because I don't want anyone to know we're here together." He shut my phone off and handed it back to me.

I gulped hard. "Why?"

"Because there's a possibility our phones are being tracked."

"What? By who?"

I must have looked terrified. I know I certainly felt terrified.

"Sorry. Didn't mean to come off so dramatic. By Emma's murderer."

I gasped. "What? You know who killed her?"

He put his finger to his lips and nodded.

My head swiveled around like a bobble-head toy, suddenly vividly aware of our vulnerable situation.

He whispered. "The murderer hacked Benning Brothers Nursery emails. I don't doubt phone tracking is in his bag of tricks. If they've figured out how to hack into your cloud account, they can see everything on your phone."

"Should I stop using my phone?"

"We don't know for sure, but Adrian thinks it's possible he's hacked into our phones to keep track of our investigation. Don't stop using your phone, just don't leave details in your texts about your whereabouts or the investigation. And don't reveal anything that could let him know we're aware he's tracking us."

"Great. Do you think he followed us here?"

"Not exactly."

What the heck did that mean? And suddenly I flashed on Ernie's warning. "Please don't hurt me. Just turn yourself in and I'm sure that will be favorable in terms of what charges are brought and—"

He grabbed me by the shoulders. I tensed up.

"Tory, it's me, Jake. What are you rambling on about? You think I would ever hurt you? Why on earth would you ever think that?"

"Ernie."

He released his grip and sighed. "Of course. Why wouldn't it be Ernie. He told you I was a suspect, didn't he? I thought we'd cleared that up."

I nodded. "And I didn't believe him . . . until you bring me to this godforsaken, isolated place where no one would hear me scream or—"

Jake grabbed my shoulders again. "Hey, you're spinning out. I'm Jake. I'm a PI. I shouldn't be telling you this but, I know you, and nothing but the truth will do because you can sniff out a lie a mile away."

"Thank you."

"I brought you here because it's beautiful and I feel like we've kind of drifted apart a bit and needed some quality time. Also, I'd been hired to investigate Emma prior to her murder. That's why I couldn't say much due to my confidentiality agreement."

"By who? Who hired you?"

"Chris Kringle. He thought she might be a gold digger and he feared Connor might be gullible."

"Oh. Well, that explains a lot." My head rushed with thoughts filling in the blanks like a sponge sopping up water.

"So that's why you were captured on videos."

"Correct. Adrian cleared that up right away."

"And you weren't dating Emma? Or formerly married to her?"

"What!" He shook his head. "I knew you had a good imagination but—"

"Then what did you want to talk about?"

"Us. Our friendship. Our relationship—"

"I'm not sure I'm ready for a relationship yet."

"I know. And I don't want to push you into anything you're not ready for or to rush anything. Truth be told, I'm still nursing a few wounds from my divorce and have fears of getting hurt again."

"Same, about getting hurt. But mine is about losing the person I love. And you're in dangerous situations sometimes as a PI."

He nodded. "Looks like we're kind of on the same page."

"If by same page you mean we're both scared of commitment at the moment but value our friendship, then I agree."

He sighed and opened his arms for a hug.

"Okay, now that we've agreed to be just good friends—"

"For the moment at least."

Our hug lingered a few seconds longer than a "just good friends" hug.

"Agreed, for the moment, now please tell me who the suspect is."

"Adrian has it under control."

"How?"

"He's tracking the guy."

• • •

After a quick breakfast at Clementine's, Jake dropped me back home. My curiosity had been piqued. Not only about a possible suspect, but about Emma. I Googled Emma Evans again and this time found a different site that listed several aliases as well as people possibly related to her. On this site she was listed as Emma Elizabeth Evans Levy, and also Liz Levy. Hmm. I wondered if that had been her married name. I opened up another window so I could Google some of the listed names as I went along. Again, Nicole Evans, who I'd assumed was her sister or mother, was listed as a possible relative or friend or associate. Must be her sister, because I remembered Emma sending condolences when my father died, and she had referred to when her parents had died. Hmm. Wonder if her sister could fill me in on Emma's friends and possible exes, boyfriends and/or husband?

I Googled Nicole Evans, a common name in California, with one in Santa Sofia and two in Santa Barbara. The one in Santa Sofia was ninety-six years old. Not the right one, unless maybe she was her grandmother, and maybe she'd lived with her at some point?

The first Nicole Evans in Santa Barbara had a picture with her LinkedIn account. She was a Black woman who, judging from her college graduation date, was in her mid-fifties.

The second Nicole Evans in Santa Barbara was listed as Nicole E. Evans. For a second I wondered if the E stood for Emma and whether Emma had gone by the name of Nicole at some point. I stopped and pondered this for a minute. I knew kids from high school who had changed their first names while in college. One had used her Japanese middle name, and another now went by her Korean middle name. So maybe Emma had done the same thing? Maybe her birth first name had been Nicole and then she had started to use her middle name, Emma, as her first name when she got older. But no evidence of a Nicole Levy. Only Emma Levy and Liz Levy. Hmm.

I tried Googling Nicole E. Evans by itself and nearly fell off my chair when I saw the first entry of my search results.

Chapter 22

I sucked in air as I read the first few lines from the Wikipedia summary. "Nicole Erin Evans, aka Nicole E. Bubb, aka Nicky Bubb, was the wife of Lyle Bubb, a plumber convicted and subsequently exonerated of her murder based on the work of the Justice Program led by UCSB's Professor Barry Hayes. Lyle Bubb's conviction was vacated and he was released after spending fifteen years in prison for a crime he had always claimed he didn't commit."

My heart felt like it was skipping beats as I quickly skimmed the page. "Her sister, Emma Elizabeth Evans Levy, aka Liz Levy," leapt out from the page. Oh, my God. Liz Levy must be Emma Evans's married name. Nicky Bubb was Emma's sister and Lyle Bubb was Emma's brother-in-law. I bet Emma had gone by her middle name back then and then switched back to her first name and maiden name after the murder to keep out of the public eye.

I fell back in my chair. Emma's brother-in-law was Lyle Bubb. The same Lyle Bubb the Justice Program had exonerated by overturning his conviction for the murder of his wife and Emma's sister, Nicky. Ashley must have known all of this.

I'd only recently been paying attention to the Justice Program case. Ever since Emma's murder. Wait. I bet that's why Emma and Ashley had a relationship. I called Ashley.

"Hi, this is Ashley. I can't come to the phone right now."

Grr. "Hi, Ashley. Call me ASAP please." Then I texted her. *Hi, Ash, I just figured out why you and Emma knew each other because I found out Emma's sister was Nicky Bubb. Since I found out on my own, maybe now we can put our heads together and brainstorm about Emma's murder more.*

There were several photographs in the Wikipedia entry. One was of Nicky Bubb. She looked a little like Emma, dark hair and light eyes. There was a mug shot of Lyle Bubb from when he was arrested fifteen years ago. He was an average-looking guy, with a bewildered look on his face. Another shot taken at his release dated two days ago revealed a totally different demeanor. He had a winsome smile, although I detected a sadness in his eyes.

I leaned back in my chair and thought about the irony of Lyle Bubb finally being released after being falsely accused of his wife's murder, only to find that his sister-in-law had also been murdered. What were the odds of that? How awful to have his loss doubled, something that triggered more relatability to his situation than I cared to admit. What a horrid coincidence. And it was too bad Emma's sister was a dead end in terms of helping us find out more about Emma's killer. I shook my head at my insensitive word choice. I stared into space, reviewing my newfound information for another few minutes. Iris started hopping around to signal she wanted out. Otis kept rubbing against my leg.

"Okay, you two, you win." I picked up Otis and rubbed his tummy. After a minute of tummy rubs I set him down. "Okay, your turn, Iris. Let's do a couple of laps in the backyard."

Iris galloped to the rear of the yard right when I opened the door. She rushed back to the driveway gate as I started my laps. I zoned out and thought again about what a shock it must have been for Lyle Bubb, upon his release, to discover his sister-in-law had been murdered. I wondered if he had any other family. I remembered Ashley telling me they hadn't heard from him since he'd been released. She still hadn't heard from Barry since he'd gone missing either. The cops seemed to be sticking to their theory that Barry was possibly negotiating with Dwayne Rudders to turn himself in since, apparently, Rudders had had second thoughts. I made my way around the backyard's perimeter another time and then stopped in my tracks. I called for Iris to come inside and I ran in and closed the door behind her.

A minute later my phone vibrated. But it wasn't Ashley, it was Jake asking me to call him. Ugh. We'd spent the whole morning having a bonding moment, which was fine, but now I wanted to focus on finding Emma's murderer and I knew he'd just tell me to stay out of it.

I pulled up a chair and Otis jumped on my lap. I stared into space and then stood up abruptly. "Oh, my goodness. I think Nicky and Emma's murders might be related."

Otis meowed as he plopped to the floor. I tried calling Ashley again. This time she picked up.

"Thank god. Why didn't you call me back? I left you a message and I texted you."

"Slow down. I just got out of the shower and didn't have my phone. I have a hot date. Or rather a coffee date. It's with the Calvin Klein model."

"Glad you're meeting in a public place. Just be careful. But this is important. I know that Emma is Nicky Bubb's sister."

"Good work, Sherlock. How'd you crack the case?" She chuckled.

"By Googling. I found Emma listed as Emma Elizabeth Levy on a site. I figured Emma must have been married when Nicky was murdered, and she must have gone by the name of Liz Levy. That's why Emma Evans wasn't mentioned in any of the recent articles about Lyle Bubb, right?"

"Ding, ding, ding. We have a winner. Seriously, Tory, good deduction. I hope you understand now why I couldn't tell you how I knew Emma. She'd gone to great lengths to distance herself from the past. We even had trouble finding her at first because we only had known of her and her sister as Liz Levy and Nicky Bubb, not Emma Evans and Nicole Evans. Once the results of the new DNA test we did on the cloth found at Nicky's crime scene came back, and the results revealed the DNA wasn't Lyle's, we wanted to let Emma be one of the first to know since she claimed from the start that Lyle was innocent. She had pointed the finger, as did Lyle, at Nicky's ex-boyfriend, Dwayne Rudders, so when the DNA came back ID'ing Rudders, we knew she'd be thrilled. Not only was Lyle going to be finally released and exonerated but we were close to putting Rudders in prison for a very long time too."

"I have so many questions."

"Of course you do. But like I said, I've got a hot date. Adrian has been so busy that he even put off the dinner he promised me to celebrate my birthday. Which is fine, but it shows you where his priorities are."

"Catching a murderer is pretty important and affects everyone's safety."

"Oh, I know. I'm just nervous and really don't want to go, but I feel like I should put myself out there. Don't want to put all my eggs in one basket."

"Hear anything from Barry?"

"No, it's been five days now and I'm starting to really get worried. No one has heard from Lyle Bubb either. I have a bad feeling."

"Sorry. I hope Barry shows up soon. I can't imagine why he hasn't contacted anyone." Actually, my imagination had many scenarios, all gruesome. "Do you really think meeting some weirdo for coffee is the best choice right now? Especially with Barry, Bubb, and Rudders all still MIA."

"Rudders's lawyer keeps saying he's working out the details to turn himself in, so I don't think we have to worry about him right now. Before Barry went missing, he mentioned that Bubb would take some time to decompress with his family before emerging in public. And Barry . . ."

"Barry's still missing. Forgive me, but whenever anyone disappears, I might get a little panicky, based on my past experience."

"Sorry, Tory. Calm down. There've been no signs of foul play I'm aware of. And just between you and me, I've gotten a couple of missed calls from his cell phone. So, I'm sure he's fine. Maybe he's laying low so that negotiations with Rudders and his lawyer can proceed without any outside distraction. And for the record, the so-called weirdo I'm meeting is very hot, and has a good reason for meeting in person today. He said he's going out of town for Christmas, so this was our last chance to meet before then. I told you he's not been tagged by the Valentine Vigilantes as a problem either. You're the one who should be careful, playing detective, when both Adrian and Jake have warned you off.

You're the one with the stalker. That condo break-in and the drone surveillance."

"Surely, Barry must know everyone is worried sick over him. Why wouldn't he leave a message?"

"I don't know. Honestly, when I think of possible reasons it gets very dark." She paused briefly. "But please, do be careful. Don't forget Ernie told you to be careful too. But then, he thought Jake was the real killer."

"I'll be careful. You know me."

"Okay. I'll call you after I meet this guy."

"Looking forward to it. Have fun and be—"

"Careful. I will."

I went about my day and took Ashley's advice to calm down to heart, reading to Iris and Otis while I enjoyed a cup of tea. After their story Iris and I went for a walk in the backyard. When I passed the spot where the drone had landed, I stopped to think about what had happened leading up to that uninvited landing. Ashley and I had been at the condo earlier when someone tried to break in. Then the drone had landed later that night, when Ashley spent the night because her tires had been slashed. The next morning the guy, who we suspect was Rudders, was pleasant and nonthreatening to me as I stood at the half-open door with Ashley out of sight behind me. Hmm.

I started to head back inside and froze. "Ashley!"

Iris looked at me and cocked her head.

All the stalking had occurred when I was with Ashley. None of them occurred when I was by myself. In fact, when Rudders, the supposed stalker, came for his drone, he was more concerned about his broken drone than he was about me. I snapped my fingers. "Because he's not stalking me, he's stalking Ashley. Oh my god, I've got to warn her." It was so obvious, but we had so much going on we hadn't noticed what was right in front of us.

I called Ashley but her phone went to voice mail. I left a message asking her to call me. Next, I called Adrian but got his voice mail too. And I left another message requesting a call back. I started to text Jake and then remembered what he'd told me about the hacker. We could leave messages and text, just don't reveal anything that could let him know we're aware he's reading them. I texted Jake and told him I needed to talk about our relationship, hoping he'd figure out that since we'd spent the morning doing just that, he'd know something was up. He was a private investigator, after all. Any PI worth his salt should be able to pick up nuance.

I clicked onto the Find My iPhone to see where Ashley was. It looked like she was at Starbucks. Her hot date was in full swing apparently, and she was too into it to check her phone. The texts I sent her were marked unread.

My phone vibrated. It was a text from Ashley. *The strangest thing ever just happened. Ernie texted me to meet him up at St. Nicholas Vineyards. He said it had to do with the Justice Program case.*

My heart pounded hard as I read her text. Ernie? St. Nicholas Vineyards? What was going on? I looked at the Find My iPhone app and she had moved. She was on the Avenue heading north now. I hesitated before texting her back. Jake had made me so paranoid about hacking that now I was suspicious of every message I got.

As an alternative, I decided I'd follow her from afar. I rushed out of the office. I was about to get into my car when I saw Connor at the tree lot.

He waved to me and jogged over. "Hi, Tory. How are you today?"

"I'm fine, thanks. My aunt Marian told me that your family owns St. Nicholas Vineyards and Winery. I'm surprised you aren't working at your winery tasting room, partaking of all that holiday cheer, instead of manual labor at the tree lots."

"First, as a landscape architect I'm sure you'd agree, it doesn't get more festive than being surrounded by beautiful Christmas trees at Christmastime. Nothing says Christmas more than a Christmas tree lot."

"Totally agree. But that's my bias."

"Plus, the tasting room is closed right now for renovations. We had bad roof leaks in November after the rains and quickly got a new roof so we're watertight before the next big rain. Now we're fixing the water damage, hoping to finish by Christmas so that we can reopen for our busiest week, between Christmas and New Year's."

My heart stopped. "You're saying the tasting room isn't open today?"

"Nope. Hasn't been since that November storm."

I looked at my Find My iPhone app. Ashley was heading up the hill toward the winery.

"Connor, I need your help. And your drone."

"How do you know I have a drone?" His eyes widened.

"I saw it in your truck. That's a longer conversation. But right now, I need your help because Ashley is supposedly meeting someone up at your tasting center. She's headed there now. I'm going to follow her but I'm not as fast as a drone, nor do I have a bird's-eye view."

His gaping mouth gave away his confusion. "Sure. Okay. Actually, it's in my truck. I'll head up there right now."

"Okay, why don't you follow me."

I got in my car, and before turning on the engine I left another message for Jake. By the time I'd passed the Starbucks, Ashley's phone was showing her halfway into the foothills headed toward the winery tasting room. I headed into the foothills after her. The more I thought of it, the more I thought I'd risk the hacker and text Jake. I pulled over. Connor dutifully pulled over behind me.

Just wanted to keep you in loop. Ashley texted me she's meeting Ernie at St. Nicholas Winery tasting room. Something to do with Justice Program. Connor said tasting room closed. I'm on my way there now.

I continued up the winding roads, with Connor following me. His following skills were impressive. He kept up with me but didn't hug my tail. I'd always appreciated drivers who were good in a convoy. The higher up I climbed, the more isolated it got. As we approached the winery, I pulled over and decided to text Jake again. On my phone screen, all my messages were marked "Undeliverable. Try again." I cursed at my phone carrier. Not the time to fail me. I tried to send them again and crossed my fingers.

There was a tap on my window that startled me so much I got a kink in my neck. "Connor. You scared me half to death."

"Sorry. There's a back lot where we can park. It's not known to the public, so I think that's our best bet. That way we can observe the winery tasting room without being observed ourselves."

"Great idea. Thanks, Connor."

"I'll lead the way."

I gave him a thumbs-up.

A sign pointing to the left directed me to the vineyard parking lot. Ashley's car was parked at the far end near to the entrance of the tasting room. But there was no trace of her or of Ernie or of his car anywhere. Connor hung a right. We circled around to the back lot surrounded by a tall hedge. We parked, partially hidden by the hedge but not totally. I tried texting Ashley again but got no response. Connor got out of his truck and ran over to my car. I opened my door and got a call.

Jake was on the phone. "Tory. Good. I got you. Where are you?"

"Can we talk safely?"

"Yes."

I exhaled loudly. "Ok, good."

After I filled him in, I felt better.

"Good work. You'd make a good PI."

"I'm just trying to save my best friend."

"Help is on the way. Just stay put."

If Jake had really known me, he'd know that was impossible while I knew Ashley was in jeopardy.

"I know that's impossible for you so please be careful and watch yourself."

I smiled. He got me. I felt seen. I'd have been overwhelmed with emotion in reaction to this touching moment, had adrenaline not been pumping through my veins like a burst dam.

"Don't worry. We'll be careful." I suddenly felt stronger and full of energy.

"We? Who are you with?"

"Connor Kemp." I glanced at Connor and his gaze was on me.

"What? Tory, be careful."

"Don't worry. I'm always careful. Why would I worry with Connor?"

Static blasted in my ear and the line went dead. I held up my phone to Connor. "Great. I swear I'm going to switch to another provider. This one keeps dropping my calls and I never can get Wi-Fi or get my texts to send when I need to."

"My phone's in my truck. Do you want to use it?"

"No, thanks. That's all right. We need to focus on Ashley and Ernie right now. That was my PI friend and he's alerting the cops."

"The cops? What did you have to involve them for?"

"What?"

"Sorry. That was my PR role talking. As you well know, all businesses dread bad press."

I nodded. I agreed about the bad press. What I didn't like was seeing the mirror image of myself concerned about business repercussions when lives were at stake. He was just being honest. It didn't mean he felt any less compassionate about Ashley and Ernie. He could be both, compassionate and worried about business repercussions. And just like that, I realized something. I could feel all the emotions at once. Feeling one way one second did not necessarily negate another emotion I felt the next second. I could be forgiving of Connor for having mixed emotions. I should treat myself with at least as much forgiveness.

"No worries, Connor. I totally get it."

Connor smiled. "Thanks."

I pointed toward the tasting room. "What are we waiting for? Let's get this show on the road." Who was I?

We crept back to the tasting room parking lot, hugging the hedges that bordered the lot. I peeked out from behind the hedges, wondering where Ashley was. I was still trying to figure out why she was at the winery and why on earth Ernie would have wanted to meet her here.

As if on cue, a car got closer and drove by inches from the hedges where we hid. The car parked next to Ashley's car. Ernie got out of the car. He headed toward the tasting room. What was Ernie up to?

I was about to suggest to Connor that we use his drone to spy on the tasting room when a gunshot pierced the silence. Connor and I both flinched and exchanged terrified looks. My first impulse was to make a run for it in the opposite direction, but after a few seconds my concern that Ashley might be hurt outweighed my fear.

We continued to creep toward the tasting room, where it seemed the shot had come from. Connor motioned me to follow him and then made a run for it to a low wall at the other end of the lot. But I'd already headed to the other end of the lot in an attempt to get phone reception. All of a sudden another shot sounded. Dwayne Rudders emerged from behind the low wall and he grabbed Connor by the arm.

"Where's the girl?"

"What girl?"

"Don't play coy with me. That Benning girl."

"I don't know."

"I knew that shot would get all the rats out of the bushes. I'll come back for her after I secure you." With that, he marched Connor back toward the tasting room.

I'll tell you where she is, hightailing it to her car. I jumped in my car and turned on the engine before I even closed the door, which I then slammed and locked. I peeled out of the gravel lot like a maniac, only glancing in my rearview mirror before the drive curved to see Rudders glaring at me and then roughly pushing Connor back toward the winery.

I rounded a curve and glanced back, pretty sure Rudders decided not to follow me. At the next curve, Jake was heading toward the winery. We both pulled over. He was out of his car before me.

"Adrian and his team are on their way. Where's Connor?"

"Rudders got him."

"Okay, let's go try to see what's going on."

I jerked forward in consternation, and from the look on Jake's face, I assumed my expression fully conveyed how absurd I considered his response. "Are you crazy? He's got a gun."

Jake opened his jacket to show me his holster. "So do I."

I gulped hard, which manifested as a convulsive jerk, since my whole body was already shaking like Jell-O. We stuck to the perimeter, staying close to the bushes so we could duck into them if needed as we edged our way to the winery. And then we saw it. The damn drone. It rose up from the winery building and headed our way. Jake and I clambered into the dense bushes, parting the lower branches and crawling underneath, ending up about six feet from each other.

The drone skimmed overhead and made a big circle around the parking lot and then took off down the drive.

Jake shouted to me. "He's looking for us."

"Why? What's he going to do with the drone? It's not a heat-seeking missile, is it?"

I prayed Jake would laugh at my comment, but he didn't.

"I don't know. I doubt it. Although Rudders is a techie whiz kid."

The drone had circled back and hovered over Jake in his red sweater.

"I think it sees you, but I don't think it sees me."

"Right. He doesn't know you're still here, mainly because of your camos. Let me take the heat now as a decoy and you can sneak up and see if you can find Ashley."

"Roger that. Also, maybe next time you'll think twice before questioning my fashion choice."

"Not now, Tory. But one more thing, in case everything backfires. I meant to tell you earlier today, but Adrian told me not to. But I trust you."

"Backfires?" I was glad he trusted me, but then I wasn't the one with all the secrets.

"No time to explain"—he pointed to himself—"about me and Emma's murder." He whispered. "I didn't mean to . . ."

The drone had moved on after hovering over Jake but was now circling back.

"I need to go before it sees you too."

What? "Wait. Finish what you started to say. You didn't mean to what?"

The drone was back. What did Jake not mean to do? Kill Emma? Was it true? Was Ernie finally correct? Like a blind squirrel finding a nut once in a while, maybe this time Ernie picked the right suspect? Why Jake had chosen this time to tell all was beyond me. Better late than never? I was totally confused.

Jake stepped out closer to the road and the drone hovered above him, leaving me stunned, my mouth gaping. Then Rudders emerged from the winery with a gun. He pointed it at Jake.

He ran over to Jake. "Your nosy girlfriend got away, but we'll catch up with her later."

I couldn't believe my eyes. And my ears were on fire. Nosy girlfriend? I definitely took umbrage at the *nosy* but was somehow vaguely intrigued being referred to as Jake's girlfriend, since he'd just moments ago seemed to confess to Emma's murder. Murderer's moll might be more accurate at this point. I watched as the hovering drone, Rudders, and Jake made their way back toward the tasting room. I followed at a safe distance as they disappeared inside.

The tasting room had walls of glass which made for easy viewing of what was going on inside. The first thing I saw were four people sitting in chairs in a semicircle. On a coffee table in front of them were several bottles of wine. With several wineglasses. But no one was drinking. Rudders, who held a gun, was pacing around the room. Ernie stood behind the chairs. My whole body relaxed when I saw Ashley sitting in one of the chairs looking alive and well. Also seated were Jake, Connor, and an older Black gentleman I assumed was Professor Barry Hayes. A mixed feeling of relief and anxiety overcame me.

Rudders had his back to me, waving his gun around like he was ranting.

I got closer to try to hear what he was saying.

"Okay. I know the cops are on to me. Apparently, they thought they could outfox me. Trying to do a sting. Two here among you, in fact, fancy yourselves as Butch Cassidy and the frigging Sundance Kid."

With that he moved quickly behind Ernie and Jake. "Hands up, both of you. The only thing I hate more than a cop is a double-crossing cop. You're nothing like your father back in the day. But now he's gone soft. Raised a soft son too."

I had no idea what he was talking about. Ernie was a double-crossing cop? A sting?

"Let me tell you all a little story. About fifteen years ago I had a no-good girlfriend who dumped me for a no-good guy. No one dumps me. Especially for a no-good guy. When I tried to talk some sense into her, she got mouthy to me. We'd been drinking, and one thing led to another." He started to cry. "I didn't mean for her to die. I really didn't. But alcohol does weird things to me, makes me do things that are wrong."

Good to know, given the empty wine bottles scattered around. Duly noted.

"One of my poker buddies happened to be a cop. Eddie Gomez. Good guy, bad cop, luckily for me. My old girlfriend's frigging sister tried to get me arrested even though she knew I didn't mean to kill her sister. But my friend Eddie managed to sweep her and her testimony under the rug, because he was friends with the prosecutor, who owed him one. We needed someone to be the fall guy, and who better than the chump who stole her from me in the first place. That's right. Lyle frigging Bubb. The perfect sucker. He took the rap for me. All was good until these frigging university lawyers with their Justice Program matched my DNA to Nicky's death. Then Eddie Gomez, my *former* friend, ratted on me too. That was it. Something snapped. I tried to talk to Liz, she thought she could hide from me by changing her name to Emma . . ." He paused to gloat for a second. "Anyhow, I tried to explain to Liz how her sister's death was a mistake. She said I deserved to go to prison and die. I just lost it. She called me weak and said Lyle Bubb was the real hero. I've been looking for Bubb ever since he was released but couldn't find him because that coward has been hiding from me. Anyways, we have everyone else here who tried to ruin my life. The professor, his lady lawyer friend, who both helped to free Bubb and charge me with murder. Shame about the intern, but she tried to call the cops on me when I was asking around about Lyle."

He took a swig of wine directly from one of the bottles on the table while still pointing his gun at Ernie and Jake. "So. Who's going to be first on the firing line? We'll have our own execution party. Sorry I can't offer you wine. I'm the only one who'll be drinking."

He drank another swig of wine. "Now, who should I start with? I think the son of the double-crossing cop is the one I hate the most. Get over there." Rudders pushed Ernie against the wall and grabbed hold of Jake's arm while trying to take aim at Ernie. I needed to make my move now.

I ran in front of the window, banging on it. Rudders quickly turned and Jake and Ernie both lunged at him. There was a scuffle with the three of them fighting for the gun. I dashed into the tasting room as soon as Jake and Ernie piled on top of Rudders, but he wasn't yet under control. In the chaos the gun went off and the force of the gunshot, coupled with Jake and Ernie on top of him, made Rudders loosen his grip but not let go of the gun. He was bucking and spitting and squirming. I grabbed his hand and dug in with my nails and he howled in pain, relaxing long enough for me to gain possession of the gun. With Rudders now disarmed, Jake and Ernie corralled him without fear of getting shot and soon had Rudders under control.

The next minute, Adrian and several uniformed cops arrived to take Rudders away. After Rudders was taken into custody, Ashley ran into Adrian's arms and Jake and I hugged.

And wonders never cease, Ernie and I hugged. He had tears in his eyes. "Thanks, Tory. You saved my life back there. I'm forever indebted to you. I don't know how I can ever thank you enough."

Adrian came over with his arm around Ashley. "Tory, Ashley tells me you saved the day. We needed that extra time you bought us by distracting Rudders and saving one of our officers, Ernie, and all these innocent people."

"Well, I saw he was drinking and having difficulty standing without swaying so I hoped if I could catch him off guard, he wouldn't be able to shoot straight or recoup quickly. All I can say is, thank goodness for St. Nicholas wines."

Chapter 23

I looked longingly at the racks of wines behind the counter where wine samples were usually served. "How I wish the tasting room wasn't a crime scene right now."

Ashley chuckled. "That makes two of us."

Jake smiled. "Make that three."

Adrian clapped his hands together. "Hate to be a party pooper, but all of you need to give your statements before you do anything else."

Professor Hayes was happy but shaken. Adrian said he wanted him checked out by the medics and then would get his statement after that.

Ashley, Jake, Connor, Ernie, and I all gave our statements at the police station. Jake stayed at the station and told me that he and Adrian would try to join Ashley and me later. Ashley and I exchanged knowing looks. We both knew we'd be lucky if we even heard from either one of them, given all the work involved at the crime scene. We decided to pick up food, go to my place to eat, and then crash.

We needed comfort food so we both agreed on Santini's pizza on the Avenue. We ordered it with everything on it.

Back at home Iris and Otis gave me a nice welcome. Both were at the door when I opened it. I knew Iris sensed I'd been through an ordeal. She licked my face when I crouched down to pet her, as if I were a newborn puppy. Otis rubbed against my legs and circled me as I tried to walk, making me nearly trip over him.

When Ashley arrived a few minutes later, they extended an equally warm welcome to her too. On Ashley's heels came the pizza delivery guy with our pizza.

Ashley's eyes widened. "What size is that? And how will you even get that box in your refrigerator with the leftovers?"

"Leftovers?"

We both burst out laughing as we poured some red wine into my largest goblets and each grabbed a piece of pizza. We moved into the living room with our plates and goblets to feast while we reviewed the last few hours.

I nudged an errant mushroom from my plate back onto my pizza slice. "So when did you know it was Dwayne Rudders behind everything?"

"I didn't know he was responsible for Emma's murder, to be honest. We knew he killed her sister, Nicky, and that he had framed Lyle Bubb. That was a two-fer for Rudders. He killed Nicky, who'd rebuffed him and married Lyle Bubb. And he got rid of Bubb by pinning the murder on him."

"Yeah, I remember you telling me that. How did Rudders manage to pin the murder on Bubb again?"

"Having a corrupt prosecutor running for office on a law-and-order campaign looking for a slam dunk case at the time helped."

I nodded. "That's right. I still don't understand how Rudders hacked into our email system."

"Being a tech wizard helped him a lot. He's a smart guy. Too bad he didn't use his brains for a good cause instead of evil. But he had mental issues that plagued him all his life, a narcissist who couldn't handle being thwarted. When he found out Bubb was exonerated because of new DNA test results, Rudders played along like he was going to turn himself in, but he must have been having a major meltdown psychologically."

"He never planned to turn himself in, did he?"

Ashley shook her head. "No, he didn't. He wanted to find out who had ruined his perfect plan. So, he started bugging Emma, asking her if it was her who got the Justice Program on the case. Now, Emma had always suspected Rudders and had defended Bubb. But Rudders was Nicky's ex-boyfriend from a few years earlier. The main suspect from the start for the cops was her husband, Lyle Bubb."

"I'm all too familiar with the police suspecting the spouse. Ernie thought I'd killed Milo at one point."

"Speaking of Ernie, ironically it was his father who actually was the main driving force behind getting Bubb convicted. He was the cop in charge of the investigation."

"That's what I pieced together from Rudders's rant at the tasting room. Had there been any evidence supporting Bubb's arrest?"

"Not really. That's the thing. Quite the contrary. There was evidence pointing to it not being Bubb, uncovered by Ernie's father, that the prosecutor failed to mention."

"That's so corrupt and inhumane."

"Tell me about it. Ernie's father knew the prosecutor was sitting on evidence to clear Bubb, but Ernie's father was also an alcoholic desperate to hold on to his job. When he approached the prosecutor, the prosecutor threatened to badmouth Ernie's father to the higher-ups in the department."

"So, kind of like blackmail."

"Uh-huh. Sadly, Ernie's father could barely keep his own life together, let alone help poor Lyle Bubb."

"That makes me feel so sorry for Ernie now. Learning how stressful his life must have been growing up."

"I know."

"So how did Ernie figure into Emma's murder? I thought he was convinced that Jake was a suspect."

"Promise you won't get mad?"

"Um, maybe. It depends. Why?"

"Because Ernie was part of a sting operation Adrian set up with Jake."

"You knew?"

"I just found out when Barry went missing. Adrian suspected he'd been kidnapped or worse by Rudders as a payback for setting Bubb free and naming Rudders as the prime suspect. Adrian had already pieced together with Jake's help that the murdered Justice Program intern from Santa Sofia was probably murdered by Rudders. Adrian didn't like the pattern when Barry went missing because he thought I might be next."

I reached out and squeezed her hand. "Oh, no. That must have scared you so much."

"Ya think?" She laughed and took a sip of wine. "Especially since Emma had told me Rudders had contacted her and threatened to hurt her if she said anything to hurt him and get him convicted."

"Yikes. So then you must have known it was Rudders who killed her all along."

"That's the thing. I didn't at all because I was under the impression he had more or less been watched twenty-four-seven once we figured out that Bubb had been wrongly convicted. I thought there was no way he could have gotten near a relative of Nicky's without being detected by the cops watching him. But mistakes unfortunately happen and somehow there was a lapse in his surveillance. His communication with Emma had slid through the cracks. Adrian said he thinks Rudders hacked police emails and misdirected police personnel purposefully so he could leave his house undetected because no one was watching him that morning."

"Wow."

"He followed Barry and the other kidnap victims with his drone, and it was me he was after at your condo and your house with the drone. The drone crash was actually a good thing that he hadn't planned for. When Ernie came over to look at it that morning, he placed a tracer in it so they could then track Rudders."

"Irony. The worm turns."

"Yes. Then all he had to do was lead them to the winery, where he was keeping Barry. Also, as was Rudders's way, he was hoping to frame Connor for everything since he was holding Barry hostage at St. Nicholas Winery."

I gave Ashley a nudge. "You never told me about your hot date with the Calvin Klein Santa guy."

"I got stood up because you were right, that was a fake account that Rudders had created to mine data from unsuspecting women who swiped right, like me. More of Rudders's tech knowledge used for evil purposes."

"Wow. That was my gut feeling all along."

"Yup. Gut feelings rule."

We each ate more pizza than usual.

I chuckled. "Speaking of gut feelings, oof, I'm stuffed."

"Me too. But it was so good. And at least there are some leftovers." Ashley threw the leftover pieces on a large plate, covered them with plastic wrap, and put them in the refrigerator.

"Thanks, Ash."

I'd had just the right amount of wine. Enough to wash down the pizza and to take the edge off of a harrowing day. Iris and Otis were content after they were fed. Iris sprawled out asleep on the floor and Otis curled up in a ball on a chair, happily snoring.

"So where are you with Adrian right now? You two make a good team."

Ashley smiled. "Thanks. I wish he would have clued me in sooner but, overall, I think he handled everything well considering all of our professional constraints. What about you? You and Jake make a pretty dynamic duo too."

I chuckled. "We did okay. I don't think he'll ever tease me about wearing camo again."

• • •

Two days later Ashley and I met for coffee at Starbucks.

"I wish their Santa Barbara court appearance wasn't tomorrow morning. Jake told me Adrian stayed with him last night and they had a lot of work to do before Rudders's arraignment."

"I'm totally bummed they won't make the party. I don't know why they couldn't prepare here, go to your Christmas party tonight, and then drive down early tomorrow morning."

"Agree. But it is what it is, I guess. Hey, I'm going to head over to the Hotel Santa Sofia early to make sure everything is on target, especially since Sadie's doing the catering. Do you want to help me?"

"You got it."

Since the hotel had kindly made an exception to their no-outside-catering policy for Benning Brothers' annual Christmas party, so that Sadie's Seafood could handle the catering this year, I wanted to make sure everything went smoothly. To add to the pressure of pulling off a perfect party, I'd also increased the number of attendees, having extended last-minute invitations to the Kringles and the Kemps and their Santa's Helpers tree lot employees. They all felt like extended family now, given what we'd all been through together.

Ashley had promised to meet me at the hotel at four and, true to her word, she pulled into the lot at the same time as I did. We parked next to each other in the parking lot near the lobby.

"You look drop-dead gorgeous." As soon as I said it, I apologized. "Let me rephrase. You look gorgeous and I'm glad you didn't drop dead after being held hostage by a murderer."

Ashley laughed. "I'll take a compliment, any way you phrase it." Her dark green velvet off-the-shoulder dress showcased her fit figure. She tossed her curls. "Thanks, Tory. It's also comfortable. Always a plus. You clean up pretty well yourself."

"Thanks, Ash. I'm a sucker for velvet too." I adjusted my black velvet tuxedo-style dress since its faux jacket top was a bit low-cut.

Ashley stuck out her lower lip in an exaggerated pout. "I'm still disappointed Adrian and Jake had to go to Santa Barbara for the case."

"I know. Of all the days. But I'm grateful we're all alive, to be honest."

"Not going to argue with you there."

"At least they offered a rain check for next weekend."

The Spanish Mediterranean–style Hotel Santa Sofia stunned in December. The meticulously maintained property literally glowed with a million white twinkle lights that were wrapped around its palm trees, trimmed its hedges and white stucco walls, and outlined its red-tiled rooftops. Even before setting one foot in the lobby, the two-story glass windows revealed the majestic twelve-foot noble fir that could easily qualify as one of the most beautiful Christmas trees in the world.

"Wow. That's got to be the prettiest Christmas tree ever. I might be a tad biased, since Benning Brothers has been supplying the hotel with a twelve-foot noble fir for as long as I could remember. Or *fir* as long as I could remember."

Ashley chuckled. "Ha. Good one, Tor."

"This year's tree looks prettier than any other in recent memory."

"Don't you say that every year?"

I laughed. "Maybe."

Our party was located in one of the hotel's small ballrooms, resplendent in evergreen wreaths, poinsettias, and a smaller version of the lobby tree. French doors lined one wall that opened to a small courtyard decorated with cedar garlands and lighted twig reindeer of varying sizes. Heaters were dotted around the perimeter of the brick patio to fend off the frosty evening air.

Sadie's staff was already busy setting up. A wave of relief swept over me as I watched the hotel staff set up the outside bars. Before I knew it, an hour had gone by, guests began to arrive, and waiters were walking around offering trays of hors d'oeuvres. A long buffet table had other appetizers. Oysters and clams on the half shell, jumbo prawns, and three different types of clam chowder, Rhode Island, Manhattan, and New England, served in easily portable tiny mugs. Sushi was also passed on trays, as well as smoked salmon canapés, and caviar-stuffed baby potato halves. Calamari, mini lobster rolls, coleslaw, and fries were arrayed at another table.

"Oh, my goodness. So glad I wore a material that has some give in it."

I giggled. "Me too."

We took a walk around the courtyard. The bartenders were busy still setting up some stations. We swiped two glasses of wine as one server passed us with a tray.

I took a sip. "So good."

"Why, thank you."

I whipped around to see Connor Kemp with his mother, father, and grandfather. We made introductions.

Marissa Kemp smiled warmly. "Sorry we got off on the wrong foot, Tory."

Chris Kringle stepped closer with his eyes twinkling. "We sent some of our best St. Nicholas and Frost wines over for tonight as a peace offering."

I held out my hand and he hugged me instead.

"Yes. So nice to finally meet you all under happier circumstances. We've all been under a lot of stress lately.

"Think nothing of it. I'm just glad we were able to get justice for Emma."

Christmas songs started to play over the music system. The trickle of guests soon mushroomed to a crowd of friends and family. I caught up with my aunt Marian for a while. Then my friend and hairdresser Philip strolled in later, having worked late at the hotel's Zoe Stella Salon. Before I knew it, the tables were being converted to dessert tables with arrays of Christmas cookies and miniature servings of trifle.

Someone tapped me on the shoulder. When I turned around it was Jake.

"What are you doing here? I thought you had an early court hearing tomorrow."

"We do. But we decided to drive back super early tomorrow morning."

"I wish I'd known. I would have saved you some of the entrées."

"Oh, don't worry, we caught the servers when they were clearing the tables. I'm happy to report I had lobster rolls, clam chowder, and the best jumbo prawns ever. Also had a couple of raw clams."

"Oh, good. We? Is Adrian with you?"

"Yep. He's here somewhere."

We twirled around in search of Adrian and spotted him talking to Ashley across the ballroom.

"What a great surprise. I'm so glad you both decided to come after all."

"I also wanted to finish our conversation."

"Which one?"

"About Emma. You know now I was hired by the Kemps to make sure Emma wasn't a gold digger. As it turned out, Emma was so preoccupied with seeing justice served for Rudders, she couldn't focus on a relationship with Connor, so they broke up amicably."

"Yes. I can certainly relate to that."

Our gazes locked for a few seconds.

"Adrian actually explained all that in detail," I said. "I only wish you could have told me earlier so that my imagination didn't get carried away. But I know now why you couldn't. One slipup could have jeopardized Adrian's whole operation and Rudders could have ended up hurting more people. I get that. Now."

"Good. Because I didn't want you to think our talk on the hiking trail was just me saying words that I thought you might want to hear."

"Okay."

"I meant it when I said truthfulness and transparency are vital to trust. And trust is the foundation of good friendships."

"I totally agree."

"And relationships."

Uh-oh. "Yeah, about that."

"I know we agreed to take it slowly because we both value our friendship."

I nodded.

"But that being said . . ."

"Yes?"

He stood close enough that I could smell the alcohol on his breath. "I'm not sure I really meant what I said."

My face felt on fire and my stomach flipped. So what did he mean? He didn't want to be friends anymore? "I'm a bit confused."

"That trifle was loaded with alcohol, wasn't it?"

"It had sherry in it. Why?"

"Combined with a glass of wine on a previously empty stomach I'm just feeling its effects right now. Anyway, I know I've had a bit to drink, but I swear it's not the booze talking. And when I said we should just be friends for the time being, I meant this year. And not to say there couldn't be exceptions to our agreement. So, I wanted to tell you that I'm going down to Los Angeles for a few days to spend Christmas with my family."

Adrian called from the doorway. "Yo, Jake. We have an early wake-up. Let's get going."

Ashley was standing in the doorway too. She was smiling and had her arm entwined with Adrian's.

"Be with you in a minute, Adrian." Jake turned to me. "Look, I just wanted to—"

I smiled. "What are you doing for New Year's Eve?"

His head bobbed up and our gazes locked again.

"I think I'm coming back to Santa Sofia to see you."

I laughed. "Good answer. We can talk more then, about exceptions, time limits, and extensions to our agreement."

He gave me the biggest smile. "Definitely."

We hugged. It was a long hug.

He hugged me a little tighter before we separated, then again, our gazes locked.

He took my hand and held it as we faced each other. "Merry Christmas!"

I squeezed his hand. "Merry Christmas to you too. See you in a few days."

"Try to stay out of trouble in the meantime."

"Oh, believe me, I will. I've had enough excitement for the year, and then some."

We hugged again and our cheeks brushed. His eyes twinkled when he said goodbye.

I sighed with satisfaction. Now, not only did I have a date for New Year's Eve, but the way things were going, I think the new year was going to be happy and bright.

About the Author

Judith Gonda is a mystery writer with a penchant for Pomeranians and puns, so it's no surprise they pop up in her amateur sleuth mysteries featuring landscape architect Tory Benning. As for the hot buttered lobster rolls, black tea, and California wine that also pepper her pages, they can be traced to her growing up in Connecticut, London, England, and the San Francisco Bay Area.

Trained as a Ph.D. psychologist, she taps the knowledge gained from her time spent conducting research at USC, heading a human resources department, and running focus groups as a jury consultant to inform her characters and plots.

Judith currently resides in Southern California with her architecture professor husband and her two rescue Poms/surrogate daughters. Her two human daughters, a landscape architect and a TV writer, live nearby. All, along with crime stories in the news, have inspired her books.

To learn more about her upcoming releases, please visit her website at judithgonda.com.

Made in the USA
Las Vegas, NV
22 September 2021

30897336R00134